BEST LITERARY TRANSLATIONS

Best Literary Translations 2025

CRISTINA RIVERA GARZA,
GUEST EDITOR

Noh Anothai, Wendy Call, Öykü Tekten,
and Kọ́lá Túbọ̀sún
SERIES COEDITORS

DEEP VELLUM PUBLISHING
DALLAS, TEXAS

Deep Vellum Publishing
3000 Commerce Street, Dallas, Texas 75226
deepvellum.org · @deepvellum

Deep Vellum is a 501c3 nonprofit literary arts organization founded in 2013 with the mission to bring the world into conversation through literature.

FIRST EDITION, 2025

Support for this publication has been provided in part by grants from the National Endowment for the Arts, the Texas Commission on the Arts, the City of Dallas Office of Arts and Culture, the Communities Foundation of Texas, the Addy Foundation, the Marin Community Foundation, and a generous anonymous donor.

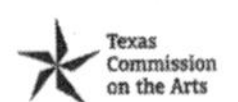

Print ISSN: 3066-4209
Online ISSN: 3066-4454

BLT series cover designed by Zoe Norvell
2025 cover designed by Jen Blair
Interior layout and typesetting by KGT

PRINTED IN CANADA

In memory of

Refaat Alareer (1979–2023)

and

Jerome Rothenberg (1931–1924)

TABLE OF CONTENTS

Coeditors' Introduction

As the four of us were working on this second edition of Best Literary Translations, we found ourselves returning to a perennial question about literature in English translation. Why do some source languages appear in our nominations again and again, while others don't at all? To state it more broadly, why does the publishing industry continue to focus on literature written in only a scant handful of the world's nearly seven thousand languages?

In the fall of 2023, as we were busily reading nominations for the present volume, our Coeditor for Asian Literatures, Noh Anothai, shared an interesting case from Thailand. The most recently elected Thai government was finally planning to invest in Thai literature as a form of "soft power, which, in this context, means branding cultural products and practices for foreign consumption, to encourage tourism and investment in the country. Whereas a previous government administration had limited its focus to Five Fs of fashion (in the form of traditional textiles), festivals, fighting (*muay thai*), film, and food, this successor insisted that it would be more forward-thinking in its conception of Thai culture and how to market it to the world.

When the National Committee for Soft Power Strategy released its proposed numbers, however, they were not at all forward-thinking. Out of a staggering budget of US$ 1.4 million, 72% was allocated for modernizing Bangkok's central library into a "Book Landmark," with an updated catalog system and facilities. Another 22% was to be divided evenly between coordinating a book fair "at the national level" and both domestic and international "book weeks." A meager

US$ 114,000, less than eight percent of the total budget, was apportioned for sending a Thai delegation to the Taipei Book Exhibition, Asia's largest book fair. There, presumably, Thai authors were to make significant contacts with foreign publishers and pitch their manuscripts by whatever means they could.

"If you're in the book industry and didn't yell out in frustration . . . then I say you must be, if nothing else, a masochist," responded Thai scholar Chitti Phalangsri (in Noh's colorful translation). The proposed budget would do little to nurture a genuine culture of reading, which could in turn bolster book sales and attendance at book events of all stripes. More glaringly, the budget also lacked any explicit provision for the translation of Thai writing into more widely read languages—essential for any international appreciation of it.

We coeditors shared a sigh of recognition: as translators, we have all seen this before. As we wrote in our introduction to the inaugural *Best Literary Translations 2024*, all too often, translators' on-the-ground work is overlooked, as if books magically emerged into new languages *ex nihilo*. This chronic oversight often manifests (as in the Thai example) as a lack of funding and dearth of institutional support for the work that translators do, which hampers their efforts to bring literature in other languages to the world's attention.

A 2024 study by Wellesley College sociologists Markella Rutherford and Peggy Levitt, and student Erika Zhang, "Whence Three Percent? How Far Have We Come toward Decentering America's Literary Preference?" demonstrates how very limited the "world literature" presented by U.S. book publishers is. The study's authors assert that "translated works in English are relevant because of their potential to alter or decenter the cultural understandings of globally privileged readers." The study reviewed nearly 8,500 books in translation (fiction, poetry, nonfiction, and children's literature) that were published in the U.S. between 2008 and 2020. They found that *nearly half* (45%) had been translated from just three languages:

French, German, or Spanish. Only 20% had been translated from non-European languages. In the U.S., more books are translated from French than any other language, and 80% of those books are by French or Canadian authors, leaving just one-fifth of the publishing pie to Francophone authors from another forty-three countries.

The authors of "Whence Three Percent?" offer solid proof that supporting literary translators and publishers dramatically expands the possibilities of "world literature." For years, Argentina, Chile, and Mexico have funded both translation and foreign publication of their nation's authors. In stark contrast to the French example, the study's authors found that close to half (46.7%) of the books published in Spanish translation were from those three countries, while less than 30% were from Spain. And that support has led to tangible change—even among large, commercial publishers. A U.S. reader picking up a big-press book translated from Spanish is just as likely to encounter a Latin American author as a Spanish one.

Here at Best Literary Translations, we know that without the labor of translators and the editors who publish them, no literary work in any language has the hope, nor any national literature the chance, of aspiring to the status of a "world literature." Defining that term is tricky; we think of it, in the broadest sense, as works of literature read widely beyond their language of origin. And so we honor both translators and their U.S. publishers.

Of course, more specific (and more insidious) forces account for the lack of translations out of many languages. In our first two years of publication, we have received only a handful of submissions translated from African languages: Bété, Malagasy, Old Egyptian, Reunionese Creole, Swahili, and Tigrinya. (And we have been very grateful to receive them!) Our Coeditor for African Literatures, Kọ́lá Túbọ̀sún, wonders if the pressure on African authors to write in English has stymied original compositions in local languages, as evidenced in the nominations we receive. He reflects on this state of affairs:

The image that flashes to mind for most people who hear "African writer" is that of an "African writer in English/French/Arabic, etc"—but mostly English. The most successful writers from the continent, including Chinua Achebe, Buchi Emecheta, Wole Soyinka, Ama Ata Aidoo, Léopold Sédar Senghor, Chimamanda Ngozi Adichie, and J. M. Coetzee, to name only a few, have practiced their craft within the vehicle of colonial languages. Those who have rebelled against it—by which we usually mean one prominent person, Ngũgĩ wa Thiong'o—have come to this juncture after years of practice in the colonial tongue. All that cultural production in English and other hegemonic languages has not only conditioned the world to expect that from the continent, it has also conditioned African practitioners themselves about what is appropriate to produce, practical to publish, and feasible to sell.

African writers who achieve book publication have generally gone through Western education, earned readership in a Western environment, and depend on this competence to carry the weight and depth of their experience. In many cases, there is no large audience for work in their local language, because of sociopolitical limitations, lack of publishing resources, economic power, or negative attitudes toward that local language caused by the dominance of English and postcolonial government policies. Sometimes, the language is limited to the oral spaces, and writing/publishing is therefore an unwieldy imposition. For these reasons and more, very few spaces exist to publish the African-language works that defy the odds, which leaves precious few original works to be translated into English. Things are changing slowly, and the internet is presenting a workable alternative. It is our hope, in the long term, that Best Literary Translations not

> only encourages *translation,* but also *original writing* in those languages that will eventually demand translation for wider readership.

In the past two years, this anthology has included works originally written in thirty-two languages, selected from nominations that have spanned eighty-two languages. Yes, there have been many submissions from Spanish, French, German, and Italian—nearly 40% of all the submissions we receive—but we're pleased to have read work from a diverse range of languages from around the world. Despite the many difficulties that can hinder their translation, twenty-three languages are represented here in *Best Literary Translations 2025.* Featured in these pages are not only works from languages that have been underrepresented in U.S. publishing, but some that have been actively persecuted, such as the Uyghur of Adil Tunaz (translated by Munawwar Abdulla), the Faroese of Kim Simonsen and Lív Maria Róadóttir Jæger (translated by Randi Ward and Bradley Harmon), the Tu'un Savi of Florentino Solano (translated from Spanish by Arthur Malcolm Dixon), and the Ukrainian of three different authors, among others. That some of these works made it to publication at all—much less into our nominations and eventually into the pages of this anthology—is a testament to steadfastness of the authors continuing to write in those languages, the dedication of the translators working urgently to amplify their voices, and the solidarity of the editors who published this work. Best Literary Translations celebrates their successes and honors their ongoing struggles.

To that end, we encourage literary journals to continue seeking out translations from less frequently encountered languages. Please waive submission fees, when necessary, for the opportunity to share this work with your readers. Journal editors and translators, please continue to nominate work during our annual submissions period each autumn. For our part, we coeditors will continue to advocate for the work that translators and their publishers do and look forward to even more, and even more diverse, submissions with each new edition of the anthology.

Finally, book publishers, please look carefully at what you find on these pages. Seek out these translators' work. Consider publishing the books they so diligently translate and champion. According to the Wellesley study we referenced earlier, small, independent presses produce 60% of the fiction in translation published in the United States. We suspect that percentage is even higher for poetry. Small publishers, we salute you! Commercial publishers and university presses, we beg you to follow their lead!

With these entreaties, we welcome you to the second edition of Best Literary Translations, our dream for an annual space to celebrate literary translations in English, published in literary journals with U.S.-based editors, during 2023.

We extend a warm thank you to everyone who supported our first edition, *Best Literary Translations 2024*, and helped make this second installment possible. We particularly want to thank the patient and committed staff at Deep Vellum, as well as a generous benefactor who has made our work as coeditors possible. Finally, we enthusiastically congratulate Cristina Rivera Garza who, in the midst of preparing this volume with us, received the Pulitzer Prize. We thank her for the thoughtful selections that fill the following pages—selections by a multi-genre author, a multidisciplinary artist, and a devoted educator who understands very well what it means to live, as she calls it, an "accented life."

Noh Anothai, Coeditor for Asian Literatures
Wendy Call, Coeditor for Literatures of the Americas
Öykü Tekten, Coeditor for Middle Eastern Literatures
Kọ́lá Túbọ̀sún, Coeditor for African Literatures

Guest Editor's Introduction

A STACKING OF TRANSLATIONS AND THE AFFECT OF THE HERE-AND-NOW

> Podríamos imaginar una transmisión de flujos de energía y materia. Como si pudieran existir diferentes procesos de traducciones en múltiples direcciones. Como "un apilamiento de traducciones" en el que, por un lado, afectamos a la materia, pero al mismo tiempo nos dejamos afectar. Se produce un diálogo.
>
> —Bustos + Galay, "Ánima," *El sonido de las plantas*

Marc Liblin was six years old when he learned a completely unknown language in dreams. No one spoke this language in his small village in the Vosges region and, despite his lifelong efforts to find an interlocutor, he failed, repeatedly. Even researchers at the University of Rennes proved incapable of deciphering or translating this dream language. Then, living already in another city and about to lose all hope, something remarkable happened. Marc performed a monologue in his dream language at a bar near the docks, surrounded by men from Tunisia. The manager, a former member of the Navy, turned around as soon as he overheard him. "I know this language," he said, interrupting the event. "I remember it from one of my journeys in Polynesia." Excitedly, he informed Marc about a nearby woman, a military widow, who spoke his dream language. Marc rushed to her door and, realizing they understood each other, his life changed. Their lives changed. Forever.

I recalled this fragment in Judith Schalansky's *Atlas of Remote Islands* quite often as I read these pieces in translation. It was not that I miraculously became fluent in Arabic or Ukrainian or Icelandic, but rather that I recognized, with that whip of intimacy that often gives out goosebumps, the act of translation: my language and theirs. The language we shared, regardless of the languages we spoke, when the doors flung open, and we finally met each other's eyes, in awe. Unlike Marc Liblin, I didn't learn this language in dreams or isolation, but there is a dream-like quality to the mode we employ when we are half ourselves and half not ourselves, becoming something irreducible in the process. Could it be that translation is a zone we incurred, unsettling our understanding of who we are and what we do here—and how malevolent and malleable this "here" truly is? It could be.

Translation as a site of irruption and contestation, I salute you.

For the past thirty years, I've led an *accented* life, living in translation and writing in a translation mode from within the United States, the second-largest Spanish-speaking country in the world. As one of the fifty to sixty million Spanish speakers and one of the twelve million Spanish-English bilinguals, I have resided and toiled in a land wounded by the 1848 Guadalupe Treaty, which turned the flow of a meandering river into a rigid boundary. During the mid-nineteenth century, teams of Mexican and United States engineers, soldiers, astronomists, and surveyors traversed the land, laboring to translate the words contained in a political treaty into the territory itself. Words were transmuted into geodesic monuments, wire fences, migration booths, and walls. Words metamorphosed into stone and metal and cement, clearly demarcating a neocolonial zone only some were permitted to cross.

In the beginning was translation.

I was born on the Mexican side of the U.S.–Mexico border,

within the twenty-kilometer radius known as the northern border strip, which, at least throughout the mid-twentieth century, facilitated movement for residents across the borderline. Adults in my family ventured to the Other Side quite often, whether to purchase pieces of rusted machinery for growing cotton or to obtain the weekly pack of groceries. Children visited less frequently, remaining in homes where Spanish was spoken but where most commodities bore English names and TV programs played in English nonstop. I soon learned that the language I spoke at this juncture on Earth came with heavy burdens but also with a vengeance. Everything I said could be turned against me. Everything I said could become otherwise. I could be myself and my double, simultaneously, switching back and forth. I could hide, and I could mock. I could curse, unbeknownst to my neighbors. At its very heart, translation is a wound, as Johannes Göransson and Joyelle McSweeney suggest in *Deformation Zone*, a proliferation of bodily openings that confounds the outside and the inside, making it unclear what the separate languages are, or were.

Gloria Anzaldúa, the Chicana writer who was born only miles away from my family home, although hers lay on the U.S. side of the border, spoke of the unequal relationship of English and Spanish as a form of linguistic terrorism. While she described the existence of at least nine different types of Spanish-English border languages, she was painfully aware that, to employ Deleuze and Guattari's terms, the "power takeover by a dominant language" forced many to bury at least half of themselves, rendering them half-silenced too. More than a cultural affair, Anzaldúa understood this takeover as a material conflagration, one in which dispossession and accumulation, racism and misogyny and homophobia, not to speak of the implementation of industrial agriculture in the region, played key roles. I believe that Gloria Anzaldúa would have agreed with Mixe linguist and language activist Yásnaya Aguilar Gil when she reminds us, from the stance of the present, that languages do not die, they are killed. Literally.

South Korean poet and translator Don Mee Choi has revised and retranslated Walter Benjamin's famous dictum—translation is a mode—to make it account for the "interconnected histories of imperialism, colonialism, and militarism, and . . . economic interdependence," that underlie translation practices worldwide: translation is an anti-neocolonial mode, she has argued. For, as in the story of Marc Lublin, the forces that account for the unlikely encounter between the speakers of a language one of them might have acquired in dreams, are revealed, perhaps even propelled, by the unremitting journeying of military machines across the globe. What was a member of the French Navy doing, one may ask, far away from home, in Polynesia? What kind of life did an uprooted military widow, unable to speak her language, lead in France? Translation both embodies and manifests the colonial history of these encounters. Translation announces and denounces—as the pieces included in this anthology confirm, from Palestine to Iceland, from Mexico to Indonesia—regardless of the topics they explore.

In *Translation is a Mode = Translation is an Anti-neocolonial Mode,* Don Mee Choi also diverges from two pervasive notions of translation. On the one hand, she not only questions the idea of mother tongues as seamless entities devoid of internal conflict but also, perhaps fundamentally, the very belief that they exist at all in the first place. In the context of the United States military incursion in South Korea, and before the combined onslaught of militarism and neoliberal devastation forced Don Mee Choi´s family into exile, she acknowledges that, as a woman, as someone always already "expelled from power," as she notes, "even within my so-called mother-tongue, I was already born with a tongue with a task to translate . . . " In her perspective of the takeover of dominant languages, gender and class manage to designate some of us as originary motherless translators. Similarly, pieces written originally in Tu'un Savi, Mapudungun, or Asturian included here shed light on the colonial histories of Spanish and the devastating effects on Indigenous languages and their practitioners throughout the Spanish-speaking world. They are testimony to the resilience of ways of life and modes of expression that have survived 500 years of continuous colonial expansion.

Don Mee Choi compellingly introduces the notion of a translation as an operation in opacity. In mapping the paths of neocolonialism, this translation practice mirrors states of incomprehensibility that migrants and nomads are all too familiar with. She pretended to be a foreigner even before she became one, she concedes. "As a foreigner, as foreign words myself, I seek incomprehensibility—a mirror image of myself. I seek mirrors through which I can also traverse, in order to map out the neocolonial history of my home, to translate myself." Similarly, Johannes Göransson and Joyelle McSweeney speak of translation as "a wound that makes impossible connections between languages, unsettling stable ideas of language, productive ideas of literature." Translation complicates things, in the sense in which Emily Wilson speaks of Odysseus as "a complicated man" in the opening line of her version of the *Odyssey,* for example.

Of all the books published in the United States, only 3% are works in translation—an infamous number that has endured, and a stark reminder of the dominance of English-language literature. Reading, a creative practice commonly associated with a pair of people, gets suddenly crowded when translation intervenes. Reading in translation makes it evident that, in writing as in life, we never work alone. There was once someone else, at the beginning of it all, and there is someone else now, hovering quietly over my shoulder as I flip the pages and nod in conformity or squint in disbelief. What was this like in the past? What other form could it take in the future? Translation takes time, and it is time, concentrated. This is its gift. There is always something more: an excess, a disturbance, the opacity that embodies mediation. The acknowledgment of this mediation reminds us that writing is a material practice: we must break through. There are bodies involved.

Translation warns us that there is always work to be done. As it unfinishes the text, leaving it open to the elements, translation lures us. In contrast to absorption, translation instills a basic critical awareness: we are not on a journey into the past, seeking to access the stable core of the original; rather, we are creatures of our present, rooted in and reading from the stand of the here and now, collectively shaping this here-and-now as we tread onward. It takes thousands of years for the light of the stars to reach the Earth. Although we admire the beauty of stars, it is their light that we crave. Could it be that translation is this luminescence touching our skin, making tangible contact, sheltering us? It could as well be.

Translation is generative, too. As English-Spanish translator Max Granger once told me: "Translation can erase the more radical meaning of words in service of readability and the rules of a given language, but it can also work to represent those meanings when we find creative ways to allow the source language to influence and change the target language, and thus, perhaps, to change how we think and act in that language." When collaborating on the translation of a piece on gender violence, in which the role of the perpetrator, *feminicida* in Spanish, was of significance, we both concurred that the term "killer" was inadequate. A killer is a criminal, but a femicider, a term still relatively unfamiliar in English, specifically denotes a criminal who targets and kills women because of their gender, reflecting the basic definition of femicide in penal codes throughout Latin America. Femicider, a vocable that might have initially seemed awkward or incorrect to readers in the Anglophone world, was the precise term needed to convey the structural nature of this crime, holding both patriarchy and its perpetrators accountable. Uttering the term femicider in English may as well contribute to a more open discussion about the silent epidemic of gender violence that, at least in the United States, claims the lives of three women every day. Translation is always political.

In *Anima,* a site-specific sound piece that Bustos + Galay (Javier

Bustos and Julian Galay) first performed at the Theater San Martín in Buenos Aires during the International Festival in 2020, they blended writing, improvisation, and sound art as they strove to translate the language of plants. They believed, with Murray Schafer, that listening is a way of touching from a distance. Using an electromagnetic microphone to "auscultate" a branch from the Pehuén-Có region, they were convinced that they could sense the forest where it originated, as if the branch held the memory of its surroundings. They attentively listened to this language and translated it so that it could resonate in human ears. But their curiosity went further. "We are interested in plants," they remarked (in my translation), "precisely because they are plants, because they articulate things we cannot hear." They thus aimed to preserve the inherent plantness within the plants, despite all interventions and against all odds. "We don't know what plants and stones sound like, and that's why we use fiction and poetry." Perhaps, as with the plant kingdom, we need fiction and poetry and nonfiction in translation to approach an enigma as an enigma, with no resolution in sight.

Cristina Rivera Garza
Berlin, April 1, 2024

Mother Tongue

Adil Tuniyaz
translated from the Uyghur by Munawwar Abdulla
Four Way Review

We were born like gold
on this sparkling brown land.
It fell, ringing
from the mouth of an Uyghur angel,
its music sunk into our ears.
Oh, mother tongue,
we became wanderers,
and have moved far from your horizons.
Opium poppies
bring the scent of the seas,
thoughts kept moist for a while.

I have left the radio on.
It speaks
in the wind.
Cool orchards,
oil, sandy mountains
a group of people whose colors have drained,
dead still cities and winter pastures.
I drank coffee
and cried.
The ocean waves entered my home.

Translator's Note

I was first asked to translate a number of Adil Tuniyaz's works from a member of Steppe Space, an online intercommunal platform showcasing Central Asian art and culture. It's unlikely that I may have come across this particular poem of his otherwise. Adil Tuniyaz was imprisoned in 2017 as China began its campaign to re-engineer Uyghur society through concentration camps, prison sentences without trial, and many other invasive means to control Uyghur movement and thought.

Tuniyaz was a journalist, poet, and bookstore owner who was swept up in the mass arrests of public intellectuals and academics. He had been accused of promoting terrorism and religious extremism, perhaps because he had studied literature in Saudi Arabia for some time. A close look at his poetry provides a different story. As I read more about his life and influences, I began to appreciate his love for his own deserts near Kashgar, so removed from any ocean, as he, perhaps, sat in the foreign deserts of Saudi Arabia. Perhaps, unlike the Arabic words that fell from the angels that conveyed the message to the Prophet, we'd inherited our own beautiful language, which we had moved far away from, both physically, in this new land, but also politically, as China enforces their "national language" in favor of Uyghur as the language of instruction at schools, and disappears writers and publishers like Tuniyaz.

It struck me as ironic to translate "Mother Tongue" into yet another foreign tongue. Each line takes us further away from our homeland. Together, we look back to the horizon we were born to, he in a foreign land, I in a foreign language, coffee in hand and an ocean at our doorsteps.

Tumbleweed

Ao Omae
translated from the Japanese by Emily Balistrieri
The Kenyon Review

In the sleepy West, a run-down bar is turning sepia colored. In front of it, two men turn their backs to each other and begin walking. One step, another—they silently take their distance. Time audibly stops. Sweat drips down a forehead. With the sound of their breath, the two men whirl around—drawing the guns at their hips—and shoot. A moment later, one of them turns back and walks off into the desert. The gunman left behind stands stock still, but a few seconds later his knees crumple, and he falls to the ground. A hot, dry wind blows, and one of those tangled spheres of dead grass so familiar in Westerns—me—goes futilely rolling along. Cut to the victor walking off into the shimmering sunset. Fade to black. The credits roll. My name is there.

That was the end of this week's *Fury in the West*. I wanted to get to the wrap party as soon as possible and soak in one beer for every stalk I had broken. Finally, Viewer Appreciation Month was over. I wish they would quit doing these live public broadcasts. Well, I get how production feels, not being able to trust a one-time shoot to a rookie tumbleweed. But they forgot to fetch me every time I tumbled, so I rolled and rolled, sprinkling my seeds everywhere.

I had arrived at the studio four hours before rehearsal, and getting blown on by all that hot wind upset my stomach. I decided to slip off the set and get out of there. I'm the leading man in the biz, so no one stopped me, and I left.

It was summer. The asphalt burned my belly. I wanted to make a dash for the loo, but I've never had very good chemistry with the wind, so I ended up getting carried down the road. And it was a highway, to boot. No, that wasn't a problem—thanks for your concern, though. I'm a lot bigger than I look on the screen, so cars don't hit me. I was stuck in a traffic jam, so even if I did get hit, I would just lose a few dozen arms and legs.

The driver in the car behind me was honking at first, but then he noticed it was me in front of him. After a few moments of what was probably hesitation, he got out of the car and came to ask for an autograph. If I refused, there was no telling what he would write about me later on social media, so I signed for him with a smile. Then, taking advantage of my good humor, other drivers came out into the street, and the traffic jam got even worse. "Hey, are you trying to turn this into 'The Southern Thruway'?" I said, but they just laughed instinctively, and didn't rib me like, *This is actually the central part of the country!* (despite the fact that they probably didn't even know who Cortázar is). They were the same as the yes-men and the sponsors. At any rate, they flashed their yellowed teeth just because the words were coming out of my mouth and happened to be directed at them. But this was serious. I was surrounded by people, and soon I wouldn't be able to move at all. *Are you telling me I should soil myself right here? I've been constipated for a month!* But then a meteorite hit, the air pressure sending all the people flying all over the place, and I found myself in front of a supermarket. I was saved.

I know that meteorite well. Back when she was in *Armageddon* she was doing bit parts, but now everybody wants a piece of her. *She made time in her busy schedule to come rescue me?* Maybe I'll treat her to a parfait later, I thought as I headed toward the supermarket to use the loo. But the automatic door wouldn't react. The door wouldn't open, but it was leaking strong air-conditioning. The temperature differential pushed my bowels to their limits.

Just as I was thinking, *Well, it's pretty common to see excreta in front of supermarkets. Plus, I've got all the grass I need to wipe with,* about to give up, a young child walked by. He had come to return a shopping cart, but instead I had him give me a lift back to his guardian's car. His mother got out of the car and started kicking up a fuss. Me, a kidnapper? It seemed like she didn't know who I was. Apparently she lived under a rock. When I did my famous line—"Whoooosh" (the sound of the wind blowing)—and gave her an autograph, she finally seemed to figure it out, at which point she duct-taped me to the top of her car in a way that brooked no argument and took me to her house.

The road was all cracked up due to the meteorite's impact, and the vibrations were no joke—it seemed like I was finally going to have an accident. But then I noticed some of the townspeople who had begun to evacuate reaching out to me for help, and I decided to hold it together. With a tranquil expression, I shared one strand, then another, of my body. I just hope I was able to be of some small solace to them . . .

By the time we reached the woman and her son's house, my body was half its original size. I lost even more when she removed the duct tape. The blessing in that curse was that I was able to fit smoothly through both the front and bathroom doors and give my flesh over to sheer bliss. More of my body came off with my gold brick, and it seemed like the toilet would plug, but since the family hadn't hit on the idea that water might be a precious resource in the near future, I could flush multiple times.

When I went into the living room, the boy was sitting in the dark, watching TV at point-blank range. The sound was muted—perhaps the woman had turned it off—and the colors of the sky being destroyed and the red of the flames bathed the boy's face. I noiselessly sat in a chair. The woman brought three glasses of iced tea from the kitchen and set them on the table. Then she said,

"I'm Erica."

"Thanks for saving me. My name is—"

"I know. You gave me your autograph before."

"I'm just a humble tumbleweed. And the kid?"

"Luca. Hey, why don't you come over here and have some iced tea?" The boy was absorbed in the TV broadcast and didn't seem to realize he'd been spoken to. "He sure didn't get that from me."

"Where's his father?"

"I've been trying to call him for a while now . . ."

"I'm sure he's all right."

"You're single, right?"

"Oh, I had work today. I take my ring off when I have work. Or rather, I used to."

"What's that supposed to mean?"

"I'm in the middle of a divorce."

"I'm sorry."

"It's OK. One day after work there was a younger guy from my agency pulling up his pants, that's all."

"Your partner was human?"

"She's the one in spy movies who always gets her car, bike, mobile phone, or whatever stolen by the protagonist. I'm sure you've seen her."

"I can't believe it! How could she do that to a guy like you!"

I couldn't say anything more, and Erica just looked at me. Our glasses were sweating. "Isn't it hot in here? The AC's broken," she said, flapping her T-shirt back and forth. I caught a glimpse of her cleavage. She picked up her iced tea, and I could hear her throat noises clearly as she drank. There was lipstick left on the glass. A drop of sweat rolled down her neck. She licked her lips. Then I heard a car pull into the gravel driveway. "Luca, Daddy's home!" Erica said, and went with the boy to the door.

I took a sip of iced tea and said, loud enough for Erica's husband to hear, "Man, you really helped me out. Thanks for letting me use your bathroom. I guess I'll be going now." I stood up to leave, but before I could, a man came into the living room, leaning on Erica. He seemed injured and was holding a hand over the left side of his face.

"Ayanokoji."

Because of the injury, I couldn't tell who the man was, but he knew my real name. I had the feeling I'd heard his voice somewhere before. "It's me," he said, bending his right arm. I know only one guy with a right elbow that dirty.

"Ken."

My voice was shaking. I never thought I would run into Ken in a place like this.

"Huh? You know him?" said Erica as she brought over some disinfectant she had grabbed off a shelf.

"Yeah, we went to the same university." Ken moved his hand away from his face. Luca was enthralled by the sight of the blood and tried to touch it, but Erica brushed his tender hand aside. She dabbed at Ken with a cloth soaked in the disinfectant. He writhed.

"Hey, are you OK?" I asked. "Your arm is hurt too. Do you want to stabilize it with my stalks? You know how sturdy they are."

But Ken said, "I don't need your filthy grass. It's crawling with bacteria."

"Are you still holding a grudge about back then?" I wasn't.

"Why are you here?"

"Like I said before, I borrowed the bathroom."

"You came all the way out here to use the bathroom?"

"What are you trying to say?"

"Stop it, you two," said Erica, and she wrapped another cloth around Ken's forearm. "I don't know what happened between you guys, but you're both tired."

"Are you fighting?" asked Luca.

A beat later Ken said, "Sorry, I'm on edge because of the meteorite. Ayanokoji and I were in theater club together. When we joined, I was getting more attention, but right around the time we turned twenty, his arms and legs started going plant, while I stayed human. I couldn't stand that he was getting ahead of me as an actor, so I quit the club. Happens all the time."

Erica said, "Honestly," to hold him back.

"I know. It's ancient history. It's great that we've met again. You should relax for a while." Ken got up to leave the living room, and his eyes said to me, *Don't say anything more than necessary.*

It was still evening, but darkness was gathering in the rip the meteorite had made in the sky, so we ended up turning in early.

Before accepting the plastic sheet I would use as a blanket, I thought of suggesting that we gather food and water, but I figured neither Erica nor Ken would want me taking charge like that.

I never imagined a meteorite would fall because of circumstances involving my defecation. I thought of all the people I'd seen on the way to this house: a mother wailing the name of her child, someone getting swallowed up in a crack in the concrete and crushed, a man who had embraced his lover just as a rock came sailing over and killed him instantly. Some corner of my brain wondered if we were filming. Someone would fly up to space and stop the violent meteorite attack. Damage would be kept to a minimum, and the people would stop overconsuming and focus on the life in front of them, walking off with their eyes on the sunrise. My name would be in the end credits. Then the people would leave the theater, go to sleep still a little wound up, and upon waking, they would have forgotten all about the movie, and their humdrum lives would begin again. But that's not what was happening. All night long, my eyes saw flames, and when I curled up in the plastic sheet and looked out the window, the transmission towers that had always been an eyesore were gone.

Morning came without me getting a wink of sleep. When I opened the front door, I could hear the birds chirping as they pecked at the insects between blades of grass. The sky was so blue it seemed like someone had gone over it with a paint roller, and the air smelled fresh. There was no wind. I wanted to scream. I wanted to cry. *What the hell!* The world was so peaceful, it didn't seem to care that we were all going to die. I smelled cigarette smoke, and when I turned around, Ken was there.

"Look at this, Ken."

That alone was enough for him to understand what I meant.

"But soon the panic from the city will come here too," he said, approaching me.

"Do you have somewhere to go when that happens?"

"I don't know."

"Want to come to my vacation home? It's on an island, so I'm sure we'd be safe once we crossed over."

"I'd rather die."

"Hey, don't come too close. I'll catch fire."

Ken flicked his cigarette away and dug in his breast pocket for another, but the box was empty. Crushing it in his hand, he headed for the car parked in the yard.

"Where are you going?"

"I'm just getting a cigarette."

The car's windshield was spiderwebbed with cracks and covered in bloody handprints.

"How are your injuries?"

"Fine." He lit the new cigarette.

"I told you to stay back."

As I said it, I remembered the old days. Ken would often smoke next to me. Back then my body was more warped than ever, because he would always lean into me. I looked forward to admiring myself in the mirror after he left. His body heat became a part of me.

"Let me see." I tried to touch him, as if my body were replaying old memories, but he jumped away.

"I have a family! And you're married too." My tips burned on his cigarette ash.

•

I tried to leave before Erica and Luca got up, but as I was gathering grass that had fallen around the living room, Erica stopped me. "It's too dangerous for a tumbleweed to go out alone. You'll get ripped to pieces. And with things as they are, I could use another man around." I think she wanted Ken and me to go back to the way things used to be. But if that actually happened, she was the one who would get hurt.

They didn't need to worry about food or water. There was more than enough. This was the kind of family that had duct tape at the ready. And I could survive as long as I had a little water. I started sleeping in the yard that night. "It was really nice of you to find a plastic sheet for me and all, but it seems sleeping closer to nature is just better for me. Plus, this way I can also stand guard."

As the days passed, I started spending not only my nights but most of the time outside. "Won't you dry out?" asked Luca, worried, but I was a ball of dry grass to begin with.

Ken wasn't very happy about it, but I knit hats for Erica and Luca out of my body. I messed up on the sizing, and Erica's went down to her eyes. "Ken may be a grouch, but he's actually really happy to see you. He talks to the water because he thinks it will make it taste better. Right, Luca?" Luca poured water over my head with a green watering can shaped like an elephant.

Sometimes Luca napped on me. At first there was a streak where he did it every day, but once he got used to me, he went back to the TV even though it didn't turn on anymore. He was sitting there watching it as if he were appreciating a pitch-black abstract painting when Ken grabbed him. Luca kicked his legs and screeched cheerfully, acting the child as Ken lifted him up to sit on his shoulders. Ken's arm seemed to have fully recovered, but he still had a scar on his face. Luca touched it with his tender hands. Frankly, I hated seeing them like that. But I stared, unable to look away. I can't carry someone on my shoulders like that. Where are my shoulders, even? I couldn't have a baby with my wife.

After I had completely transformed into a tumbleweed, I thought I wanted to be at least a little ordinary, and I married my wife without saying a word to Ken. I don't think I did him wrong by that. Ken has a wonderful family. But that marriage was a mistake for my wife. It was a mistake for me.

I was waiting. I was waiting for the wind to blow. Just watching the sky. As the tranquil days continued, I was the only one still waiting for destruction.

The sound of laughter came from inside the house. Ken was laughing in an open way I'd never heard from him before. The light of his family leaked out and soaked into me. I'll never bathe directly in this light ever again. I'll never laugh with my wife. I was always drunk. She didn't do anything wrong. She even wanted to stay with me after she walked in on me sleeping with that younger guy. She broke all the alcohol bottles in the house for me. I hid the shards in my body and went to sleep with her. I hurt her. Irreparably. There's a restraining order. My vacation home on the island has been seized. Maybe that's why I snuck out of the studio. No one has come looking for me. I'm alone. The laughter on the other side of the windows pummeled me. Those people had something I would never have again. They were laughing so happily.

In the middle of the night, after everyone was asleep, the wind blew—whoooosh. Countless dark shadows were headed this way. Tumbleweeds. The seeds I'd spread along the road had grown up—that much time had passed. The tumbleweeds came into the yard and surrounded me, closing in like a tightening rope. The neck being strangled was mine, but I wouldn't be killed. I reached my hands out, and my doubles reached their hands out; we tangled—the only sound was of plant matter rubbing together—and became one. Eventually I was as big as a planet. I was big enough to cover everything. I could crush it all.

I sat perfectly still like that, waiting for a meteorite to fall. I waited for rioters to come from the city. If they came, I would mow them down. If a meteorite fell, I would make a dome over this house and protect Ken's family. I was glad he didn't end up with me.

But the meteorite never came. No rioters, or anything else either. When Ken and his family woke up, they came outside to talk to me, but the countless tumbleweed consciousnesses swirled within me, and I couldn't speak well. The family decided to keep an eye on me, but nothing changed. By the time they realized something needed to be done, I had forgotten how to talk. Erica tried to cut me up with a knife, but Ken stopped her. Rain soaked into me, making me heavy, and I was too big to dry out completely, so I was too massive to move or be moved; just as words invite more words, my grasses tangled up even more, and I grew so hard you would never have guessed I was a tumbleweed.

Luca tried to climb on top of me. He fell from about a third of the way up, and the left side of his body was paralyzed. Clenched in his hand was the watering can. Ken tried to set me on fire. Erica was crying next to him. She didn't try to stop him. I wanted him to burn me. If it was him killing me, I could accept it. I wish that had happened. He kicked divots in the yard and in the driveway. He burned the hats made of my body right in front of me.

They went away. The cracked car was left behind with the house. I fell into a long slumber.

•

There's a curved wall before my eyes. Behind me too. All around. It curves in toward me. When I look up, there's a circle of blue sky. Someone is trying to trap me. They're trying to cover me with a dome. Why? Maybe a museum? How will they introduce me? The World's Biggest Tumbleweed. A Once-Famous Actor. As the visitors gaze up at me, my old movies will play. In the sleepy West, a run-down bar is turning sepia colored. In front of it, two men turn their backs to each other and begin walking. One step, another—they silently take their distance. Time audibly stops. A chunk of concrete being welded overhead falls and stabs me. It's no meteorite.

Translator's Note

"Tumbleweed" is the titular story in Ao Omae's first print collection, published in 2018. (Incidentally, he once said he never really decided whether the Japanese title should be read *Kaitengusa* or *Kaitensō*, but I'm team *Kaitengusa*.) I came to the book via Saki Souda's fantastic cover, and was immediately hooked by the way Omae's stories had my emotions vibrating at unfamiliar frequencies. I'll never forget being at an event featuring him in conversation with Akutagawa Prize–winner Ryohei Machiya, and Machiya calling him "a shooting star pinging rapidly between the poles of beauty and pain." It felt like such an apt description.

Translating this story was mainly a lot of fun. I enjoyed writing Ayanokoji's hard-boiled voice and capturing the cinematic cuts seen through the narrative lens. None of the other stories in this collection have appeared yet in English, though I've translated a couple from Omae's 2019 flash fiction collection *Watashi to wani to imōto no heya* (A room for a crocodile, my sister, and me).

Nuigurumi to shaberu hito wa yasashii (*People Who Talk to Stuffed Animals Are Nice,* tr. me) in 2020 marked a new direction with the gender- and contemporary society-focused themes of the titular novella. He continues to write about social media, comedy, and masculinity in a way that resonates with anyone trying to be kind in a world that often chews people up and spits them out. While "Tumbleweed" no longer feels like his most representative work, I cherish his weird early stories and hope that his inclusion here will help bring more eyes to his output as a whole.

"Apple-Flesh," an excerpt from the novel *Deportation*

András Visky
translated from the Hungarian by Anna Bentley and Jozefina Komporaly
World Literature Today

506
forced abode comes with forced labor, only they had omitted to inform us of this, nor is there any mention at all of it in the deportation order, which simply does not provide particulars about, does not raise the issue of, does not give a name to, does not go into what the punishment will consist of, leaving no doubt only as to the fact that it concerns manifest criminality and the legal use of force

507
but then this is, after all, understandable, the Party being tied up with the creation of a new heaven and a new earth, having embarked on a large-scale, truly cosmic project, there is no time for formalities. God, for example, had promptly failed to make the grade and had been officially thrown out of the Universe, there'd been a sudden increase in the number of black marks in the class register, more and more unexplained absences. Where is God, the people asked, raising their eyes to the heavens and they had every right to do so. Not here, that's for sure, they concluded, pointing around at the camp, and when He was called up to the front of the class, which He was every day, He'd just stand there at the board, lost-looking and silent, crumbling the chalk like He'd

wet his pants and been found out. He could no longer be tolerated, that was clear, a Party order was issued stating there was no God, and He, too, was officially notified, You don't exist. Keep your head down if you know what's good for you, all right God-bod, it's over

508
work sets you free, forced labor most definitely, no doubt about that, what does it free us from? well, from ourselves, that's what they thought it up for, that's what we're in need of. The Party may, quite rightly be thinking that, while the people it is dealing with may be ideologically misled, they are, in their own way, intelligent, they realize the position they are in and won't quibble at being forced to work, they will, without putting up any particular resistance, march out in neat columns on a daily basis to build a new heaven and a new earth

509
perhaps we'll realize that organized work is for our own good, that the Party, for its part, is generously attempting to reeducate us, is generously placing its hopes in us, including Mr. Goma the writer, General Praporgescu Commander of the Royal Lifeguards, oh, and let's not forget Marino the liberal arts scholar, and, yes, the two pale widows, Mrs. Lilica Codreanu the Iron Guardsman's wife and Mrs. Maria Antonescu, wife of the fascist Marshal. If anyone should happen to resist or attempt to escape, he or she will, for their own good, be shot, and will end up being put with the others who failed the grade over in the same corner where the nonexistent God is already standing

510
in the spirit of reeducation, everyone is driven out daily to work somewhere or other. In neat formation, you leave the camp, you leave your children and the invalids, if there are any, to fend for themselves, and you work until you can barely put one foot in front of the other. The

children go out and stand in front of the barrack, all seven of the camp's children, which is us, they wait until you march out with the others in the direction of the ferma, seven rickety, knock-kneed children, the pale glow of their swollen knees stays with you until you are far away. At the end of the day you need somehow to get back to these children, but by then you haven't the strength to walk, your ability to put one foot in front of the other has evaporated, to put one foot in front of the other, that's right, it's become a fixed phrase, it would be good to manage at least that till the end of the day, and to make it back home

511
lean on me, ma'am, urges Professor Balotă, offering himself to her, now then, up you come, coaxes Madam Nadia the pilot, who, gripping both her hands, pulls our mother up from the edge of the ditch, you needn't worry about Nicu, Júlia, I should know, adds Nadia and laughs. Nicu Balotă goes bright red, he suddenly has no idea how to take hold of our incapacitated mother. In the end, he decides on her waist, puts his arm around her and gently eases her toward him, that's it, that's it, says Madam Nadia, beautifully done, and to think I'd given up on you completely, Nicu dear

512
our mother had a horror of being touched by any man she didn't know, any man other than our father. We couldn't begin to imagine how she had touched our father when he was still unknown to her, and she to him, this unanswered question led us to the possibility of our having been born of a virgin, all seven of us were virgin births, no question, and what's more, we increasingly had to reckon with the probability that our mother's own conception had been immaculate too

513
our mother finds it difficult to expose her chest, for example, before

Romulus the medic, and when he places his naked ear against her naked skin, the little blood she has remaining drains from her face, picture a stethoscope, ma'am, when you see my ear, Romulus the medic tells our shrinking mother encouragingly, and there spreads across her face that childlike, boundless beauty of hers, and truly, a miracle is taking place, Romulus's ear is pleasantly cool, like the eardrum of a stethoscope, though it could have been red-hot like our father's.
Our mother is visibly reassured by this metallic coldness, people have been created in such a way that they cannot listen to their own hearts

514
oh yes, it's God she ought to be leaning on at this point, thinks our mother on the edge of the ditch, but then God would have to exist. That would most definitely be the solution, if He were here in the camp and she could lean on Him, and it's no excuse to say the reason he's not here is because He's everywhere, everywhere is not the same as nowhere. Whatever the case, it's possible she would feel less horror at God's deathly touch than at Professor Balotă's, but she'd also settle for Abraham's encircling arm, to be quite precise, for Abraham's unfathomably extensive bosom into which the angels took the vagrant Lazarus all covered in sores when he handed his soul back to the Creator, the same Creator who, as we have seen, is so clumsy in His handling of the affairs of the poor, and who doesn't exist of course, a fact that has now come to our attention too, by way of the new Party decree from Bucharest promulgated in the camp

515
Professor Balotă speaks Hungarian to our mother, he understands *our* language too, and at least as well as Dukát the Franciscan. Mr. Pali Făgăşan can also handle Hungarian to some extent, when he puts words together, he makes pretty good sense, he butchers Hungarian, says our firstborn sibling Feri, but I'm puzzled by this butchering of

Hungarians because Mr. Făgăşan the radio repair man is especially fond of us, he definitely isn't butchering the handful of Hungarians that are here. Now Marin the pickpurse and Livezeanu, *they'd* butcher them soon as touch them, but then they beat anyone black and blue who gets in their way, doesn't matter if they're Hungarian or Romanian, or Russian, like Nadia, or a Jew, like Saul Făgăşan, or a Lipovan, like the eternally drunk Danube fishermen, as for us, says brother Feri, we butcher Romanian. What does he mean, we butcher Romanians, tell me a single one we've butchered lately or ever for that matter. I don't like any of this, but that's not important, I'll understand this too, when the time comes, and if I don't, then I don't

516

Madam Nadia speaks to us children in Romanian, to my mother, though, who can't speak Romanian despite all her best efforts, she speaks German or French. Mother waves her hand dismissively, that's all in the past, as useless as having a sixth finger. Nahdge-ah, my dear, imagine, I can't for the life of me remember what the Italian for ceiling or window is

517

Nahdge-ah, that's how our mother pronounces Nadia's name, and this sweet softening of the central sound magically makes Madam Nadia the pilot all the more beautiful. The language of captivity isn't Hungarian, nor is it Romanian, says our mother, and least of all is it French or German. Now Major Livezeanu, he really does speak the language of captivity, and we, too, will be broken in somehow sooner or later. The country, they say, already speaks the brand-new language of captivity fluently, we're the only ones who still haven't learned it, that's why we've washed up here in the camp, the best thing would be to regard our time here as an intensive language course, as time in a state captivity-language school

518
our mother has been assigned to work in an enormous granary, she has to shovel wheat from one end of the building to another and back again. Golden grains, dust rising and falling in the harsh sunlight and the sound of Mimi Vaida's deep coffee-house singing voice: breath-taking, murderous beauty in the forty-degree heat of the Bărăgan, and this beauty does regularly actually relieve our mother of her breath. Every day, pain lurks in her chest, keen lightning bolts slice through her left arm, and for a while she is able only to hold the shovel in her right hand, she scrapes clumsily at the fresh, still-damp wheat, then, when she can't stand it any longer, she goes out in front of the store-house in search of shade, she ducks behind a burning-hot trailer and massages her chest over her heart with a damp rag, then somehow she pulls herself together and goes back to the steaming mounds of grain to shovel

519
think yourself lucky doamnă, they say to her, seeing how slowly she's getting on, she's got it pretty good, the granary's one of the best places to work, she shouldn't be fussy, but if she's more interested in digging irrigation channels, the work Aurél the architect and Praporgescu the Lifeguard Commander have been assigned to, she only has to say, it can be arranged. The country's coat of arms has golden ears of wheat twined around it, it's a great honor to work on the ferma, and, well, manual labor liberates a person from spiritual torment, that's why the poor are blessed, doesn't she know. She ought to be grateful then, that she's happier than she's ever been, happier even than in the encircling arms of Livezeanu, perhaps. She should beat any thought of sabotage out of her mind and if that doesn't work, they'll be glad to step in and beat it out for her right away

520
in front of the barrack, Professor Balotă hands our mother back to us. Our mother can't walk, just staggers, her feet weaving about like Livezeanu's and Marin the pickpurse's do when they're drunk, she looks like she's saying something over and over, but no sound comes out and we have no idea who this continual stream of talk is directed at, she looks at us, counts us up, is glad to see us, to see that we're there all seven of us, and heaves a sigh of relief. Nadia looks in for a short while and says something to the sisters. Sister Lídia and sister Máriamagdolna get the tin bath out. Us boys have to go outside the hut, we stand around at a loss, listening to the water sloshing onto our mother's depleting body

521
soon Nényu turns up too, on Romulus the medic's advice, she has stolen some nice-looking apples from the model farm for our mother's haphazardly skipping heart, she wipes them carefully, then pushes shiny iron nails into their flesh. When the apples have absorbed the iron, she grates two of them, stirs the fresh, iron-soaked, rust-red apple-flesh into some crumbled rusk, and after the bath, spoons it into our feebly protesting mother

Translators' Note

András Visky's novel *Deportation* made a great splash when it came out in Hungary in 2022 and swiftly garnered several prizes. Anna read it with interest, having already worked on the excerpt here entitled "Apple-Flesh" back in 2019, when Visky brought it to a literary translators' workshop in Budapest. Jozefina, whose connection with András goes back a couple of decades, has published a critical anthology focusing on his *Barrack Dramaturgy* as well as a translation of his drama cycle *Stories of the Body*. Like *Deportation*, the former deals with Visky's childhood experiences, as a member of the Hungarian-speaking minority, in the Romanian Gulag of the 1950s. Despite the privations suffered by the protagonists and their appalling treatment by the guards, the novel succeeds in being uplifting, thanks to the love and faith that infuse the child's narrative.

On a linguistic level, there is a challenging mix of ideological turns of phrase, biblical language, legalese and the child's attempts to make sense of idiomatic expressions. Add to this the narrator's regular use of Romanian words. These were not translated or marked out in any way in the Hungarian original and enable the reader to share in the narrator's experience of this multilingual environment. The Romanian language itself plays a decisive role in the children's camp experience, as they grapple with it at school and are tutored by other political prisoners. In this excerpt, therefore, we retained doamnă (Madam) and ferma (farm), only translating terms when we felt the reader needed help, e.g. in the case of remorka (trailer). This is a collaborative translation, combining Jozefina's knowledge of the Romanian language and history and Anna's native-speaker feel for how to render this layered text into a version that could be enjoyed by readers of English with no immediate experience of totalitarianism.

a moving grove

Iryna Shuvalova
translated from the Ukrainian by Uilleam Blacker
Words Without Borders

go escape while you can go escape
buy tickets for the last water train
which as it subsides reveals
curbs pavements the riverside
the anatomy of the sinewy city that lies
naked and unfamiliar like a man in your bed
go—escape while you can

take all your belongings
everything that's yours
split lips cut knees
the cracked jar of a head from which
memory slowly seeps and all you can
leave just leave behind
the evening lights in the windows
the beloved exposed throat of the sky
the smell of the subway the lead of the river

go and don't come back have no doubts that's how it is
to fall into the bottomless well of a body
to throw yourself like a comb over your shoulder
to sow yourself across a field so that a host
of warriors might grow

this is how the needle passes
through the needle's eye this is how the forest
shall come up to the walls

and start to tremble

Translator's Note

Working with Iryna Shuvalova is a pleasure—she is both completely involved in the process (as a talented translator herself) and completely respectful of my role as the translator. (Perhaps also a consequence of her own experience!) It's a privilege to have her on hand to provide insights into the poems. She uses many subtle cultural or historical references, and these can be easy to miss; 'a moving grove' contains nods to Slavic folklore, Greek mythology, the Bible, and Shakespeare, for example. But she always makes these things her own, inflecting them in unexpected ways—it's important to be alive to that as the translator. She almost never uses punctuation, which produces a deliberate fluidity and ambiguity. We sometimes become unsure as to what exactly the relationships are between nouns and verbs, or where clauses begin and end. It makes the poems exhilarating and a little disorientating. Ukrainian lends itself to this because of its more flexible grammar and syntax, but it can be a challenge to reproduce in more restrictive and precise English. Perhaps what I was most eager to preserve in this poem, however, was the sense of urgency felt by a person who is forced to flee their home and is suddenly faced with the physical and mental chaos of displacement. There is a powerful sense of the physicality of the move, of the bodily longing for the lost home city, but also of the way in which displacement affects the mind and the memory. It was important to make it punchy and rhythmic and driving, like the original; I hope I achieved that.

Come wilderness into our homes

Daniela Danz
translated from the German by Monika Cassel
Poetry

break the windows come
with your roots and your worms
spread yourself over our wishes
our waste-sorting systems our prostheses
and outstanding payments
cover us with your rustling greenery
and your spores cover us that we may
become green: green and reverent
green and manifest green and replaceable
come weather with your storms
and sweep the slates off the roofs come
with snow and hail smash
through the collective sleep
we are all enjoying in our beds
our worn rationalizations come ice
and form glaciers over the shadow banks
and our drive for liquidity
come through the cracks under the doors
you desert with your sands fill
our desolation up until it forms into a solid mass
rise up over the search-and-rescue teams
and our growth compulsion trickle into
the control panels of the missiles

and the missile defense systems into
the think tanks and the hearts of internet trolls
just leave the hedgehogs with their
snuffling so that it may calm us
come rising sea levels
up over our shorelines both the developed
and the undeveloped the homey
lowland areas wash
jellyfish into our soup bowls
and ramshorn snails into our hair
as we swim in each other's direction panicked
with our yearning for one another
because almost nothing is left because it's all gone
and thoroughly soaked through with regrets
finger-pointing and tranquilizers
come earthquakes shatter the apartments
which we built on the foundations
of how we always did everything
come tremors fill the mine shafts
the end of work and
the literature of redemption bury anger
and affection and all manner of added values
swallow up the memories come tremors
hurry so that the bedrock covers us
so we are covered with water desert weather
and over everything that which covers all the wilderness

Translator's Note

"Come wilderness into our homes" is the second of three poems that open Daniela Danz's 2020 *Wilderness (Wildniß)*. All three poems describe and invoke, in incantatory fashion, the collapse of civilization as nature demonstrates that our sense of control is an illusion. In a recent essay, Danz notes that "wilderness is [. . .] a creative force, both life-giving and life-taking, and [. . .] remains what we yearn for, the counterpart to our 'culture,' the adversary we so deeply desire." We can see the speaker's pull toward this "adversary" as she welcomes rising sea levels and the havoc they wreak. How to capture in translation this voice that seems to call for the very erasure of subjecthood, speech, and memory?

The invocation is a single, breathless sentence with additive syntax, the anaphora of "come . . . " elaborated with clauses enumerating details of our dissolution. The exalted diction of this mode contrasts sharply with the flat, quotidian vocabulary of the "civilization" that nature erases—often to almost comic effect. I used sound and syntax to create a comparable energy in English, often by maintaining equivalent patterns by breaking lines in syntactically unexpected places. Yet there's a risk, when intentionally breaking a line in an "awkward" place, that it will simply read as an "awkward" translation—the structure of the whole translation must support those choices.

I'm not the first person to say it, but I see translation as the most intimate act of reading possible. Translating Danz takes me deep into my internal wildernesses, until I'm ungrounded, not unlike what Danz says of Hölderlin, her greatest influence, entering "the impassable wilderness, that within him and that of the new era." Where is my language, indeed, between these two poems, one that I've read with such attention and one that came (in part) out of me?

Kaddish: For Miklós Radnóti

Radu Vancu
translated from the Romanian by Sean Cotter
Words Without Borders

My love after you pulled my body from the common
grave you found in my front coat pocket the notebook

with my last poems It was wet From the wet earth And from my body
that rotted & soaked the paper You dried them in the sun You sat

by the notebook & you waited for it to dry to see if the
poems could be read I thought you watched my body

evaporate from the notebook It evaporated from the poems And it was
a little strange that poems could appear only if my body evaporated

from them It was springtime I evaporated quickly & the poems
started to appear You read them & I watched you at the same time from

the air above where I had evaporated & from the common grave
where I was left & from the poems You didn't cry But I did You were

surprised to see the notebook wet again You started to blow on
it On me The more you blew the wetter the notebook got You
put it

in your pocket The heat of your body made me evaporate much
faster than the sun did The way sometimes I evaporated

from the sun & little death that rose together on your
face when you came When you took it back out just a minute
later perfectly

dry you didn't understand it I don't either my love I am
looking at you from the common grave Or maybe from

the poems In fact from both The air around you is me If
you feel the air & light suddenly make a kind of wet salt don't

be afraid It's just me It's just a poem

*

(If the light cries at what I write
it doesn't mean that I'm alive)

*

I could avoid remembering you my love but
simple things aren't worth doing Simple is a heart

when it dies it dies Simple is a brain
when it stops it stops

But a common grave is never simple Here everything simmers
even the blood Like in poetry Like in love You

were always our common grave my love In the first
seconds we went even further than blood

*

(Just because I write these poems
doesn't mean that I'm alive)

*

It's beautiful, the way hearts rise over our common
grave says Miklós Shhh say the dead let's not scare them

And we forget how hearts slide past above us
like fish of light Tight lines someone shouts from the

edge You scared them off you idiot shouts another
They're not scared dummy Some hearts drift lower

nearer The dead fidget like orphans on an adoption visit
I hear her says Miklós it's you Fanni Your heart is a salmon

of light It descends among the dead & starts to swim
toward me

*

My love when my flesh melted & saturated
the notebook in my pocket I knew that I had never

betrayed you more horribly Only your flesh had I ever entered
the way I did this paper No The opposite Only your flesh ever
    entered

me so deeply I soaked & waited for the
pages to start singing right there in the grave

the common grave The way my flesh sang after you soaked into it
The way it sang ceaselessly from when I saw you at the tram
    station

near Keleti & until the bullet went in my
neck here at Abda near Győr You won't believe

me when I say the bullet passing through a brain soaked in
you began to sing But the whole common grave will be

my witness it happened So there's this small problem
the pages didn't sing here with the bones The song

would have made us forget we'd lost our flesh Like
we did before To forget we had flesh After about 2 months

they took me out of the grave You were already back in Budapest
    on
Pozsony in our bed You took out the notebook from which

I had evaporated & you put it beside you in bed & you
opened it It started to sing like a music box You

lay there & listened carefully to ceaseless singing
from then june 1946 to february 2014 when

you got up from the bed & closed the notebook & came down
    here
beside me You embraced me & we started to soak into

each other quietly like into the ground Like into paper The
    common
grave suddenly began to sing like a

music box

*

The way you made Flammkuchen & got angry at the oven that
always burnt the bottom Even though you loved crispy things

The way you poured me more coffee from the ibrik
Even though you loved coffee The way you always gave me the

bigger share of crème brûlée Even though you loved that too The
    way
you translated Nerval's *Aurélia* & you got angry that he killed
    himself

before finishing it Even though you loved suicides The way you
    tried
to moan as little as possible when you came Even though you
    loved sex The

way you got angry when I came silently Even though
you loved silence The way you got angry you were 3 years younger

than me I'm obviously the older one you said

(You were right I would die at 35 & you at 102)

All this illuminates the common grave blindingly Almost as
much as you on sad days illuminated the grave below the sky

*

My attempt to catch light in phrases. Because, as Erigena says somewhere, *omnia quae sunt, lumina sunt.*

This is why I asked poetry to take words & build instruments to capture light & beauty. A word regulator to focus their light until it becomes incandescent. Beauty is hard, as the ancient Greeks said & Yeats & Pound. But it's the only meaning I can find for literature: to capture in words light & beauty. To use words like instruments for the eyes, not the ears; like instruments for sight, not hearing.

This is why I believe in literature that *we see*, that shines on the page like the play of light.

*

I know what you're wondering Yes they shot me here at Abda
near Győr Yes here is our common grave next to the

memorial Yes Fanni found me here after 2 years & moved
me to the Kerepesi cemetery in Budapest But I am

still in the common grave in Abda I still write in the common
grave Impossible to write anywhere else I know what you're

wondering Yes And you are reading me in the common
grave And the Starbucks where Vancu writes about

us is also the common grave And the pictures today from
the Webb telescope are also in the common grave Our bones

here in Abda are no less colorful
& sexy than the pictures of a universe that's been dead for 13

billion years Hi My name is Universe & I am a common
grave Hi My name is Literature & I am a common

grave Hi My name is Radnóti We know We know the bones
shout From the pyramids to Google Photos all we've done is

invent common graves for ourselves So yes That's how it is
Beside
these poems you lie beside a common grave

When you read them you disinter someone The bones in
them were alive & will be alive again But don't be scared From

here no one can move us If you read these poems
your bones & our bones will be happy & laugh together

in their grave We will watch together someone push
select all for all the images in the world Including

the ones from the Webb telescope & the first images of the
universe
We will then watch someone push *delete forever* We will

then listen carefully We will hear without much work how the
    bones
yours & ours laugh together here in the common grave

Translator's Note

Few recent books of poetry have made as much of an impact in Romania as Radu Vancu's lament for Miklós Radnóti, *Kaddish* (Bucharest: Casa de editură Max Blecher, 2023). Winner of two major literary prizes, shortlisted for two more, and reviewed in print, online, and over the radio more than thirty times, the book's retelling of Radnóti's story has demonstrated the social value of poetry, and the practice of the compassionate imagination. Radnóti, a Hungarian Jew, was murdered by the Hungarian Army in 1944, while on a forced march away from the Allied forces. A year and a half later, when the mass grave was exhumed, Radnóti's last poems were discovered inside his jacket. With horror and humor, Vancu's collection reimagines Radnóti's biography, his marriage with Fanni Gyarmati, and his murder and afterlife, as it questions the value of poetry in a world that includes mass graves.

I first heard Radnóti's story from Zsuzsanna Ozsvath and Frederick Turner, my colleagues at the University of Texas at Dallas. English-language readers should read their translations of his work in *Foamy Sky* (Princeton University Press, 1992). What attracted me to Vancu's work was not the revelation of this history but *Kaddish*'s resemblance to translation. While the poems do not bring Radnóti's own poems into Romanian, and while Vancu's loose couplets and edgy enjambments are far from Radnóti's aesthetic, Vancu's extension of his imagination to place his creative self in dialog with the suffering of a Jewish victim of fascism seems to me to embody the best impulses of translation. Without confusing himself with Radnóti in a maudlin manner, Vancu sits in a Sibiu Starbucks and employs his poetry in the service of a voice from another religion, language, and moment in history. In bringing these poems to English, I am learning from Vancu's example.

[THЭ ЯOOM]

Natalia Rubanova
translated from the Russian by Rachael Daum
128 LIT

"Our country needs you to set records!" They're everywhere, the cancerous cells of their speech: a model—smiling unnaturally, adeptly adjusted to the electorate's conception regarding the reproduction of the species, that is to say, motherhood (a colorful blouse; an apron; *natural,* barely perceptible makeup, etc. etc.)—embraces her three offspring. Consider, for example, lizards of the gecko family—Sana cautiously tries on her own voice—which will delay if they don't find *the second* 0.5, the unfertilized eggs which offspring will later hatch from; some like it hot foязэвeя![1] If only human females were capable of doing the same, the question of sperm quality would fall away entirely; however, if you know how to p r o p e r l y stimulate the unfertilized egg cell, it will start to divide—madness!—in a manner identical to our embrion. Such is the immaculate conception: but what, then, is v i c e, Mr. Deus? Calling coitus—any coitus, not necessarily mechanical—"lowly," "sinful," Thou automatically signest the verdict on Thine own offspring (who are, we observe, rather unsightly): well now! And Thou art imperfect, and Thine own program crashest: perhaps our little balloon is one of Thine many drafts, perhaps Thou simply t r y e s t to rewrite it all . . . In this, frankly speaking, sordid little business I am merely interested in the issue price: how many more litres of living blood must be transferred to Thine heavenly account, and perhaps by

1. As a result of parthenogenesis, only females are born.

legal processes—that is, by not going *AWOL*—to minimize the costs. That is, essentially, all.

Sana spreads her hands, and then, as though trying on something other than her voice, lightly does a handstand on the gymnastics bar.

There's no shadow on this planetling: nowhere to hide. In *situations* like this, they advise imagining a room. Or something like that: a bird-house, a burrow, a porch—whatever you have—and run, oh! Run, even if you only have one leg: never mind that *they* can't tell the prosthetic from the flesh, never mind: you'll get used to it soon, too.

So, run—no more breaks, enough experiments *in vivo*[2]. In the meantime the choice, as they say, is there (even if, on closer inspection, you have long been pinned): crawl, begone! Sperm—a sticky viscous murky slime, smelling of raw chestnuts, in every milliliter of which a hundred million living squirts amuse themselves with an *escape* attempt—behold the p r o g r a m Allegro barbaro[3], which you fear to read between the notes, despite your considerable age, just as you still fear the dark corridor, where there is: a boney hand—Yaga's? Kashchey's? The sorceress Bastinda's?—a rustling, tears on your little cheeks, "*Grannyyyyy!*" A boney hand, *they* say, is an archetype, tears dropped, last year's snow melted, and you never learned the most important thing.

I'll—*who's there?*—tell you about it: raw chestnuts, му dэaя, give off chlorine.

Imagine: excess is an essential condition. Thus, s/he is in a vast, luxuriously clutterless, absolutely white space, triggering no internal hysteria. Everything reflects here like proper mirrors, like in that film

---

2. An acute experience, without anesthesia.
3. B. Bartók's "Barbaric Allegro."

s/he peeped—"Quick, go back to sleep!"—during childhood: enfilades of rooms, the chiming of antique clocks, a beautiful and, naturally, unhappy неяоIne ("with long slim fingers and such pain in her eyes, that . . . "), pressing an unsent message to her bosom; and still these white dresses, corsets, parasols, all these ribbons and hats—and, naturally, wicker chairs (from the props department): white wicker chairs on a summer veranda.

The room. You have to imagine the damn room very clearly, come on! Okay now: in the center—a formidably sized divan (excess as an essential condition), covered in a snow white comforter.

The window is flung open: the wind rustles the curtains. Let's even say: *the finest, most innocent curtains.* Which, of course, is even worse. But—let it be, let it be so! Let the wind rustle *the finest, most innocent curtains,* it's not like this never happens. A few times s/he watched as the wind did that to the finest, most innocent curtains! Some sort of good fortune: you find yourself in some sort of perfect place, you're lying on some sort of perfect surface, and the air . . . Isn't that so? Are you ashamed? Relax: trying to translate jackal dreams to the dreams of the human embryo is a fool's errand for bewildered professionals, who document at which age you deigned to masturbate.

Now, give it a rest and don't ask any needless questions: we had a good half a page, huh? A real conglomeration. Well, come on then, let's go: Ready, set . . . Action!

Act like no one's home.

Translator's Note

This excerpt, "[тнэ яоом]" ([the room] in the Russian original), features the starting pages of Natalia Rubanova's 2013 novel *Spermatozoids,* which she considers her masterpiece. Among the accolades she has accumulated for her writing is the Nonconformism Prize—and this excerpt is a good example of why.

Casting her net wide, Rubanova draws in scientific fact, refers to pieces of classical music, makes allusions to Slavic folklore. She jams English words and letters between her Cyrillic ones. She forces the tempo with spaces lodged within words. Rubanova is a classically trained pianist, and she uses her background in music to play with tempo, strike dissonant chords, thunder through the mind of her reader. The result feels like a fever dream.

The attempt to cast a similarly functioning English is, of course, a challenge: in translating this excerpt, I mirrored Cyrillic letters into English words (visible in the title of the piece), consulted the King James Bible, revisited ghost stories. Rubanova's English is limited, but she is responsive, kind, and trusting with her text in translation. Occasionally in our work together I will read aloud from my translation, and her comments on the tempo and musicality will influence the next steps of my translation.

I have had the pleasure of working with Natalia Rubanova's writing for a number of years. I am pleased that, still, when I sit down with her texts, I never quite know what I'm going to get. What a t r e a t .

W for War

Fatemeh Shams
translated from the Persian by Armen Davoudian
Poetry Society of America

I wasn't a helmet
I wasn't a boot
I wasn't a bullet
I wasn't a tank

I wasn't a commander
I wasn't a private
a minefield, barbed wire
I wasn't a fort

I was a piece of a photograph
in the left breast pocket
over the warm blood
of a soldier's burst heart.

Translator's Note

Fatemeh Shams's "W for War" pits the power of the word against the sword. The speaker of the poem is not a tank, a bullet, or any other implement of war. It is, instead, a photograph—or rather "a piece of a photograph"—found in the pocket of a dead soldier. A portrait of the soldier's loved ones, a partner, or a family member, the photograph does not exactly represent or depict war, and yet it is undeniably affected by war. This photograph, representing war only indirectly, stands in for it in the same way that "W" can be said to stand "for War." The photograph shares, with poetic language, this strange mixture of directness and indirection: like a photograph in a breast pocket, the poet's task is to witness and record, close from the heart.

Loom

Florentino Solano
translated from Tu'un Savi to Spanish by the author and from Spanish by Arthur Malcolm Dixon
The Kenyon Review

My first word was "huipil."

Before I could walk,
my mother put a loom at my waist and told me,
"Weave your future with it."
And I started weaving time:
sometimes I stitched the future,
sometimes the past;
until one day, finally,
I learned to spin memory
to hide the pain.

Translator's Note

Florentino Solano is from the town of Metlatónoc in the state of Guerrero, Mexico. Metlatónoc is a community of the Ñuu Savi people, often called "Mixtec," whose name for themselves could be translated into English as "Rain People." Their name for their language, Tu'un Savi, could be translated as "Rain Word."

In 2021, Florentino received two of the world's most prestigious prizes for writing in Indigenous languages: the Indigenous Literatures of the Americas Prize (PLIA) for his nonfiction chronicle *Yaa táxá'á kàà tùxìi / La danza de las balas* and the Nezahualcóyotl Prize for Literature in Mexican Languages for his poetry collection *Tákúu ndi'i tachi si'í yu / Todas las voces de mi madre,* which includes the poem published here.

Like most of his readers, I came to Florentino as a translator. Like most writers working in Indigenous languages, at least in Mexico, he has assumed the double-duty of translating his own work into Spanish, such that it might be accessible to both a wider readership and prize-granting institutions. So, when translating Florentino, I know I am translating a translation.

This is central to my process. I know, because Solano says so, that the Spanish does not quite capture the Tu'un Savi. At the same time, I know every word in Spanish represents a choice on his part, and I seek to respect his choices. The result, in my estimation, is a translation that hews close to the previous link in the chain, trying to gather up all it can of its syntax, diction, and sound while knowing it can't carry everything.

I hope I have helped some small measure of "Loom" to weave out of one language and into another, like weft over warp, and I invite my fellow translators into English—from the Spanish or, I hope, from the Tu'un Savi—to add their own pick.

Instructions

Yordan Eftimov
translated from the Bulgarian by Jonathan Dunne
World Poetry Review

Stick your chin in the sand
to feel its hardness.
Now swim in it—
it is soft as air.
Breathe through its interior—
it is hollow.
Immerse yourself to the waist,
then to the neck.
Finally leave a straw
for looking in.
Dig yourself out—slowly.
Scoop two handfuls of sand,
generously pile them up, level them off,
and put them in your mouth.
Chew.
Then spit
without helping yourself with anything.
Let every grain
stuck to your lips, your eyes,
remind you how you went from being soft-bodied
to being a killer.

Translator's Note

Since the poet and I are both Classicists, I find his clear, direct style (and mischievous sense of humor) easy to follow. I have the same relationship with another Bulgarian poet, Iana Boukova, who also studied Classics. The poem is a succession of imperatives (using the informal "ti", not the polite form "vie"). That is, it is spoken to a friend. There are rarely more than five words to the line. It describes the process of burying yourself in the sand, then chewing two handfuls and spitting them out, to remind yourself where you have come from. Perhaps the main difference between the two languages is the way Bulgarian uses prefixes ("*na*tupchi", "*iz*ravni") where English uses an adverb or a preposition ("pile *up*", "level *off*"). It is amazing how much information the Bulgarian language can insert before a noun ("the long ago forgotten, much missed and difficult to understand once told to me by your uncle premise"), a construction that English almost always replaces with a relative clause. (Thank God for relative clauses!) Word order, of course, is different ("mek e", "soft [it] is"), like Yoda in *Star Wars*. And Bulgarian can omit the "of" between two nouns ("dve shepi pyasuk", "two handfuls *of* sand"), as it will omit the indefinite article "a/an" before a noun ("ubiets", "*a* killer") unless it wants to specify the number. I changed the ending slightly. In Bulgarian, it reads: "from soft-body / you have grown up to killer". I like the repetition in English: "you went from being soft-bodied / to being a killer".

Time Delivery

Hisham Bustani
translated from the Arabic by Thoraya El-Rayyes
Pilgrimage

I. WAITING FOR 0.01 SECONDS TO LAPSE

1

In her time zone, it is now eight minutes past midnight.

My world is one hour later than the actual time, and it never arrives. I wait for it, on a chair in the garden: now, she is going to send me a message but my phone is lying dead next to me. In a little while—I tell myself—her name will appear in my inbox, but letters fall without forming her name.

Without arriving. They never left to begin with, for them to arrive.

I leave myself in the garden chair, and go for a short walk. Nothing happens. Nothing at all. Me and the man waiting resemble each other. I circle him, contemplate him.

In the past, when I got hit by a car and hovered outside my body, I saw—from above—that body flung onto the asphalt, unmoving. And I saw those who gathered around him, and the ambulance, and the splattered blood.

Now, this body is not like that other. I am not watching myself from afar. That was me, and I am me: unseparated. A mirror of time is the translucent barrier between us. Time that is equivalent to precisely, exactly, one hour. One hour.

Tick.

Tick.

Tick.
Tick.

2

An hour is sixty minutes, and a minute is sixty seconds, and a second is split into infinite segments, and during that time, momentous events occur.

The universe exploded and expanded a million, million, million, million, million times during 0.01 seconds, and here I am sitting in that endless hour between a Beast of Doubt and a Beast of Waiting.

A distant heat pierces my eyes. I open them quickly: the sunrays of noon strike my pupils and I do not see a thing. It is now eight minutes past noon in her time zone, and my sun has started to descend. I am still alive but I am dying. I will join my phone that does not ring.

3

A few days ago, she told me that her lips had fornicated with someone else. That their red snakes had embraced as they went in and out of the two caves fitted together. Maybe he had licked her lips and held the lower one of them with his teeth, sucking it like I do to her. "Only for a couple of minutes . . . " she said, but I remember that the entire universe had formed in those 0.01 damn seconds. How many 0.01 seconds are there in two minutes?

4

There is a sound muddying the purity of my silence.

Tick.
Tick.
Tick.
Tick.

The walls are bare, and there is nothing under the couches.

Tick.

Tick.

Tick.

Tick.

I turn the drawers upside down, I root through the closets, I scatter the books.

Tick. Tick. Tick. Tick. Tick. Tick. Tick. Tick.

To the toolbox then. I lay myself out on the kitchen table and begin to saw a straight opening in my forehead, inserting a screwdriver and slanting it once, twice, three times—and the two halves separate. The sound becomes clear: Tick. Tick. Tick. Tick.

I take the clock out and hang it over the bed, then sit and sift through books of poetry and philosophy, looking for that phrase about memory remaining as an echo in the heads of the defeated, but I do not find it.

5

Tick. Tick. Tick. Tick.

She asks me: Then what?

I, too, am awaiting the explosion.

II. DESCENDING INTO THE ROCKY ABYSS

New Year's Eve had turned old, and so I awoke from the glasses of vodka that had played with my head to find a hand playing with my hair. It's her again. I used to know her, she visited me last New Year's Eve. She spends those decisive moments with me, between sobering up and the break of morning, then disappears.

"I don't have anywhere to stay."

I knew she would say that sentence and then—enchanted—I would be drawn along, out the bar door behind her.

The faint drizzle falling from the miserly sky made us hurry a little. Where will I find a pharmacy open at this hour? My penis, about to become erect, was occupying my thoughts. And the girl, was anonymous—I do not know her name and only see her at this particular time of year. I had to be careful. Where will I find an open pharmacy?

We get to the car, I opened the door for her and she stepped in like a queen and smiled, then we drove along a path covered in stones. As far as I know, we are in the city. A city that has a name—Amman—whose streets are paved with asphalt and covered in holes and speed bumps.

The stones were new.

There was no one in the street except for us, and the street was narrowing, constricting, besieging us from every direction as if we were moving in a tunnel. We are in a tunnel, and the car is panting and stumbling and choking.

Amman, city of stairs. This thought returned to me when our path ended in stairs.

"Alright, let's go down . . . "

I knew she would say that sentence then, bewitched, I would be drawn along out the car door after her.

Hop . . . hop . . . hop . . . She started to jump down. And what I saw was no ordinary stairway: every stair was lower than the one before it by the height of a single person. Every stair was suspended in the air like a floating platform surrounded by nothing. There was a lone railing at the right of the stairs, but: if the first stair was attached to the railing, then the next would be three people wide away from it, then the distance would alternate until the end. Beneath the stairs was an abyss embellished with protruding rocks, ensuring that a fall would not be a contemplative experience or one that was painful merely because it was terrifying.

Hop . . . hop . . . hop . . . Here she is jumping like a mountain goat, like a child playing hopscotch in front of the house. As for me, the vodka in my head tells me: don't do it.

I assure myself that I am rational, and that my life is more valuable than a woman who suddenly appears to me once a year then disappears. More valuable than a penis wrapped in a condom, more valuable than the magic drawing me along by my shirt collar. That is what I said, and when I decided to listen to myself, people appeared behind me walking towards the stairs with heavy steps and a light wind started to blow, sending plastic bags and newspaper sheets flying.

The arch-backed old woman was able to jump on to the first stair by leaning against the railing but her next jump became impossible so she got stranded.

The Egyptian labourer—taken with his own agility—jumped one stair, then another, then another, then was betrayed by a newspaper sheet stuck on the edge of a stair that was far from the railing. Under it was empty space and he fell in. From him came the sound of three screams after three collisions, so that my heart turned into a vast room with horrifying echoes ricocheting off its walls.

As for her, she beckoned me to come along. She had reached somewhere around the middle of the stairs, while at the bottom of the stairs, a shop appeared lit up with the logo of a snake and chalice. It too beckoned me to come along.

The old woman sat on the first stair, spread out her sheet and started to beg. The New Year's Woman continued her descent and disappeared. The stones turned back into holes in the street, and as for me, a noise of some sort is muddying the purity of my silence:

Tick

Tick.

Tick.

Tick.

The hands of the clock move towards me with sharp nails, ready to kill. I am between the pincers of Tariq bin Ziyad: the stairs of the abyss before me, and the clawed fingers of time behind me. There is nothing for me but a collision.

The hands of time.
Tick. Tick. Tick. Tick.
She asks me: Then what?
I, too, am awaiting the explosion.

III. THE INEVITABLE AGE OF SAND

A sea of sand surrounds me. I cannot see its individual grains and my hands cannot push aside its clumps.

The tide of this sea attacks sometimes when I am sitting on the balcony, turning a demitasse of coffee and finding shapes on its inside walls. There, too, I see sand surrounding me and I suffocate though I know I am sitting on the balcony watching cars and smelling their exhaust fumes.

It might not be sand. It might be exhaust fumes that surround me. It might be the grounds of coffee gathered in my cup that surround me. It might be the rays of the sun condensed into granules of light that surround me.

There is someone else with me. Is that also me? Could it be that I am sitting with myself? But the other person sits in the opposite chair, puts one leg over the other and jiggles the first. Could it be me? I don't know. The olive tree opposite our house is laughing at me/us, so she hits it—the woman standing under it with a stick. Then I hear the groan of the olive tree as its fruits fall on pieces of cloth made to gather all that pain.

Next to it, I hear another olive tree in pain. Its screams are a few more fruits falling on a piece of cloth in the street. Do you hear it like I do, you sitting opposite me in the chair on the balcony? They will compress those screams in glass jars with salt and water.

Salt.

Sand.

Coffee.

Exhaust fumes.

Smoke.

And we all get pickled in that glass jar.

I am going to tell him what I think of him. Him, sitting opposite me in the chair on the balcony. I don't know if he will like what I am going to say. He is not that important. He can go to hell. Who said I am capable of feeling anything towards another thing? But his presence terrifies me, awakens in me that particular instinct: survival. Does he want to kill me? Does he want to crush me? Will he swiftly bring his shoe down on my head? Slowly, I started to creep along the wall, then started to crawl.

Ah, he has gone. But I am still pulling myself along the floor and have become convinced that the ceiling of the world is right above my head. When I raise my arms, they collide with the ceiling. It pains me that I am confined in that narrow space which is as tall as I am. I am short, but nevertheless my head keeps colliding with the ceiling of the world when I try to stand up.

I tried to push it. To lift it. It would not budge but dropped towards me, cramming me in even more. Anger will not do me any good now as I will be crushed between sky and earth and in that narrow space—shrink, becoming shorter.

A clock is ticking somewhere, every movement of its arm makes me feel my height being pressed down. I will return to my bed of sand, I know it will swallow me and that this warm vortex will take me below.

But at least my height will stay as it is, or even increase a little.

Tick. Tick. Tick. Tick.

It is a sand hourglass. It is not supposed to make noise. But—oh, misery—here, everything is possible.

Tick. Tick. Tick. Tick.

She asks me: Then what?

I, too, am awaiting the explosion.

IV. AT THE STATION

So, we have to die here . . . as we wait for a country that does not arrive.

A country? It is you who names the country. You who blows the spirit into it. You who fashions it into a pillow for your head and a mattress for your body.

I tried. I grasped handfuls of earth and smelled it. I played hide-and-seek with the neighbors' children. I visited my grandmother every week—she used to make me cake. All of that didn't mean a thing. And there, where there are no children, grandmothers, or earth, it also did not mean a thing to me. My real homeland is: waiting.

Listen: I was born in a lemon tree. Can you believe it? I mean that my first memory was between its branches, and they told me that after my first year they dripped lemon in my mouth. "These countries melt iron, so how about what they do to people?" My father used to say, and squeeze the sour liquid, passing it to me. That is why my skin thickened and I stopped complaining.

You listen: There is a sun that sets, and there is a man standing inside a plate of mountains—he is me. One of them poured soup over my head. One of them shot at me, and many stabbed me in the back. Look at it, riddled with holes like a sieve. I hear the melody of a funeral. The bugle call of last return. Do you remember it? They used to play it as The Leader watered The Tree of Life, accompanied by wind instruments through which ran the breath of a bunch of clowns. Maybe one of them took a piss in the gold-plated watering jug. Listen, don't talk to me about sour lemons and thick skin. My hand is a crystal cup, and my mind is a time bomb.

Tick. Tick. Tick. Tick.

Can you hear it?

Then what are you waiting for?

I think the situation has become clear. I am awaiting the explosion.

Translator's Note

I am lucky enough to be a native speaker of both English and Arabic. As a teenager, I used to watch American movies on Jordanian television and I was preoccupied with the Arabic subtitling. Much to the annoyance of anyone watching with me, I would start a running commentary of all the subtitling mistakes. Having a native understanding of the cultural connotations of literary works in both languages is a privilege many literary translators do not have.

The things I struggle with most when translating from Arabic are word order and musicality. Arabic sentences tend to begin with action and the reader has to continue reading to know who does what. I think this structure creates a kind of tension in the act of reading. It can be difficult to translate this feeling into English.

Arabic also flows more smoothly than English does. There are diacritical marks at the end of Arabic words that make nearly every word end with a vowel. Each word sounds as if it flows into the next. This can make it very hard to retain the musicality of the original Arabic work, which is particularly problematic in translating Hisham's work. Initially, I try to do as much as possible on my own as I would like the translation to reflect a reader's perspective on the text, rather than the author's. For words or phrases that I find challenging, I go back to Hisham and discuss several alternative translations. I would find it difficult to finish the translation without these conversations; they have become an important part of my process.

This story references Tariq bin Ziyad, an Umayyad Empire Islamic military commander. Upon the arrival of his troops on the shore of the Iberian peninsula, it is said that he burned his ships and in a speech to his soldiers said, "Where is there to escape? Behind you is the sea, and before you the enemy. There is nothing for you but steadfastness and patience."

Not Just Passing

Heba Abu Nada
translated from the Arabic by Huda Fakhreddine
ArabLit and *Mizna*

Yesterday, a star said
to the little light in my heart,
We are not just transients
passing.

Do not die. Beneath this glow
some wanderers go on
walking.

You were first created out of love,
so carry nothing but love
to those who are trembling.

One day, all gardens sprouted
from our names, from what remained
of hearts yearning.

And since it came of age, this ancient language
has taught us how to heal others
with our longing,

how to be a heavenly scent
to relax their tightening lungs: a welcome sigh,
a gasp of oxygen.

Softly, we pass over wounds,
like purposeful gauze, a hint of relief,
an aspirin.

O little light in me, don't die,
even if all the galaxies of the world
close in.

O little light in me, say:
Enter my heart in peace.
All of you, come in!

Translator's Note

I first came upon Heba Abu Nada's work after she was murdered on Oct. 20, 2023 by an Israeli airstrike. A video of her reading a short poem posted by people who knew her kept popping up on my social media timeline. I was devastated by the loss of this brilliant young poet and felt guilty for having only learned about her so late. This is a guilt we, across the Arab world and the world, all share towards Gaza. Heba lived most of her life under siege and the entire world was silent and complicit.

In November 2023, *Protean Magazine* editors Jake Romm and Dominick Knowles proposed that I translate a poem by Heba and, in that, I found a calling. Heba's poem "I Grant You Refuge" circulated widely. I started getting emails from all around the world asking about Heba and her poem, and expressing admiration of her unique, measured, yet defiant poetic voice. I was devastated. Heba should have been receiving these messages, not me. She should have been here to see the light she brought to the world in the darkest of moments. I lost sleep for days until I was finally able to connect with her family who were sheltering in Khan Younis. Her sister Somaia responded to me with graciousness and generosity. I shared the translation and asked for her permission to translate more. Somaia is intent on publishing all her sister's works once the horror in Gaza ends. I would be honored to play any role in that. May Heba's voice resonate forever and may Palestine soon be free.

Two Notes on The Scream

Edvard Munch
translated from the Norwegian by Eirill Alvilde Falck
The Kenyon Review

Sketch 2367

I walked along
the road with two
friends—then
{I walked} the sun set
Suddenly bloodred
Skies
~~—and I felt~~
~~as a gasp of melancholy~~
~~—a sucking pain~~
~~under the heart—~~
I stopped, leaned
against the fence, tired
as death—over the
blue-black fjord and city
hovered blood <in> blazes
My friends walked
on and I stood
lone, quivering
with anxiety—
and I felt coursing through
nature a gre{a}t
unending shri{e}k

Note 69

One evening I walked
along a road with On one side
the city and fjord—
~~—The Sun set—the Skies~~
~~. . .~~ I was weary and ill—I stood
staring out over the fjord—
and let my friends walk on.
The sun set—and the air—hued
red—as blood—
—I felt a shriek—pass
nature—I nature—I felt
I heard a shriek—
—I painted this [painting]—I painted
the air and skies as blood—
—the painting {s}Shriek!—in the frieze of life.

Translator's Note

During a tour of Edvard Munch's home and studio in Åsgårstrand, Norway, the guide described the transformation the house underwent after Munch's death. Munch, who spent his final days in Oslo, had left the Åsgårstrand home unkempt: floor strewn with clothes, little bottles in disarray, an anthill in the attic so large it threatened the structural integrity of the house. Munch, I learned from the guide, had been aware of the anthill and let it be; the ants, he told friends, were good company. Mice were equally welcome. He intentionally left his kitchen cabinets open for them when he traveled, lest they go hungry.

I understood why the museum staff had removed the anthill and the rodent snacks. But why had it been necessary to tidy the bottles? Hang his clothes and hat on hangers, neatly arrange his desk?

When I read Munch's journals, at the archives of the Munch Museum in Oslo, I was transfixed. Most of all, by the series of painstaking attempts he'd made at capturing the experience that birthed his most famous motif, *The Scream*. In translating the journals, I sometimes imagined the pages as rooms in the Åsgårstrand home. I imagined what I would and wouldn't do if I'd been tasked with opening the home to visitors. I imagined, or couldn't at all imagine, closing the cabinets.

An excerpt from *A Plan to Save the World*

Hassan Akram
translated from the Arabic by Ibrahim Fawzy
Consequence

> "If you want to save the world, you should first take care of your money." —My grandmother

I was born in the midst of an endless war. I grew up and reached the height of a tall sunflower, and the war was still going on. Or if it had ended, another one must have taken over because I never noticed. That's why I devised a plan to save the world. For a start, gunmen from every corner of the world would be gathered. They'd then get crammed into huge barrels and pushed down a cliff. This plan would hopefully bring my people back to life. If it worked, I'd wear my rain jacket and stroll the streets. The sky wouldn't be enveloped in dark clouds, nor would we come across colonizers' eyes peeking out of high-speed jeeps as they shout, "Get outta here!"

I don't particularly mean this ongoing war. I mean all the wars I witnessed or heard about and the wars yet to come. "If the man couldn't find anyone to argue with," my uncle once said, "he would start arguing with himself." I dare not claim to hold the keys of wisdom, for my years are still tender. Honestly, I never admire this serenity always striking me. It is as if our bodies and minds have ripened, under the heat of war, before the time is right. So here we are, old children, and we have the right to plan to save the world.

The saga of the long war haunts me. It goes with me everywhere.

It shares my food. It nests in my head. I find it difficult to sneak away from it. This saga clings to me like a faithful shadow, woven into the fabric of my very being. My mother narrated my very first days in this world meticulously. I was born in the attic at dawn. I was adorable and healthy except for a big nose inherited from my father and a slight outward curvature in my feet.

Families usually name their newborns right away. The first child may have his name even before the parents are married. During their clandestine rendezvous, six months before marriage, my auntie and her husband had agreed on the name of their first baby. In my case, I was born nameless and remained so for two whole days. My parents didn't even take a minute to think about my name. Wars divert people's attention away from everything but to reflect on how to elude the clutches of death. I can't remember my first encounter with this world. The lightness of my heart had filled my soul until my name, heavy as a stone, came crashing down upon my chest.

My elder uncle named me when he came over to congratulate my parents. Once arrived, he asked my name. Surprised that I hadn't yet been named, he gazed at my countenance for a little while. "Hassan," my uncle turned to my father standing by the door and said, "This name absolutely fits him but for his big nose."

This was how I got my name and grew up, catching up to my big nose till this very moment I'm writing down these words.

•

My mother had joined the university to study English literature, but unfortunately, she didn't complete her studies. Her father recommended her husband, and she just said yes, having no other option. She gave birth to me and my sibling here in Basra, Iraq.

Our house was big. My mother was responsible for all the housework: cleaning the house, feeding us, caring for my brother and me, and on top of all that, tolerating our whimpering. Whenever I felt hungry, I'd get into the kitchen and neatly write "hungry" on the wall with chalk. Sometimes, though, I would just write the letter H. I was in awe of her patience. She'd tell me that the food would be ready in a minute and would wipe the "hungry" off the wall. When she returned home late one day, I knew she had visited our neighbor's house to wash dishes and clean the floor. She told me that she did so for her brother Sa'doon.

Our neighbor was an officer in the Iraqi armed forces. That day he had the military unit head over for lunch. My mother begged him to ask the head to drop the charge of dereliction of duty from her brother, who had fled the war. Our neighbor agreed, but only if she would wash the dishes and clean the floor after the party.

"Why do you do it?" I asked.

"I don't know! It seems that a woman's job entails enduring humiliation for their children and siblings," she said in a sorrowful voice.

I usually helped my mother do housework. I adored her lovely smile whenever I collected bread from atop the wicker mat. We had two ovens: one was metal in the small yard behind our home, and the other was made of mud bricks built on the roof, where we'd grill fish.

Stuck with nothing to do, I'd pick up the phone to call my grandmother. I'd try for twenty, thirty, forty, and even a hundred times until I'd finally hear my grandmother's voice on the other side. Hearing her voice, I'd call my mother to come in so they could talk. I'd hide behind the door, eavesdropping. My mother would bewail her wretched state. She didn't only wash dishes and clean the house, but she also fixed the holes in the walls, reconnected broken electric wires, raised chickens, and even washed my uncle's clothes as we lived in the family house. "Why should I do all these tiring tasks?" My mother would ask. My grandmother, unmoved, would narrate her story, which seemed to be a story of all women. In her youth, she was fraught with struggles and dark moments like her daughter's. She'd wrap up her talk to remind my mother of me and my brother. My mother would let out a warm gust of air from her lungs, uttering: "Nothing compels me to endure throughout this period, except for these ladybugs." Most likely, we were those ladybugs.

One night, my father came home with red eyes, singing in a broken voice. When my mother confronted him, he punched her in the face, leaving her crumpled on the ground. My mother cried and cried until she got tired and fell asleep. Hidden under the blanket, my brother and I fell into a deep slumber.

•

The way to school hinted that we were on the brink of war—sandbags in the entrances of buildings, some of which would surround a firearm aimed at the sky. With our teacher Mr. Hady we would do daily morning exercises that weren't just physical movements but a way to gear us up for war. Mr. Hady would say, "We are all willing to sacrifice our lives for the sake of the nation and its president." Sometimes he would put the president first. Even though he'd been teaching family education for the last few years, he thought he was better than that. He wore his military uniform to school and was overly attentive to his pistol. He'd sometimes pick up his gun, breathe out a puff of vapor, polish it with a tiny piece of cloth, and place it back in its holster. This regular action might have frightened my fellow schoolmates, but it never worked with me because my father had bought me a plastic pistol on Eid al-Fitr.

The country would mobilize everyone, even children, to resist the colonizer. We'd start school every morning with Mr. Hady's exercises, which he called "war exercises." These exercises would include three movements depending on our ability to endure. "Hands up. Jump. One, two, three. Jump. One two three. Jump," Mr. Hady would shout, then ask: "What would you do if you were holding a gallon of petrol and saw the enemy's tanks coming at you?"

"We'd burn it, sir."

On our way home, I saw fear in the eyes of the passersby. When I got home, I saw it in my mother's eyes.

"Mom, why are you so afraid?" I once asked, "If the enemy's jeep comes, it will be burnt."

"Who's the feeble-minded who told you that?" She asked in a sarcastic tone as she scoffed.

"Mr. Hady!"

"Oh, war ruins everything, even the teacher's mind."

At night, the first missile slipped into the river. We didn't hear it, but my father did. He had trained ears to capture the slightest sounds. He anticipated the next missile and sent us each to a different corner of the room.

"When missiles fall," said my father, "homes are stripped naked, and nothing will remain but these corners. Never leave your place no matter how loud it gets."

I didn't care. I wasn't afraid. I just wanted to piss. My mother laughed, "It's not your bladder. You're just afraid."

The toilet was outside, near the garden, and the adults wouldn't let me go. My mother brought me an empty bottle to do my business. I couldn't even unzip my pants in front of my cousin, but it got a little bit easier when she asked for one too. I ignored the sound of the explosions and my mother's praying to Allah to spare us. Since everyone was preoccupied with the war, I realized that was my opportunity to watch my cousin pee. Fatima noticed me glancing at her and pulled up her pink dress. I saw her underwear.

Suddenly, the sound of a missile shook our home. My cousin jolted and dropped the bottle. Urine splashed all over her dress. I realized war ruins everything, even the underwear.

Translator's Note

In the realm of contemporary Arabic literature, fiction emerges as a transformative force, capable of reflecting and transcending real-life experiences, especially in the midst of conflict and societal upheaval. The post-2003 Iraq witnessed a significant shift in novel writing. Pre-2003 war literature often celebrated political figures and valor in times of conflict. But, the aftermath saw a surge in literary output, with novels offering a myriad of perspectives on the enduring anguish and fear born from years of turmoil.

Hassan Akram's *A Plan to Save the World* deftly navigates the aftermath of the American invasion of Iraq, presenting a narrative that boldly defies conventional genre boundaries. *A Plan to Save the World* belongs almost everywhere. It can be read as a novel, an autobiography, and a meditation on life and war, all seen through the eyes of an innocent child. This perspective offers a fresh and poignant exploration of the human experiences and repercussions of conflict.

Akram's narrative technique is notable for its use of fragmented scenes, which offer a satirical lens on reality. This approach allows for a critique of both conventional warfare and societal conflicts deeply rooted in tradition. This satirical lens adds a layer of complexity to the novel's exploration of conflict. *A Plan to Save the World* serves as a platform for incisive social commentary, inviting the reader to deeply reflect on the profound ramifications of armed conflicts. This depth of exploration fosters a sense of thoughtfulness and reflection, making the novel a compelling read for those interested in contemporary Arabic literature.

Lili in Her Forest

Elsa Drucaroff
translated from the Spanish by Slava Faybysh
New England Review

In all the houses of the children who go to kindergarten with Lili, there's always a mother at home all day. All of them. But not in Lili's house—*her* mother leaves in the morning with her father and comes back at night. She's a lawyer. It's the 1960s.

The girl thinks her mother is beautiful and tall; she stands out everywhere she goes because, besides being beautiful and tall, she wears strange dark glasses encrusted with small pearls, and colorful clothes—*different* clothes. She especially stands out because she talks different, utters long, self-assured sentences that Lili, since she's only four, cannot yet describe as having complex syntax; Lili nonetheless recognizes the distinctive rhythms, the strange sparkle of her words, and the unsettled looks—the respect and even the fear in the expressions of the men who listen to her firm, feminine voice—the rare times Lili and her mother go out together to a department store or when they run into an acquaintance from the neighborhood. With her complex syntax, Lili's mother utters very self-assured ideas about women and their rights. Lili listens but doesn't understand much, although her mother always says that these matters should concern her; in any case, Lili's mother does not want her daughter's hair to be uncombed; she does not want her daughter to get her lacy pink dress dirty if she has Sunday visitors; and she had Lili's tiny earlobes pierced with gold studs, against the feeble objections of her husband.

In Lili's house, there may not be a mother there all day, but there *is* a woman all day. Lili's mother calls this woman "the employee" and speaks to her with the formal *usted*. Everyone else calls her "the girl," "the maid," or "the servant," but in Lili's house, these words are pooh-poohed and are considered expressions of social injustice. Lili's mother instructed her that she should use the formal *usted* when speaking to this woman who is always in their home, because even if in many other homes (so says her mother) they use the informal *vos* and call "the employees" any old thing, in their home, they say "employee" and use the formal *usted*. Therefore, Lili says *usted* to Mirta, who is there all day and has her own small bedroom and bathroom past the laundry; and she also says *usted* to Ester, who only comes and does some work a few times a week, and then leaves. Mirta and Ester clean, iron, and cook. And they take care of Lili.

Although there's not much to take care of. On schooldays, they take her to kindergarten in the morning. Lili's mother chose this school because it has an extended day schedule. This expression, extended day schedule—Lili's mother likes it a lot, and she says it so enthusiastically that Lili thought it was a marvel of some sort; it was like a benevolent fairy wrapped in a pink silk dress, with a crown of sparkly fragrant flowers on a long mane of hair. But then she was disappointed: extended day schedule just meant there was a classroom and a yard, and she had to spend long hours with other children who all looked alike but didn't look anything like her; and she received orders from two very tall and skinny schoolmistresses who always ran after her when she escaped from the classroom—which is to say, a lot—and they squeezed her arm so hard when they caught her that they gave her bruises.

In extended day schedule, Lili sometimes tries to obey, but it always goes very wrong; and the schoolmistresses get *so* mad at her that they grab her by that very same arm and shake her hard. One time, Lili said, "You're a stupid," to one of the girls, and the girl ran straight to the schoolmistress and told on her; then the schoolmistress came shouting, "What did you say to this girl?" So Lili told her the truth. After all, this schoolmistress always said, "One must never tell a lie," and Lili merely wanted to be obliging: "Stupid!" said Lili. Then the schoolmistress raised her voice even more. "Insolent child, I'd like to hear you say it again!" So Lili obliged once more: "Stupid!" she said. "Say it one more time," roared the schoolmistress, "and I'm calling your mamá!"; and the prospect of seeing her mother made Lili quite happy, so she went and said it yet again. But even though she did just what her schoolmistress said, she did not get to see her mother; instead, she got herself another bruise on her arm and she was put in detention at recess, during which time she cried nonstop.

Although Lili doesn't use this word—because she's only four—she understands that obeying is *problematic*: not everything people say they want is what they really want. Another time, she obeyed her mother, and it was a disaster. Lili loves her mother so much; she's so beautiful, it's as if she's surrounded by an aura of light. If Lili is lucky enough to be up when her mother gets home, it makes her very happy. One time, her mother and father came home while she was having her dinner; they were carrying some bundles of flyers from the union hall where they both worked as lawyers. The flyers were calling for a general strike against the military government, starting the next day; but Lili did not know how to read, nor did she know what a general strike was. Nevertheless, Lili's mother said to her, "Tomorrow there's going to be a general strike, and all your schoolmistresses should read *this* instead of going to work." So, Lili put a bunch of these papers into her little schoolbag, onto which the employee Mirta had chain-stitched her first and last name, and in which there was always a plastic cup. The next day, Mirta dropped her off at kindergarten; Lili took out the papers and went over to her schoolmistress. "Mi mamá said that there's a general strike today, and you have to read this," she said, giving her a flyer. And during recess, she went from teacher to teacher, handing out flyers from her little pack.

The next day when Lili arrived at school with Mirta, they said the girl was not allowed in, and Lili's mother was to speak with the headmistress. Lili's mother was very angry at her because she had to take time off from work and go to the school. On their way out, Lili knew it was all her fault that she was going to have to change kindergartens, and besides that, it was going to be very difficult because there were almost no other schools with extended day schedules.

Nor could anyone get into a kindergarten at this time of year; so now Lili plays by herself on the floor, without other kids to bite, other kids who are all the same—but she does not run the risk of being obedient. Parked on the floor in her room, she thinks up stories about her toys: she talks to herself, whispers and hums, and makes the many wood and plastic objects converse with each other with different voices; she makes them fight, hit each other; she lifts them from the rug, shakes them, and scolds them; and she exiles them to inhospitable places, buries them beneath the rug, wedges them in under the feet of the bed, looks for dark corners where they'll be scared, where they'll suffer, where they'll always regret whatever bad thing they did. When she gets tired of playing like this, she plays something else: she puts one hand over the other between her legs, and squeezes hard with her hips; she rubs herself rhythmically, faster and faster, until she starts seeing strange, unwholesome images in her mind. She moves and sweats until a very strong sensation comes over her which she calls "I don't know what I want." When I don't know what I want comes, everything disappears; she herself disappears, and loses herself in herself; Lili thoroughly transforms into ignorant bliss, an infinite don't-know, yes-want; and, lost inside herself, Lili is very happy until the sensation wears off. Then she stays very still and relaxed—and sad because she knows there is something wicked and dark in this thing that she likes so much.

One time, Ester and Mirta scolded her and said, "disgusting." So she learned to do it when they were in another part of the house;

she learned to preemptively let go of herself and stay completely still, sweaty, breathing heavily whenever she heard footsteps.

This time it's already after dark when the footsteps come, luckily just after I don't know what I want has concluded; so she's waiting for them, pretending to be asleep on the rug. Mirta taps her awake and tells her that she and Ester have to leave immediately, before the shops close, and Lili is coming with. But Lili's mother said that she was supposed to take a bath that evening; Mirta remembers this suddenly and seems to be kicking herself over their lack of planning. She quickly gets Lili's clothes off, takes her to the bathtub, helps soap her up, rinses her off, and leaves her wrapped in an enormous towel while she goes and grabs some fresh clothes. Lili lets Mirta put a dress on her, along with some short socks, and her Guillermina leather shoes. Mirta works hastily. "And that's that!" she says when she's done, pulling at Lili's hair with a comb. It hurts, but Lili doesn't complain because the only thing on her mind at this moment is that Mirta forgot to put panties under her sundress. She thinks about telling her, but doesn't; she stays meekly quiet until Mirta says to Ester, "Ready? Let's go," and takes Lili by the hand, Lili without her panties. They seem very worked up about going out, and they keep talking amongst themselves about something that seems important. On the sidewalk, holding Mirta's hand, Lili is focused on the breeze caressing her vulva, and the sticky wetness between her legs.

They walk to the square, where there are no cars, and the businesses are still open for their last customers. When the two women stop to do some window shopping, Lili coughs softly and feels something open up a little down below; then she makes it open intentionally, squeezing tightly afterwards, playing. She feels as if a soft, dark snail is crawling inside her; she can feel its salty dribble, the same liquid that coats her hand after I don't know what I want; something mysterious and warm is set free between her thighs, and it is struck by a light wind when Mirta yanks Lili's hand. "Let's go, before they close on us," says Mirta, as if *she* hadn't been the one who'd stopped in front of the window.

But they don't close on them. Mirta and Ester buy something—Lili didn't catch what it was—something they must like a lot since they give little shrieks of joy. What Lili does see in this shop, into which she walked with her flesh exposed to the air, is a lady who offers her a piece of candy, and a man at the register who smiles and asks her what her name is. "I'm Lili and I'm not wearing my panties," she thinks, but she just says, "Lili," slowly; and she keeps looking at the man, who will not get any more answers from her now, since Lili doesn't plan on informing him how old she is and whether she goes to kindergarten and whether she loves her mother or her father more; Lili doesn't even listen to his questions, just looks at his friendly face and thinks, "He doesn't know I'm not wearing my panties. He keeps talking to me, and he doesn't know I'm not wearing my panties." Lili knows that if he knew, he wouldn't be talking to her this way. He wouldn't love her; he would turn red, purple, he wouldn't be able to breathe; he would be like her schoolmistress when she answered her question, like her mother when she found out Lili had passed out those flyers; he'd take away her candy; an enormous slash would cut open the kindly smile of this man, would cut open this entire shop, the street, the police officer who was directing traffic; everything would be swallowed up in a big black tunnel if anyone found out she wasn't wearing panties. But no one is going to find out, thinks Lili, and a strange and uneasy feeling of happiness tingles between her legs. No one will find out because Lili is the only one who knows. Ester and Mirta are rambling on about something at the counter; the candy lady is recommending something; the man at the register keeps pressing her with questions, and now he is saying she is shy; and Lili smiles because there's no fabric adhering to her labia, nothing to hold back the wetness, and something is happening there that's completely different from what's happening to everyone else in *their* down-belows. Lili feels uncomfortable; Lili is scared; she is happy; she is in the midst of an adventure.

When they get home, she wants to pee, and they take her to her training pot. Ester and Mirta shriek and they laugh. They are worried and grab their heads with their hands. They bombard her with questions: Why? What were you thinking, not telling us? Why didn't you say anything? How could you have let us take you out like this? Lili looks them in the eyes, watches them flail their arms about, hears them repeat the same questions over and over. She doesn't open her mouth. She doesn't have an answer to their questions, but even if she did, she wouldn't say anything. At four years old, she has plenty of experience with the drawbacks of obeying, and that evening she discovered the power of the mysterious blackness climbing inside her, towards her belly; now she knows that that power resides in secrecy.

The forest of I don't know what I want was exposed to the air, and there, in the space between her legs, it disobeyed the world. She is the master of her silence and master of her forest, and she is safe in that knowledge. From that moment, something begins.

Translator's Note

What makes Elsa Drucaroff's writing unique is that each piece of her writing is unique. It's almost as if she is five different authors at once. Her historical thriller *Rodolfo Walsh's Last Case* is written in a cinematic noir style, with short, punchy sentences, short paragraphs and short chapters, and the description is mostly "outside-in": readers have to infer inner psychological states from outward descriptions. In contrast, her novella *Birds Hitting Glass* uses long sentences and long paragraphs, and blends descriptions, characters' thoughts, dialogue without quotation marks, and action in a somewhat jumbled, half-stream-of-consciousness style that becomes increasingly surreal as the story progresses.

Therefore, one might say that, like a translation, her original work is itself a reenactment of a particular style, and my translation is a reenactment of a reenactment (which actually does not make the process any different). What I love most about "Lili in Her Forest" is the way that it seems to fuse an adult's voice with a child's voice, a voice that I have not seen replicated in any of Drucaroff's other works that I've read so far.

Before the Earthquake

Salah Badis
translated from the Arabic by Saliha Haddad
The Markaz Review

Winter became short, less than three months with rain falling only for a few days. The day I left my architectural tutorials at Bab Ezzouar University it was raining. I don't remember if it was a Tuesday or a Wednesday. I took the train. Every day the trains carry people between Algiers and its eastern suburbs, every single day—students, workers and the jobless. The trains watch them grow, fall in love, break up and then return them back drunk, sad or happy. The trains offer them empty seats, or a few centimeters in which to stand. The trains collect them from the station platforms and throw most of them out onto the platform of Reghaïa. You should all see how the train empties at Reghaïa—suddenly, all at once.

Mom left the laundry receipt on the fridge, sticking it on with a small, magnetic plastic orange. She'd done it before she left for my sister's house on Monday. This way she was sure I wouldn't forget the coat. We never neglect retrieving our things, neither clothes from the laundromat, nor the baklava trays from the baker. She also said that she was staying at my sister's, in Tipaza, until the weekend, which meant that I would be alone in our apartment.

On that first night I ate some of the lentils she'd left, and peeled two oranges. Many people avoid coffee and oranges in the evening. I never think of doing this, sleeping for me is like a train making its way through the night . . . nothing stops it.

•

I got off the train, amidst the human wave. I walked from the station to the post office, and turned left towards the laundromat. There wasn't a sunrise for there had to be a sunset; the sky was dark. When I opened the glass door to the laundromat, it was like stepping inside a dimly lit bubble of warmth.

I love Reghaïa, but it's an old love. I love what Reghaïa used to be—before the earthquake when the number of its inhabitants was small and the place calm. But now it's becoming worse every day: The sidewalks are crumbling and their tiles are broken underfoot, especially in winter. All my memories of this place are related to childhood. I feel like some kind of a cocoon has been punctured and I am waiting for the right time to fly away but I don't know which horizon to go towards, although the sea is always beautiful.

I took out the laundry receipt and presented it to the employee, who took it and disappeared behind a huge washing machine. I waited for him, with thoughts of Reghaïa swirling around my head. On my left, covering the entire wall, was a huge poster I'd never noticed before. It was of Building 15, which had collapsed in the last earthquake, and while the picture was a bit blurry because the poster zoomed onto a small picture, it was the building. I remembered it.

Mom says that I look like my father when I spread out my papers and architectural drawings in the living room, close the door, and become sensitive to the least bit of movement or noise. Maybe it's true; mothers always attributed the bad traits of their children to their fathers. But it isn't true. What I really want, is to be left alone. That's why I'm always thinking of going away.

I like being home alone for the longest possible time, even though I'm the only one living with Mom since my sister married. Particularly in winter, I feel like I'm living in a faraway place, as if no one knows me, as if my days here are stolen days from a future life.

I waited in the laundromat. I looked at the racks of clothes, hanging above the old washing machines. They resembled a dark cloud suspended from the ceiling, or a black hole, from where the dim, heavy light entered the shop and drowned everything in it. There were many pants and coats—I don't know how many exactly, but they exceeded well over a hundred.

It was obvious that these clothes were from the past. They were old fashioned, the texture of their cloth harsh. Some were patterned with small, black and yellow squares. It was also obvious that the clothes were up there because they had been forgotten. I thought of the coat my grandfather wore in an old photograph that used to be in our living room, before it disappeared at the end of the 1990s. I remember we had painted the house, and when we finished and brought the furniture back in, the photo had disappeared. That was before the earthquake.

That photograph haunted me for years. I asked my mom about it many times, but she didn't know what had happened to it. And even though we are one of those families that don't discard their possessions—unlike families who left their old clothes in the laundromat—we still couldn't find the photo. Some time ago I'd read an article about middle-class families that never throw away any of their furniture or renovate it, and keep living in houses that look like museum storerooms. Of course, Reghaïa isn't a town of middle-class families—it doesn't aspire to be. However, there are some families that were almost middle class, before the earthquake came and wrecked everything.

The employees at the laundromat have strange features. Their faces look like cheese triangles, their chins pointed, and their cheeks prominent and red. It's as if they've come from another country.

The degraded color of their hair is somewhere between blond and yellow. It looked like hair spotted with bleach. At the time, I thought it was because they had been exposed to the chemicals in which the clothes are washed, and that they would die, similar to people living in small American towns where factories have contaminated the groundwater—just like in the Erin Brockovich movie. Those inhabitants lost hair and skin and grew sick with terminal diseases.

No one remembers Building 15 today, although it was the biggest building in the town. Only people from the eastern suburbs know it, because they used to pass it on their way to the beach between Reghaïa and Aïn Taya. But it collapsed, and with it the dream of Reghaïa, which had vacillated between being a town full of workers and the displaced or establishing itself as a more stable suburb. Reghaïa had only that one tall building. But retailers crammed the ground floor with so much merchandise during the nineties that when the earthquake happened, the building seemed to crash down on itself in three distinct stages, like there was even too much for the brute force of nature to get through. Most of its inhabitants succeeded in escaping. I remember that.

Was it possible that in the earthquake the owners of all these forgotten clothes died or lost their homes? Something must have happened to them. Were they killed in an accident or escaped town? And when the police found their corpses they didn't pay attention to the small, folded pieces of paper in pockets of the dead, receipts that would have connected them to the laundromat.

When the employee came back with my coat, I gathered my courage and asked him about the hanging clothes.

"These . . . they've been here for two years." He told me. "And these," he gestured towards a row on the right of the door, "They're hidden out of sight . . . they've been here for so long . . . "

"Wow," I said.

He smiled at my bewilderment and then repeated his last words: "For so long."

This is the first time I noticed the clothes at the laundromat. I used to come and leave our dirty clothes without looking around or starting a conversation with any of the employees.

•

Why do people forget their clothes in a laundromat?

•

The problem with Reghaïa is not only did it lose its tallest building in the earthquake, even the green and open spaces that people escaped to from their falling homes on the day of the earthquake have now disappeared, and been replaced by new buildings. So where will people escape, if a new earthquake happens? And here, I mean a *real* earthquake, not one of those small quakes that happen four or five times in a year.

•

After my coat had been left with me in its transparent plastic bag, the employee disappeared once again behind the big washing machines that emitted a strong smell. Despite my increasing curiosity about the forgotten clothes, there was no plausible answer. Horrible things, which no one expects, happen to people. It was enough for someone to go into a small, old laundromat and notice all the cramped clothing from years gone by, to know that sad things happen, and happen a lot, even in the normally calm, eastern suburbs.

During that same week, I had been returning from university, with all my rolled-up sketches in my bazooka case that causes the lamest comments from passersby. Before I got home, on the school wall near the bus station of the Reghaïa-Algiers Line, I read, "10 dinars, not 20 dinars . . . these greedy people are stealing from you." Two days later, on another wall I saw the words: "*LA BATAILLE D'ALGER EST TOUJOURS LA* [The battle of Algiers continues]." That same evening as I was frying fish fingers and potatoes for dinner, I thought to myself, soon there will be a revolution in Reghaïa.

Mom called me from my sister's home in Tipaza, just to check on me. It was a very short phone call. Before I ended it, I wanted to tell her: *Stay where you are. Don't come back. A revolution will start here.* But I didn't. I ate a second orange before brushing my teeth, and sleeping.

I could hear the muffled noises from behind the washing machines and the movement of the employees behind them. Holding my coat, I peered through the glass door outside. The rain had become heavier, and darkness had fallen. The whole shop was gloomy. I felt like I was inside one of those apartments I had read about. The small apartments of the bourgeois cluttered with furniture, where families live their whole lives on the verge of suffocating. When the earthquake comes, everything crumbles. I looked at the poster of Building 15 and at all of the old, forgotten clothes. I imagined for a moment I would find my grandfather's photo there in the laundry, and the other forgotten and misplaced things that had been lost in the earthquake.

Then this idea crossed my mind: What if the laundromat employees were collecting these clothes and other things for the people who will start a revolution in Reghaïa, and it is the employees providing the insurgents with all they will need? When I was about to leave the shop, I heard the employee's voice once more. He had come out from the back and pointed at the forgotten, old clothes.

"Did you know," he said, "that these people come when the seasons change . . . they bring their laundry and forget about it . . . we don't know why . . . Dad used to say that they either went to the sea and drowned, or went into winter and never came out."

Translator's Note

When I first read هذه أمور تحدث (*These Things Happen*, Al-Mutawassit, 2019), the collection of stories in which "Before the Earthquake" was published, I wondered how the unique "Algiers" atmosphere and the vernacular in the stories would translate into English. So when the chance presented itself, I pitched this specific story to *The Markaz Review* for their themed issue "Architecture." They loved the idea and I was assigned the translation. Little did I know how hard a task it would prove to be. I was working at an 8-to-5 job that required so much mental, emotional and physical effort at the time, I had to work on the story in cold nights. But looking back, it was all worth it. I learned so much about the process of literary translation and how fulfilling it can be. I translated the first draft intuitively as the words came to me. Then I went back and started editing. To immerse myself in the setting of the short story, I searched for the places online to look at them. I also read about the real events to understand more where the main character was coming from. After sending the translated story, another process started, that of collaborative work with the editor Malu Halasa. I was able to capture the atmosphere of the story but still needed guidance on how to translate it with the right words. Through her expert suggestions and critical feedback, the story became the best it could be and was published. "Before the Earthquake" was my first literary translation and it wouldn't have been possible without the support and the opportunity offered by the team at *The Markaz Review.*

Five Phenomenologies

Lív Maria Róadóttir Jæger
translated from the Faroese by Bradley Harmon
Circumference

Phenomenology 1.8
When I Hear What I Inherit

It lurks in the body, the violence
in the living room in the carpet
in the flower pots in the armchair
I am with it
in grammatical past
I write it on paper
I pour it into the coffee cup
I weave it into a generational garland
(retrospection—paper—words—retrospection—paper—words)

It lurks in the body, he says. He stands with his back to me, leaning forward with his palms against the windowsill, looking out at the tall grass. Vigilant. With a skeptical back. Outside: trees and forest. And a vow of silence. They come in small bits, the sentences—declaratives fleeting like moths on their way up to the light, as I catch them and write his words: *Take it from me, the body reacts when you get beaten up.* Where should I hide the sentence, I ask? I can bury it down in the garden over by the shed next to the big hardwood tree so I remember where it is. I can donate it to the parish church maybe, but its walls are so cold. I can give it to the horses, the ones that walk silently in the pasture outside by the breakwater. Or throw it into the sea, so that it can wash up like driftwood on a wave that reaches gently for some other shore.

Phenomenology 1.10
Text to Nozick
Text to Sex

to be transformed into nature
into meat into coffee into dead sex
to see it
to resist
to try to read anyway
it is the transition
from adolescence to ice age
and then eroticism
swallowed by the zeitgeist

My 25th year. The year I stopped eating. I also stopped bleeding. My sex was frozen in time. I especially remember the hunger; I hardly slept because of it. I was morbidly obsessed with Robert Nozick and his counterfactual epistemology. I had no limits when it came to alcohol. I could drink myself out of sense and substance in conversations about proportions and the future of mountains—and forget my own name. Today my psyche is different. Hunger makes me sick, and alcohol leads to palpitations. The last time I got drunk was in 2017 at a bar called Psychopath. The next day I had such a headache that I could not open my eyes or talk to my child. For a whole day I asked my feet when I could move. Maybe tomorrow, they simply said. The sentence is from a book by Claudia Rankine; it is too good to be my own.

Phenomenology 1.12
Text to Shame

it comes after us again the shame
dwells deeply buried
in childhood
before you understood what it was
it surfaces
when we are adults
and should have known better

Everything that has happened comes after us again. Great-grandmother in the Salvation Army. Her diaries filled with prayer, sin and misfortune. The religious—who understood that the body leads us astray. When grandmother stood on her hands as a child and the skirt rolled down over her head—bare thighs and underwear—great-grandmother shouted: *Shame on you!* Because the will of the body had to be tamed. We also get this from Schopenhauer, the obsolete idiot. I write: *We carry shame / in our sensuous body / we try / to mix it with new ideas / but the thighs the thighs.*

Phenomenology 1.13
Text to Another Planet

the grape is produced in a laboratory in Freiburg
so that it can withstand the cold
and the darkness in this region
the wine is alive
when it goes down into the body
like in the blood
like the dreams of other planets
and new places to live

I write on lifeless paper. And afterwards on a walk out to the shoals; rocks and pebbles. All the way out to the seawall. There are other people present in the breeze. They are dead, I realize. They fly; breathing down on me as I stroll along. When I get home again, I sit upstairs in the study. There they are too, the dead. Now they breathe in the walls, in the floor, and in the letters of the books I read. When I look out the window to the east towards the forest, I see that they are indeed floating above the wilderness; they are the cottony haze that crowns the cornstalks. And farther away, over in the vineyard, they are bottled in shiny wine bottles with rosé and cork stoppers.

Phenomenology 1.14
Text to Stem

first
to be a rose
later
to be a fierce rose
something pursues
something crushes the stem

The paper is violent; it reveals consciousness in black and white. In a café with Rikke. We talk about Knausgård. Rikke says: *I've come to the part about Hitler, and I'm at a standstill.* 400 pages about the rational human being making systemic violence possible. I—I can't stop reading. It is deathly quiet outside the cafe and out in the universe. This silence that tells us the world will soon end. That moves the violence into the body with the written word. As if it were lodged there. The worst thing that happened in my life was becoming a civil servant. To obey the stupid, the man-made. That behavior is always on the way to the brink. Down in the drawer between my underwear are notes written in blue marker. And the fear of the future. I write: *We, the rational ones! / follow everything that makes sense to us / that's how stupid it is / not rose-colored / more like a broken stem.*

Translator's Note

I was both lucky and privileged to sink into the world of Germanic philology as a first-generation undergraduate at the University of Minnesota, where it was a natural progression for me—after a year of Old Norse classes taught by a hardboiled scholar who almost theologically professed that all we really needed to know lay in the words themselves—to attend the 2016 Faroese Summer Institute, an opportunity that arrived purely by chance. The rigorous philological training I had received combined with the magical month in the North Atlantic archipelago prepared me well for my tendency towards translating complex contemporary poetry.

Needless to say, the prescribed insistence to stay with the word before reaching for a dictionary became Pavlovian and has since served me well when working with Lív's poems, which I also came across by chance. Because it's often difficult to get ahold of Faroese books abroad, I first read Lív's 2020 collection *Eg skrivi á vátt pappír* (I Write On Wet Paper) in its Danish translation, which still conveyed how the poems bring thought close to the page itself. Only later did I come into contact with the rich texture of the Faroese text, and only then did I start translating the section titled "15 Phenomenologies," slowly and with patient breaks in between. During this prolonged translatorial period, I lingered with the words as I was trained, and I leaned into the juxtaposed verse and prose, letting the one help me better understand the other.

Though only spoken by some 70,000 people, the Faroese language has a rich history characterized by both tradition and innovation. Thus neither the dictionary nor the internet holds all the answers. This means that there's much that evades clarity without access to a fluent speaker, which I am not, however much patience I try to practice. Such is also the case with Lív's poetry, which unites an interest in poetic tradition via citation and intertextuality with the formal innovation evident in the "Phenomenologies" featured here. Thankfully, Lív answered my questions and clarified my confusions. Likewise, the poems were also expertly edited by Randi Ward ahead of their publication in *Circumference*.

Sueñu/Suañu

Pablo Texón
translated from the Asturian by Will Howard
Poetry

In my language
we distinguish
sueñu from suañu.
The first tethers us to the ground,
stuffs stones in our pockets
so we don't get soaked
by heavy clouds.
The second leads us
to summit
impossible peaks
skipping with joy.
There is a moment
when the day, gentle, wanes,
in which suañu takes
sueñu by the hand
and in this eclipse of strange
crepuscular splendor
a burst of lucidity breaks through
and we come home to sleep
and we bolt the door
and we bolt the doors.

Translator's Note

In 2019, the two words at the center of this poem briefly became a banner for the fight for language diversity in Spain's northern region of Asturias. The language activist Víctor Suárez Piñero posted a tweet explaining the difference between *sueñu* and *suañu*: "You can have the *suañu* of becoming an astronaut, but you go to bed when you have *sueñu*." In addition to the meanings Suárez Piñero alludes to, *sueñu* can denote "the act of sleeping" and *suañu* "the images one sees during sleep." In Spanish, all these definitions are collapsed into one word, *sueño*. "Who could be bothered," Suárez Piñero continues, "by us wanting to conserve our linguistic richness?" The tweet garnered support from fellow Asturians and speakers of some of Spain's other minority languages: Basque, Catalan, Galician.

Among those voicing their solidarity was Pablo Texón, one of a growing number of authors who write in Asturian. He shared a poem that metaphorizes this linguistic idiosyncrasy. The first time I read "Sueñu/Suañu," I was struck by its outward-facing posture—the almost ambassadorial tone of its opening line—and how it seemed to invite translation. It reminded me of the times Asturian friends had taught me new words in their language, often ones without an equivalent in Spanish, like the verb *trescombar*, which appears in this poem and whose definition reflects a central fact of Asturian life: the scaling of mountains. It means something like, "to cross over a peak, gaze out across the landscape, and keep going." The English-speaking reader can't intuit the loss of such a rich verb from the word I chose, "summit," but they can tease out the various possible meanings of *sueñu* and *suañu*. Through this process, the poem prompts them to consider the relationship between motivation and self-preservation, between the safety of home and the thrill of leaving, between dreaming and dreaming.

The Onion

Wisława Szymborska
translated from the Polish by Joanna Trzeciak Huss
The Hopkins Review

The onion is something else.
It has no innards.
Straight onionhood
all the way to onionimity.
Onionesque on the outside,
oniony to the core,
it can look inward
without any terror.

Inside us, alienness and wildness
barely covered by skin,
an internal inferno
aggressive anatomy,
but inside the onion, onion,
not twisted intestines.
Naked many times over,
suchlike to its depths.

A non-contradictory being,
a successful creation, the onion.
One inside the other,
the smaller in the larger,
and in the next another,

a third, a fourth.
A centripetal fugue.
An echo comprising a chorus.

The onion, I get it:
world's most beguiling belly.
Ringed by its own halos
to its greater glory.
Inside us—cellulite, ligaments, veins,
secretions and mucous membranes.
And thus, we are spared
the idiocy of perfection.

Translator's Note

"The Onion" is arguably the most inventive paean to a vegetable ever written. The poem was first published in the satirical journal *Szpilki* in 1974. It requires some mincing of words to render Szymborska's Polish neologisms into English.

The poem opens with a contradiction: a sentence that is not a sentence, as it lacks a verb. Respecting this verblessness, but unable to pull it off, I instead chopped out the verb from the third sentence: "Straight onionhood all the way to onionimity."

Szymborska describes the onion as a "non-contradictory being," evoking Aristotle's *Metaphysics,* but here Aristotle's Greek was filtered through layer upon layer of Polish Thomism, an allusion to arguments for the existence of God that posit God as the most perfect imaginable—and hence non-contradictory—being. The act of juxtaposing scholastic arguments over God's perfection with her own regarding the onion's perfection represents Szymborska at her cheekiest.

The phrase "non-contradictory being" is the linchpin of the poem. With that one phrase, an entire theology of onionness comes to light, evocative, in English, of all the divine variants of "omni": omnipotence, omnipresence, omniscience, etc. Szymborska's references to "creation," "fugue," "chorus," "halos," and "glory" layer whimsy and divinity into irreverent onionimity, but the sonic resonance of "omni" with "onion" was found in translation.

Here I encountered a tradeoff between rhythm and rhyme. In the third stanza, I forewent a forced rhyme in favor of prosody. To capture the rhythm of the poem, I did not translate "po prostu" (simply). In Polish, rhythm requires it. The fourth stanza allowed me to pick up on Szymborska's rhyme scheme. The pair "veins" and "membranes" was found in translation. But the true essence of this poem, the interpretive key, is its playful appropriation of scholastic arguments for the existence of God, which, in Szymborska's flattened ontology, are equitably applied to the onion.

my fish will stay alive

Dmitry Blizniuk
translated from the Russian by Yana Kane
128 LIT

just for a moment—what do they feel, the catfish and the carp,
when their pond is hit by a rocket?
steel shrapnel burst through the brick wall,
tore apart the aquarium
as if it were a paper bag of water and glass splinters.

she crashed to the floor.
across her back fanned wet strands of hair
interwoven with kelp.
an angelfish jumped around on the linoleum next to her face—
a bright comma
of life, suffocating.
but she was unscathed—not a scratch—
her legs just got stuck together, like hard candy,
acquired a dusty, blueish tint,
the color of moonlit fish scales.
she did not utter a word;
she became a mermaid, her fins in her slippers,
she crunched across the wet, shattered glass,
headed to the kitchen, poured water into a saucepan.
she gathered the four small fish and the snail,

searched for her cigarettes on the window sill;
warm wind kissed her fingers,
their webbing, the wedding ring.

my fish will stay alive.

Translator's Note

Dmitry Blizniuk is a Ukrainian poet who lives in Kharkiv, a city that has been under relentless attack by the Russian army for over two years. Blizniuk's poetry is a lens that focuses the light of life to a bright point. The horrors of the war that have invaded this life—the bombings of apartment houses and schools—and Kharkiv's indomitable resistance are now woven into his subject matter. Yet the poet's voice remains instantly recognizable: his light-gathering lens with its crystalline clarity remains unchanged. As before, his city, with its ponds and lakes surrounded by parks, is an active part of Blizniuk's inner world, not just a setting. As before, he is enchanted by a beloved woman who is both a partner in his quotidian life and a fairy-tale being imbued with life-sustaining magic. He retains his compassion for living creatures, even ones as small as an angelfish thrown out of a rocket-shattered aquarium: "a bright comma / of life, suffocating." This poet continues to write in the two languages, Russian and Ukrainian, that the current Russian regime aims to pit against each other.

I experience writing and translating poetry as a way to explore aspects of being that I am not able to access through any other means of perception. It is akin to proprioception: a way of learning about the world that integrates what is outside me and what is inside me into a single map; a way that orients me and helps me choose a direction for moving forward. As I translate Blizniuk's poetry, I find a world that is astonishingly capacious: a single moment of life, captured in two dozen short lines, has space enough to hold horror, compassion, admiration, and rejoicing.

Suzy

Clemens J. Setz
translated from the German by Lizzy Kinch
Chicago Review

Sixteen-year-old Marcel Loebl wrote his telephone number on the inside of a cubicle door in the toilet of the strip club *Bang or Whimper*. He and his friends Max and Daniel had slipped into the club about half an hour before to sneak a look at the women who drifted from table to table like silent sci-fi sentinels. They'd also marveled for a few minutes at an unexpected miracle on the metal pole—a naked woman suspending herself a meter above the ground, using only the pressure on the inside of her knees. She jutted out diagonally from the pole, a wonderfully alive snake-limb. And yet somehow the applause failed to materialise; perhaps the audience was simply too moved. At some point a man appeared. Tall, bearded and bearing a decidedly ruddy complexion, he expressed much understanding for their situation before quietly, gently and not at all impatiently kicking them out of the club.

Marcel, however, had been lucky. He had been standing a little to one side and was able to disappear into the toilets. His friends were probably waiting outside in the cold. Of course he should go and meet them—the evening was over, his eyes had born witness to the future.

Yet he had sat for a while on the folded-down toilet seat, studying the mesmerizing writing on the walls. There were all kinds of names, mostly female, below which offers were noted above telephone numbers. *Olga is a filthy fuck pig.* Or, *Anastasia will suck anything.* Little hearts, stars and speech bubbles dotted around. It was then that the idea came to him. It was not so much an idea, more a kind of vision. His mind was suddenly drawn to the woman writhing around on the pole to music, indescribably elegant and in total defiance of gravity. He knew the sight would keep him going for months. But what did she look like when she went home? Completely normal, surely. The image of an ordinarily dressed woman carrying shopping bags flashed into his mind. She locked the front door. She sat down in front of the TV. Did she have kids? What would it feel like to be her child?

I am her . . . son.

The rest followed on pretty straightforwardly. With a felt-tip pen Marcel wrote his phone number on the toilet wall. *My mouth awaits,* he wrote below it. He couldn't help giggling. His friends would think this was so gay. But obviously it was different. Then he gave some serious thought to what the woman should be called.

Someone entered the toilets.

"Look, come on out now," said the voice.

SUZY, wrote Marcel. Then he opened the door and let himself be escorted out by the man who worked for the club, even now maintaining his polite good humour.

His friends had indeed waited for him outside. It had started lightly snowing. A street lamp stood enchanted, shrouded in dancing dots, a cross between a luminous jellyfish and a test card. There was also a group of gay men standing outside the club, two of whom were kissing each other, locked in embrace. Others milled around them slowly, smoking and showing each other things on their phones. Marcel looked over at them curiously—this was a late night TV documentary come to life—yet it was still nowhere near as exciting as what he had just seen in the club. Daniel kept an eye on them, mainly so things did not get out of hand, right here right now, in the middle of the night. Daniel came from the countryside, Kitzeck. His dad was a dentist, just like Marcel's.

"Look at them," said Daniel.

"Yes," said Marcel.

The first call came early on a Saturday afternoon. Marcel was at home in his room. The phone buzzed on the desk, a private number. He studied the screen for a while and considered declining, before picking up and answering:

"Hello?"

"Suzy?"

It was a very high-pitched man's voice.

"Ah, yes, um," Marcel said, shifting his own voice higher to reach a more childlike register. "Sorry, Suzy isn't available right now."

"Sorry," the voice said.

"I am her son."

"Okay . . . That's disgusting."

A deep breath, then the caller hung up.

Marcel sat and stared at his mobile phone. Sure enough, his hand was shaking. He put the phone down. His pulse was also . . . He stood up and moved around a little. He was hot. He opened a window and stuck his head out. Guttering. Roof shingles. Cold air. The sun was behind the trees lining the roads at the edge of the estate.

"Fuck," said Marcel quietly. "Fuck, fuck, fuck, fuck, fuck . . ."

Someone had actually gone and called him. Well, what else could they have done, his number was up there on the wall after all. Marcel shook himself and giggled. It had worked. Crazy. How was it so easy? Why would people just *dial* the number, it was so stupid. Way too easy. He realized he even had something on the caller; he had been in the toilets. In the second cubicle from the left in *Bang or Whimper.* That was the only place where the number was. Unless there was someone traipsing through the loos every night, writing down numbers to copy them somehow. Perhaps they even . . .?

Marcel leapt onto his laptop. It took forever to load the browser. He typed in his mobile number, first with a dash between the area code and number and then without, then with a space—thank god, no results, oh my god. How could he have explained that? But no, it was fine, only the toilets. It really was that easy.

The phone buzzed again. Marcel took a step back. But it was just a text from René, wanting to know if it was too late to go for a smoke in the carpark. He had Ethiopian tobacco, he wrote, guaranteed to give you the runs. Marcel replied:

wicked but cant tonight got family stress

Followed by a knife written in ASCII code. René sent him a smiley with an X for eyes and a p for a sticking out tongue.

its so so so gay here, Marcel typed.

The conversation ended.

The second call came early in the morning on the day Marcel had to give a presentation about the Donation of Constantine. He was averagely prepared. According to the internet, today was also *World Opabinia Day*. Marcel had looked the word up. Opabinia was the name of a five-eyed prehistoric creature from the Cambrian period, with a prehensile proboscis and segmented, armoured skin. It lived in water, managing to survive in spite of its odd number of eyes before its eventual extinction.

Couldn't he put the bloody thing down, his dad said at the breakfast table.

Iris was fidgety and nervous because her ski trip was coming up.

"It's bad for your whole body," his dad said, "the neck vertebrae, the joints in your jaw, the vagus nerve. You even get hiatal hernias from looking down all the time. Put. It. Away."

"Yeah, I have."

"Not next to you, put it away properly!"

"Alright, alright."

At this point it started to ring. Marcel's dad exhaled in irritation and laid his cutlery down.

"'scuse", said Marcel. "But it's René. Because of the presentation."

His dad raised his hands.

Marcel went to his room to answer the phone.

"Hello?"

"Yes, hello. What's the best way to meet you?"

"Oh, I'm sorry. I am her son. She'll call you back though. Please don't tell her I picked up."

A long pause.

"Ahem. I see. No problem."

The man made the humming sound people normally make when they're about to hang up. Now Marcel had to say something quickly.

"She left her phone in my room. But I'm not allowed out of the room when she has guests. She leaves me inside all day."

The caller made a strange sound. The handset might have been centimetres from his face when he heard the voice, his thumb poised to terminate the conversation. He sighed deeply and asked:

"How old are you, then?"

"Me? Nine."

"Nineteen?"

"Nine."

"Jesus Christ. Okay. That's bad. And she doesn't let you out of your room?"

"Never if guests are around. She's very strict on that."

Another long pause. Marcel struggled not to laugh. The caller then said:

"I'm sorry to hear that."

They fell silent again. Marcel smoothed down the corners of his mouth, overcome by grinning, and thought about what to say next. So far everything had gone perfectly. He couldn't ruin it now. What he would have given to press pause on the film of reality, to think up a few sentences in peace.

"Does she treat you badly?" the man asked.

"I don't know. Not really. But . . . "

"Describe it to me."

Another pause. Marcel looked out of the window. A man was walking a pack of dogs. He had one of those leashes that splayed out into lots of small, thinner leashes. The dogs were small and thin, like rats.

"You really don't sound nineteen," the man said.

"I'm nine."

"Hm", incomprehensible crackling, " . . . really difficult, huh?"

"What?"

Crap. His voice was breaking up.

"I said: I imagine it's very difficult. Everything with your mum I mean."

"Yes. I'm only allowed out of the room in the evening."

"You can't even go to the loo?"

"I have a bucket, so I can . . . "

Marcel suppressed a lurid giggle.

"A bucket?" The man laughed incredulously. It was a sort of greasy, Beavis and Butt-head laugh. Marcel watched the cloud of dogs turn the corner at the top of the crossing. He felt triumphant, like on an autumn day when the blustering tailwind means walking down the street is barely an effort at all.

"Please don't tell her I told you, please!"

"I certainly won't be calling again," the man said.

And hung up.

Marcel was ecstatic. Later, during the presentation, he was concise, coherent, spoke faster than usual and could even answer the history teacher's follow-up questions.

After dinner, Marcel found himself thinking about the callers. He imagined their faces, their postures. They were moving through the city right now, this very second, or they were sitting at home in their bedrooms, alone. He'd put his phone in his pocket so his dad wouldn't gripe, but every three or four minutes he felt a distinct vibration. When he looked, however, there was nothing—not even a text.

They had had potato gratin. Afterwards they sat together for a while in the living room, as Iris was leaving the next morning. They discussed the final details of the skiing equipment, Iris still suffering from anxiety and looming homesickness, but nevertheless praising the various accessories she'd been lent—UV cream, goggles with adjustable colour filters, etc—though she kept interrupting herself with small, strange pauses. She often glanced at her older brother, and it was a look he recognised; he was meant to contribute something, she trusted his judgement, he was older but not quite yet in adulthood, where everything was totally different and incomprehensible and odd.

After a while Marcel got up and sat with her. Another phantom vibration. He imagined a call coming in later when everyone was already asleep, and it gave him the same sense of security he might have once felt at the prospect of an evening football match being shown on TV.

Iris looked at him quizzically. It affected him more than usual.

"Another thing I meant to say," Marcel said, although so far he had said nothing. "If you feel bad, just call me. Especially at night, that's when I'm on call."

Their mum had heard him, but pretended to be occupied with the essential task of unpacking and repacking the suitcase.

"Mhm," Iris nodded.

Marcel held up his mobile phone. Lol—what if a perv called right this second?

"You . . . " said Iris.

"Yes?"

"You have to answer though, you never do!"

"I always do. If you're having a bad time at night, bam, just call. I'm on night duty. But you won't be sick, you'll see."

She nodded again.

"You imagine things very differently to how they turn out."

The callers did not tire. One called and got angry when he heard Marcel. He threatened to lock him in a cellar and torture him. Then he laughed and began whistling a melody. Another wanted to be beaten unconscious by a "real lady". One simply said, "Oh God, the world is so fucking sick,. I'll check out then please, thank you." Then hung up. One just wanted to talk. One had a ten-year-old son and kept Marcel on the phone for over five minutes asking him various harmless questions. A very elderly man, to judge by his voice, kept coughing and asked again and again to speak to Suzy, it was very urgent, he was a regular client. Another old man (perhaps the same man with a slightly adjusted voice), assured him that the truth often lay between the lines.

Marcel lay on his bed, a few sticky goji berries in his mouth, eaten straight from the packet.

A man called in tears and asked to meet; at first he couldn't understand that there wasn't a woman on the other end, and when he finally grasped what he was being told, he sobbed—you could clearly hear his trembling bottom lip—and started apologizing left right and center, swearing it would never happen again, never ever again, before putting the phone down without ending the call. For quite a while, a strange crackling and a few occasional, distant voices drifted out from his world and into Marcel's room.

Marcel sat in his classroom, 6B in Dreihackengasse college, while a Biology lesson took place a few meters from his face. The teacher moved around a lot, spoke about grassland plants and drew a few things on the board, but none of it reached Marcel, though it did look quite interesting, that he had to admit. The teacher was wearing a blue tie today.

The phone vibrated. He checked. Unknown number, very good. When the caller hung up, Marcel sent him a text. *Call me back this evening sweetie.*

The teacher asked him what was so funny. Marcel apologised.

Iris had already been on the ski trip for three days, they had a Maths test and Daniel and Max were arguing about chemtrails. Marcel realised he could no longer summon an opinion on chemtrails. Had he ever had one? It was hard to say. It was much more interesting to muse on what the men who called him looked like. Their faces, the positioning of their fingers.

Admittedly, mostly they hung up as soon as they heard his voice. Sometimes he made it to *I am her son* before scaring them off. A few held on even longer, making his day. Most were sympathetic and concerned.

You had to watch your back, though. Now he always put his phone on silent when he couldn't have it on him, which soon sent his mum—who called him often when he was out and about—around the bend. Iris, too. She hadn't called him yet, just their mum twice during the day, and Marcel had briefly spoken to her. Everything's fine so far, Iris said, Jennifer is just a stupid birdbrain. A what? An idiot birdbrain! With her high-heel pigtails. Marcel laughed like crazy at the way his sister spoke.

"You're so great," he said.

"Hahaha," she laughed sheepishly. "Thanks." Then girls' voices called out in the background and Iris hung up without saying goodbye.

In the playground, a school boy in first year was sitting on the only wooden bench and trying to play mikado with toothpicks. Next to him, for some reason, was a bee calendar. Almost every day was strange now.

They had to interpret a poem for German homework. It was

about a fly that got squished by a man one morning. The poem was almost impossible to understand because all the word endings were wrong. *A flie I findeth in bed.* This continued the whole way through—wtf. Otherwise it was death, death, and more death; everything in German class returned somehow to death. Even when someone wrote something beautiful, it always turned out to be about dying. It was really dumb. This susceptibility had begun, to be precise, before he'd started school. Marcel's first image of death had actually been a line of poetry of sorts. He'd always misheard the lyrics from a popular Christmas carol: 'the lake rests still and gently', imagining they referred to somewhere called Still Land. Still Land, a region south of Berlin or somewhere, meaningless. A mythical place, where the dead were sent. Nature stifled by winter, branches pale with clamminess and a motionless body of water under a snow-white sky. Marcel wrote in his homework that the poem could have been spoken by a human fly. Then he set about working out the rhyme scheme.

"Hello."

"Suzy?"

"No. She's not here right now. Please don't tell her I picked up. She'll hit me if she finds out."

The caller drew snot up his nose. He stayed calm.

"Please don't tell her," Marcel repeated.

Still no reaction.

"Wow, okay," he said. "Wait a minute."

A quiet creaking could be heard.

"Please don't tell on me," Marcel whispered.

"I've just closed the door. Now we can talk."

Marcel wanted to answer but something in him held back. Something about the voice felt novel.

"Hello?" he said at last.

"Yes, I'm here," said the caller. "How old are you?"

"Ten."

"Okay. And your mum, do you live with her?"

"Yes."

"I see. She hits you?"

"If she catches me on the phone, yes."

Marcel thought about just hanging up. But something told him the man would just call back.

"Where do you live?" the caller expertly asked.

"I can't tell you that."

Marcel heard soft scraping noises. Was the caller masturbating, or was it the sound of a pencil writing? Both seemed equally disturbing. He hung up.

The phone remained silent. Marcel got up from the bed to get something to drink. Then it rang again.

He picked up.

"Hello?"

"Sorry, we got cut off," said the man. "You were just about to tell me where you live."

"My mum just came home," whispered Marcel.

"Oh," said the caller, now speaking in a low, cautious tone too. "Alright. Put the phone down. Call me later. I can help you."

"I have to go now," Marcel whispered.

Disguising his voice already felt exhausting and idiotic.

"You're not al—"

Marcel hung up.

He put his phone on airplane mode, then went down to the kitchen. His mum was still up, sitting at the table. She was flicking through a magazine. The tablet was next to her, silently playing a massage video. Marcel got himself a beetroot juice from the fridge. He mixed it with some cola.

"Sleep well," his mum said.

"Yeah."

When Marcel was jolted out of an unpleasant dream in the middle of the night—he was in a village, and after dark combine harvesters drove around the fields, thickly clouded by the brightness of their headlights—he switched his phone on again and saw that the caller had tried twelve more times. The last one around two thirty.

But Iris was coming home tomorrow.

Before breakfast an unusually deep voice called up, Rammstein register. The man reacted angrily.

"What do you mean, you're her son? Well for fuck's sake, tell her I want my money back!"

Marcel adjusted his voice and said there was no Suzy. Unfortunately she had died, of AIDS. The man laughed, jarringly.

"No. It was only ever a joke," said Marcel, "there is no Suzy."

"There is my money though," the caller said. "Just you wait, you fucking whore. I'll take everything you've got. Fucking pig."

Overall, the calls now seemed to become cruder in tone. Why might that be? The men didn't know each other, they weren't in cahoots. And yet lately they had become notably petulant. Perhaps there was something in the atmosphere, chemtrails, hard to tell. Perhaps a sorcerer was scribbling sinister, misogynist curses onto his walls, from where they radiated out into the city.

The man determined to save him called increasingly often. And yes, a few times Marcel picked up, played along for five or six minutes, reassured the unpleasantly tunnel-visioned man and said that, no, he was no longer tied up and the bucket had gone too. He could now move freely around the flat, everything was fine.

At the end Marcel spoke in his normal voice and said, okay, there is no Suzy, it was just a joke, no harm meant. But the caller—who didn't believe a word—instead answered, yes, he understood he'd been forced to say that, that much was clear, but don't worry, my boy, the truth was safe with him, he didn't have to say anything at all, he said, even in silence he could tell how much all this—

At this point, Marcel ended the telephone conversation.

What would happen if you threw your phone in the bin?

Marcel let more and more callers in on the joke over the next few days, but mostly they didn't believe him. One laughed heartily and congratulated him on the prank. He said his name was Richard and chatted away cheerfully: he was sitting here on his terrace with a glass of cider, he said, it was wonderful and then this delicious stunt here, really fantastic. All the praise seemed surreal and condescending to Marcel.

"Yes, yes," he said. "I'll get going then."

"Very good, very good," said the man named Richard. "*I'll get on with it then.* Fantastic, haha. Really top notch."

"Okay."

"I'll get on with it then, oh, how cool. How cool."

In the background for the entire call there was the sound of a baby wailing.

Marcel hung up.

The liberator got in touch again around evening. He said everything was ready. He just needed assurance the enchained boy was home alone and that Suzy would be out. He could then set everything in motion. He promised. Everything would be fine, he said. Even the weather was perfect.

The last sentence confused Marcel. He looked out of the window. It was a cloudy day, somewhat windy. The trees were swaying like dreaming giraffes.

"There's no Suzy," Marcel said. He no longer bothered with speaking clearly, talking with his mouth full. The organic apple tasted like bicycle workshop.

"Be patient."

"Hey, I'm being serious," said Marcel chomping away. "Can't we just leave it? I am sorry and everything."

"Everything is ready." said the caller quietly.

"What city are you even in?"

"In yours."

"Mhm, great," said Marcel and hung up.

Going for a walk without your mobile was lovely, it turned out. Like people in the 1980s. There were tall trees here, dripping water droplets. A sign for a law firm, the solicitor's name was Dr. Zmaj.

Gusts of wind and a squat dachshund.

In a doorway someone was hanging shirts out to dry, a pleasingly medieval sight. More people should wear white bonnets on their heads, that much was certain.

So many bicycles in the neighborhood! As if they'd been able to reproduce independently, in the hedges and bushes where they'd once been locked up.

On a leash, bucket.

Marcel walked up the steps to the castle hill. An information sign on the rock face informed him about the bald ibis that bred here a few centuries ago. Spear-shaped, strange ibis head.

A tourist's backpack by the clock tower was in the shape of Totoro.

"Hello?"

Marcel had only answered because he happened to be sitting next to his phone and it wasn't a withheld number.

"Suzy?" asked a female voice.

For a few seconds Marcel's conception of the world dipped under water. He had been ready for anything, but not a woman.

"What?" he asked.

"Ahhh, hello?" said the woman. "Who's that speaking then?"

Marcel's room was very three dimensional. Every object protruded unnaturally, like books half pulled out of the shelf. A woman. Why was a woman calling? Could it be the police?

"There is no Suzy," he said quickly.

"Excuse me? Who is speaking?"

"Sorry. You've got the wrong number."

"Hm, I don't think I have," said the caller, sounding disappointed rather than aggressive. "But who is it then, please?"

Marcel didn't say anything.

The things in the room. The sky out of the window. Spots on the wall.

"Tom Turbo," he said.

He waited. The woman breathed into the mouthpiece. Then she wheezed, laughing. Yes, she laughed a little. Then he heard a rustling.

"Hello, Tom. I am Annamaria.

"Okay."

"Wait. Don't hang up. What's your real name?"

"Bernd."

"Hello, Bernd."

"I just made it all up, all the stuff with the woman," said Marcel. "Was just a gag. Sorry."

He felt liked he'd just used the word "gag" for the first time in his life. It was such an idiotic word, like something out of a German feature film.

"Ah," the woman went on. "But you sound very friendly."

"Okay."

"I mean it!" the woman said. "I think you do."

"Okay. Great."

"Wait a second, don't hang up, will you?"

Marcel didn't reply.

"Well, just in case you feel like it," the woman said, "I'm at the city park every day at 1 PM.

I'm the one with the child. You'll recognize us right away. I've got a guitar with me."

"I see."

"Just in case you fancy it."

"Hm."

"We're easily recognisable. You sound really nice. Like a nice sophisticated youn—

Marcel hung up.

It was amazingly difficult to avoid the park. Every route home seemed to go past it somehow. It was either green on one side or the other. Well, it wasn't one o'clock. Yes, so long as it wasn't one o'clock, the woman wouldn't be there either.

What would she say to him?

Marcel imagined the conversation. Every day he ran through several possibilities in his head.

The woman said something like, "You've been conducting quite the experiment. What's it like when people call all the time?"

That is, at first they'd probably greet each other. But Marcel's imagination always jumped ahead to the most interesting part. To the woman's sentence he replied something like:

"It was really cool at the start. Like listening to a radio station from another continent. Some are sympathetic. Some are creepy. Some get excited. One man offered to set me free and call the police. Reassuring him wasn't so easy."

"Yeah?"

"Mostly they're really nice though. They feel pity. They don't want anything bad to happen to the boy."

"To Suzy's son."

"Yes, even though they don't know him at all."

Sometimes the scene turned out quite differently. There were a lot of possibilities.

—

The calls only stopped completely after about a month. Marcel took his phone with him everywhere again. The park had also lost its radioactive aura. Marcel no longer even checked his watch when he passed it. He walked more slowly too, because at some point he'd realised the woman couldn't possibly know what he looked like. The paths were always full of people, like in a film. There was always a slight smell of medicine balls in the park.

Only once did he discover her, or so he thought. The woman was sitting on a bench, a huge wheelchair next to her. I'm the one with the child. Well, who knows. In any case, there was an elongated figure lying in the wheelchair, covered up, hard to make out. There was no guitar. But the woman was holding a thin, white stuffed rabbit and moving it for the person in the wheelchair.

Everyone carries their own images into the future. Lots of horrible things happen, an accident, an emergency cesarean section and a long, dreary year in Beijing, you cheat on people, you owe them money, you fail in your relationship with your daughter, you lose your job to a nineteen-year-old, you get called up, humiliated and then, despite everything, you carry a bag of oranges across town, where your mum still lives, in this huge, half-empty housing estate, my God.

Under this ratio of compression, the image of the stuffed rabbit lasted at least until Marcel was thirty six. He still had people around him who he could have told about it, about the callers, the phone, the woman, and they probably would have believed him.

But he didn't. Perhaps that general underlying feeling lingered in him a little longer, the certainty that there had been all those people who, added together, provided a kind of layer of comfort, a sigh of relief in unsuspected places. But that, I know, is easy to say in retrospect. So let's move on.

Translator's Note

"Suzy" came from a collection titled *Der Trost runder Dinge* (The Consolation of Round Things), a wonderfully strange and consistently surprising selection of stories. Clemens Setz has a singular ability to balance irreverent absurdity with a deeply serious appreciation of his characters' struggles—the stories startle with both their surreal plot twists and their tenderness.

In my translation I tried to capture both the boastful grandstanding and the self-consciousness of teenage boys' dialogue; Marcel revels in having the upper hand, but he is also desperate to avoid humiliation. There is a cool concision to Setz's prose, akin to Marcel's desired self-image: in control, not giving too much away, aloof. Yet his vulnerability—he's a sixteen-year-old boy, meddling in an adults' world—is also apparent. The final section races through the embarrassments and failures of his later life, universalising them in the indefinite third person. When I first read it, the shift in register took my breath away, and it was the most fun to translate. I rendered the 'mein Gott' literally and left it at the end of the paragraph as in the original, because it so accurately reflected my reaction. Rather than writing "one . . . " I opted for "you," which gives the English an even more direct tone, and sought to maintain the rhythm of the original. I also took care to maintain the precision of Setz's imagery: "trees swaying like dreaming giraffes," bicycles reproducing in hedges (which often comes to mind when I see bicycles in the park).

[A woman who buried her son]

Yuliia Iliukha
translated from the Ukrainian by Hanna Leliv
Another Chicago Magazine

A woman who buried her son on the vegetable patch made a cross for him from two pine planks bound together with wire. Her son bought those planks to fix their house up in spring. But the war broke out, and for some people, spring never arrived.

Her son died instantly. The woman could barely register that.

The first two shells fell somewhere farther away. But a fragment of the third one killed her son when they were running from the summer kitchen toward the cellar. The woman collapsed next to him. She could not even scream. She only groaned, as if it was her who was wounded, and scratched the frozen ground with her nails.

When the sounds of explosions grew distant, she rose to her knees, leaning heavily on her arms. She looked at her son. Half of his head was missing. The woman crawled toward the kitchen wall and, pressing her back to it, started to bang her head, yet intact, against the bricks. She was not crying—she was only gasping and groaning. Her headscarf slipped off, and her white hair was soon dyed with blood. A neighbor who shuffled into her yard half an hour later thought she'd suffered a head injury.

The woman could bury her son only after the ground thawed. It took her a few days to dig a grave, which was not even that deep. She wrapped his body into a film her son had bought to cover the greenhouse. He was an atheist, but she made a cross for him, anyway, a thick stiff wire ripping the skin off her fingers. She used the same wire to attach a rusty metal plate to the cross where she wrote her son's name and dates of birth and death with a piece of chalk.

The woman was spending the night in the cellar when she felt a pain in her chest. She did not walk out in the morning.

Several days later, the rain washed away the inscription on the plate. The cross was left standing nameless.

Translator's Note

I first crossed paths with Yuliia back in 2019 when she curated a bilingual collection of Ukrainian veteran poetry titled *The Mark of Home*, and I was honored to translate it into English. Fast-forward three years: Russia launched a full-scale invasion of Ukraine, another grim chapter in its centuries-long genocidal war against my country, and Yuliia, along with her young son, was forced to flee their home and seek refuge in Austria. She chronicled her experiences on social media, where I followed her journey. It was also on Facebook that Yuliia began sharing her flash fiction—an attempt to capture the physically and emotionally draining experiences of women during the war. Her protagonists hailed from diverse backgrounds, yet all shared the haunting bond of wartime trauma.

Laconic and striking in their emotional intensity, Yuliia's stories captivated me, and I texted her suggesting I translate a few of them into English and find them homes in English-language magazines, to share her urgent writing with a wider audience. "A few of them" gradually turned into "all of them," and in early 2024, the collection of forty stories won *128 LIT*'s International Chapbook Contest and is now slated for publication in the U.S. English translations also helped her texts appear in Slovak, Italian, German, and French—further amplifying the voices of Ukrainian women and searching for the language to speak about the unspeakable. As a translator, I considered it my main task to properly convey their verbal brevity and emotional depth—and often devastating effect like that of the story published in this anthology. Sharing the same wartime reality with the author certainly helped. Yuliia's stories make a difficult, uncomfortable read—but serve as a poignant testament to women's experiences during war, a reality far more universal in today's world than we'd hope.

Three Poems

Saadi Youssef
translated from the Arabic by Khaled Mattawa
Cincinnati Review ("Saturday") and *Another Chicago Magazine* ("Night Flight" and "A Quatrain")

Saturday

Not a glorious morning,
but a heavy, overcast sky, black like basalt,
and miserly,
not a drop,
not a breeze.
Even the bare trees chattered their long teeth,
and the squirrel disguised itself as a bird,
and the bird put on a squirrel's disguise
and the woman who walks with a cane
pounded the concrete pavement confidently
and headed toward her demise.
The car will not come with fresh milk and eggs,
the workers will not collect our garbage,
an ambulance will not rush in.
We are fated to suffocate here today, all of us,
under an overbearing sky,
a sky crueler
than a sword.

Night Flight

These planes that creep away
in the middle of the night,
their engines off,
careless and lumbering,
where do they go?
Where did they come from?
Do they bear the names of those to be killed tomorrow and their
addresses?
Or the coffins of those killed in clandestine battles in the dark?
The villages cling to silence.
But this hidden roar infiltrates, settles deeply within,
and becomes our nightmares.
Our villages that do not see us,
our villages that will not sleep.

A Quatrain

Ash clouds veil the hilltops,
the lake almost frozen,
the birds gone.

We'll go to the village pub in the afternoon.
The beer is cooling,
the curtains are burdened with haze.

The church, as always, is on the foot of the mountain.
And on the square the soldiers are dead,
the tower a nest for crows.

An evening without anguish, or candles commemorating
another evening, and without songs.
                                                    An evening that tosses me
into a waterless desert where devastation lies.

Translator's Note

The late W. S. Merwin recalls that some of the best advice he received about becoming a poet was from Ezra Pound, who told him the following: "The way to do it is to learn a language and translate it—that way you can practice and find out what you can do with your language—your language. You can learn a foreign language, but translation is a way of learning your own language."

This very much applies to how I got into poetry. Although Arabic was my native language and I didn't have to learn it, English had become my writing language and I had much to learn and to teach myself. Translating Arabic into English became how I gained my own poetic language.

Saadi Youssef, whom I'd begun translating back in the early 1990s, was right there as part of that education—how to render the geography of memory into poetry, and how translate the cadences of Arabic that were in my "deep heart's core," as Yeats states, into the English I spoke. Little did I know then, that that was also Saadi's process. In addition to reading the Arab masters and his elder contemporaries, he also translated from English and continued to renew "his language" by lending it to many of the great poets of the modern era, from Whitman to Cavafy.

I'm grateful to be translating Saadi Youssef again, and to present his last poems to English readers. Having worked on his verse for so many years, I try to be a conduit, with the fingers clicking what the eye reads, the translation occurring like a current that runs through my perception, as I create a first draft, and as I revise until it arrives, in my words, to my satisfaction, and to where it begins to feel like an "original" in its new linguistic home.

I Write to Purge This Memory

Liliana Ancalao
translated from the Mapuzungun to Spanish by the author and from Spanish to English by Seth Michelson
Words Without Borders

I write to remember who I am, because I was born not knowing who I was.

I write to honor the kongen, owners of the water, who came to me in the voice of my grandmother, Roberta Napaiman, and that time the Ngen was the horse jutting his head out from a lake in Cushamen, the sound birthing a fear in us and impeding our games on the shore.

I write to remember the kuifikecheyem, the ancestors who once were children and crossed the rushing rivers by clinging to tails of horses.

I write for the small relief of it, like the relief my eyes feel when I look out into the distance because to be Ankalaufken is to be in the middle of the sea or the middle of a lake, the extensive plains of my nampulkafe blood that ranged from the Pacific to the Atlantic and settled in the precarity of a treaty with winka, from which it was evicted.

I write to convince myself that this is why I live in Comodoro Rivadavia, the place from where I watch the sea and its waters, which at times are silver and at other times filthy.

I write because, even like this, the machi have seen in the pewma the Ngen of this sea.

I write to return this memory to bloom.

I write to ask myself how many lots and streets have been built on this Puel shore, slapping a hand over the mouths of the machines that dug up bones buried thousands of years prior.

I write for the dead stripped of flesh and exhibited as spoils of war by Francisco Pascasio Moreno in the Museum of Natural Sciences dating back 134 years.

In other words, I write so that the names of all of those assassins don't go unpunished.

So I mention Rauch the Prussian, who slit our throats to save bullets for President Rivadavia, I mention slaughter and the arrival of Rosas at Choele Choel, I mention military ranks generals coronels terror and winka barbarians who raped women, who shot prisoners, and who began separating children and women as slaves, before Julio Argentino and his photo on the hundred-peso bill.

And I add to Roca Julio: Rudecindo and Ataliva, and other names that knot my stomach like Sarmiento, Villegas, Levalle, Winter, Racedo, Uriburu, Laciar.

I write because, escaping horror, my people fled farther south, farther into the mountains, abandoning their homes, their seed and harvest, their animals.

I write because I want to remember the children who saved themselves by covering themselves in coats and those who in the frenzy of the flight fell from horses and weren't with their parents when they stopped and didn't light a fire to avoid being spotted by soldiers.

I write because they were caught and herded like animals for hundreds of kilometers, and some were abandoned along the way, left there to bleed out after being castrated or after having their Achilles cut.

I write to discover their faces covered in tears and blood from the blows, in the splatter from the cuts to their flesh, in earth after their long march.

And I write so that there's a map that records this genocide.

I write to not forget those who died on the high seas, heaped and sick on the ships that carried them to ports of family dismemberment still with us today; I write for the desperation woven with moans and cries.

I write because they didn't know their destiny before arriving at the concentration camps, the ranches, the sugarmills, the yerba plantations.

I write because I'm not a Ñanko who can soar past this misery.

I write for those tortured by hunger in the concentration camps of Fortín Villegas, Valcheta, Chichinales, Malargüe, Rodeo del Medio, Villa Mercedes, Tigre, Isla Martín García, that island where those sick with smallpox also were dumped.

I write for the relatives never heard from again, displaced from Rosario, San Miguel de Tucumán, Río Cuarto, Córdoba, Ingenio San Juan, and for those enslaved by Rufino Ortega in Mendoza and by Rudecindo Roca in Misiones.

I write to protect myself from the death that surrounds me when I don't know what to do with the fatigue, the shame, the lack of a will to live.

I write to purge this memory.

I write because I already learned defeat and I know that even when defeated one can write, to circle around events and put a name to those who had none.

I write for those who went crazy in witnessing the assassination of their children, and for the children they let die of hunger and thirst, and for the children they stole.

I write for those who were cleaved from their names and condemned to ignore their kupalme.

I write to remember the names of our Spirits, to reassert their power over foreign religions, so that their God will judge Bishop Aneiros and the priests who witnessed the horror but said nothing.

I write so that this memory doesn't stagnate.

I write because I wasn't the Nawel who consoled and accompanied those who couldn't escape the horrors; I'm no luan or choike to nourish them.

I write so that this memory flows and becomes again a single river with recent memory.

I write, then, for the scraps of land returned by the new state as if they were charity, and for those displaced from those lands because the rich always knew how to manipulate their laws.

I write for those whom the ranch owners trapped within wire fencing to strand them without water, without grass for their animals, without firewood, and who were finally thrown off the land they'd clung to by their fingernails, their heart, and their hope.

I write for those swindled by winka who lied about the numbers in their bookkeeping, and for those who paid that fraudulent debt with their land and were left with nothing in return.

I write for the children who had the Mapuzungun silenced in their mouths in civilizing, evangelical schools.

I write for those murdered in city police stations, so young they hadn't even had the time to learn their origins, killed for carrying their people, for their faces, for their surname.

I write for Rafael Nahuel and Camilo Catrillanka, shot in the back by the Albatross Group and the Jungla Comandos, respectively, assassinated for reclaiming this memory that clings to Wall Mapu, to the language of the Spirits.

I write for the machi condemned to be driven from their rewe and their lawen, their Newen incarcerated so that the claws of forestry, mining, and hydroelectricity could dig in, destroying what little we had left.

I write out of the fear that the Ngen of the mountains, the hills, the stones, the waters, will grow tired of the prolonged heresy and abandon us.

I write because the Ngen still live, in the taüles and their language, the sound of the kultrun, the cycles of the mapu, and the rains.

I write to know what death and what life I come from and endure.

Notes on the Translation

Here are definitions of Mapunzungun words that appear in "I Write to Purge This Memory":

Choike: American ostrich
Kultrun: a percussive instrument used in spiritual ceremonies
Kupalme: family origin
Lawen: medicine
Luan: guanaco
Machi: a person with knowledge to act in the many spiritual dimensions constituting the territory
Mapu: land
Mapuzungun: the language of the Mapuche land
Nampulkafe: traveler
Nawel: American tiger; one of the forms adopted by the Ngen
Newen: spirtual force
Ngen: a spiritual entity that cares for specific people and places, sometimes becoming visible by adopting various forms
Ñanko: eaglet; one of the forms adopted by the Ngen
Pewma: images in dreams that carry messages
Puel: Eastern (Puelmapu is the land to the East, occupied today by the Argentine state.)
Rewe: a place specifically designated for communication with other dimensions
Taüles: from "taül," a ceremonial song (Hispanicized and pluralized in line with the rules of Spanish-language grammar.)
Wall Mapu: the land of the Mapuche people
Winka: foreigner

Translator's Note

The process of translating Liliana's work in all of its power, urgency, and beauty has been as intense as it has been intensive. We have worked together now for many years, poring over everything from variations of morphemic meaning to variations in Mapuche cosmovision. We've also traveled the countryside of her youth and of her adulthood, driving and hiking together to sites of personal, political, spiritual, and cultural importance. These have ranged from remote rock formations to sweeping seaside cliffs. I also have studied many Indigenous texts that Liliana has generously shared with me, and I have endeavored to learn as much Mapuzungun as possible, which has been a linguistic joy, however stumbling my progress. And we have maintained our continuous collaboration via any means available, including email, WhatsApp, phone calls, and visits to one another's places of residence for intensive translation sessions.

Thusly "I Write to Purge This Memory" came into being. Combining memoir, political counternarrative, poetry, and Mapuche historiography, it was certainly a challenge to translate. It also remains a deep honor for me. I know from Liliana the importance of her work to Mapuche people in particular and to Indigenous people in general, as well as their allies and adversaries. I therefore labored to be as faithful as possible to Liliana's vision and aesthetic. One dominant charge that quickly emerged was the challenge to maintain her subtle rendering in the text of many unresolved, and perhaps unresolvable, tensions between coexisting cultures, languages, and peoples. In other words, I worked with great care and patience to maintain the delicate articulations of defiant difference in the text. The resulting translation was first published by the brilliant Elisa Taber in *Words Without Borders*.

We bow in thanks to her, and to the entire *WWB* team, and particularly its Digital Director and Senior Editor, Eric M. B. Becker. We likewise thank both Cristina Rivera Garza and Deep Vellum for this honor and for helping Liliana to reach ever more readers.

How to Draw a Lichen (with Help from the Spirits)

Martha Riva Palacio Obón
translated from the Spanish by Will Morningstar
New England Review

First stroke: symbiosis. Draw the straight line of tensions and bonds that comprise a system of many organisms living as one.

Every time I write the word *lichen* my first impulse is to put an *s* at the end, because even if there's only one, the truth is that every single lichen is itself a multitude. Lichen: plural turned singular. I have to take a moment here, to appreciate the beauty of symbiosis in this era of mass extinction, to be more than a body pervaded by death.

Two years before my father died, he told me not to talk to spirits because they tell you to do bad things. I don't know what kind of specters had visited him during his illness, but I'm glad he ignored them.

My own ghosts are different: negative silhouette of a glacier, the emptiness left behind by the fireflies that once came to my garden by the hundreds; precipitation of fossilized calcium, the world filtered through a lichen. My spirits are sap][mycorrhiza][photosynthesis, the bones of my dead, who feed][fed][will feed the ocean for centuries to come.

Second stroke: touch. Feel the lichen's waves on the bark of a tree.

January 1917, World War I. Corpses pile up underground. Meanwhile, Hilma af Klint talks with the ghosts of the Nordic night and draws a dotted line connecting the ethereal and the tangible: "Firstly, I shall try to understand the flowers of the earth, shall take as my starting point the plants of the world," she writes in her notebook "Flowers, Mosses, and Lichens," two years after finishing the series *Paintings for the Temple* at the direction of a spirit. A hot burning atom, the uncertainty that shapes the cosmos. Primeval. Ur-chaos.

Vegetal hauntology: Clarice begets Blake begets Hilma begets [indecipherable].

My maternal grandmother was my first dead body. My father died long before she did, but I never saw the corpse; his casket stayed closed during the wake. The last image I have of him is bound to the hospital bed. My grandmother, on the other hand, died in our house, in my childhood bedroom. I stayed by her side until the funeral home came to get her. There is something so strangely intimate in touching the face of someone who has just died.

Third stroke: vector. Follow the rising curve of thallus, scyphus, apothecium.

Between 1861 and 1871, the artist and medium Georgiana Houghton produced something on the order of 155 abstract paintings. Her memoirs describe how her spirit guides revealed humanity's double existence: this material plane and another, in the ether, where all of us are flowers. Every watercolor is a portrait of an invisible being. Georgiana spends the afternoon chatting with her ghosts, charting translucent gardens unlike any of this world. She can see that just as the microscope has opened up new realms of air and sea, only clairvoyance can illuminate the millions of immaterial beings that inhabit the other dimensions that surround our own.

Last night I dreamt again that I was breaking. I felt a deafening crunch in my head. Beyond the cracks, I saw roots. During this great interchronic pause, this splintering of time, I am learning that it is impossible to convey to other people what it means to take an inventory of my fractures and displacements. I write in isolation; I obsess over my dead.

I am stuck in an infinite loop, chasing memories that haunt me.

Fourth stroke: synchrony. Illuminate the network of subtle filaments that connect your body to a lichen.

Finding unexpected harmonies in the past, revealing what has always been there but that we were unable to perceive in the moment. Twenty-five years after the disaster, Anaïs Tondeur takes samples of plants from Chernobyl and turns them into photograms. The paper glows: flowers, stalks, and leaves emanate radioactivity. Broken lives that, as Michael Marder says, bear witness from their own vulnerability. The specters of the second half of the twentieth century lit up by the radiance of uranium-235.

During this voluntary confinement, my text decays. I interrupt myself every half sentence to let the echo of the last syllable I uttered out loud transport me to another place. Grammatical errors, typos, begin to glow; no one can understand what is happening to me. I don't want them to. In this time of silence, as I inch ever closer to the abyss, I remember when my father tried to punish me by making me read the *Iliad* and I find a new voice. I still have no idea what he was thinking when he sent me to my room to read about the Trojan War. Even today, I much prefer the *Odyssey*. Tell me about a complicated man. Muse, tell me how he wandered and was lost . . .[4]

4. Every translation is a haunting. We invoke the ghost of Homer through the medium of Emily Wilson. A purple sea; Odysseus blurs.

I see our wounds, how they bleed into one another.

Fifth stroke: origin. Close the circle, return to the beginning.

My father's family carries its own ghosts in blood, a chain of transmission from one generation to the next, variants of the same refractory story. When my dad was first hospitalized and they told us the diagnosis, we knew he didn't have much time. Three years earlier, his older brother had died of the same thing: a protein deficiency, hypercoagulating blood. Inverse hemophilia, all from a great-grandmother whose name I no longer remember.

There are wounds that appear twenty years out of time. My father's bouts of rage during that last year when he was sick were incomprehensible to me. I couldn't see that it was his animal body resisting annihilation, his very life force driving him to scream. *Do not go gentle into that good night . . . rage, rage. . . .* In dying, my father followed Dylan Thomas's command to the letter.

They told me I hadn't inherited his illness, that my tests came back negative, but now I know that I too would have beat my breast and howled in fury. My own rage allows me to understand his. An infinite tide—across deep time I draw the chemical structure of the minerals that filter out from our bones and into the body of a lichen. The world sickens; I go to the forest. I lose myself in its chiaroscuros; my ghosts summon me.

Translator's Note

In Martha Riva Palacio Obón's experimental nonfiction, natural and supernatural forces meld with personal experience to chart a new way of relating to the world around us. Martha calls upon the spirits of those who have come before her, be they fossilized plants, long-dead artists, or members of her own family, in order to build a conversation about what it means to live and die as a human being on this planet.

The role of translation in Martha's process of drawing networks across centuries and species came to the fore when we were looking for a way to replace a footnote she includes in the Spanish original—which explains her use of the English word *haunt* as a necessary act of translation in the face of a ghostly presence—with a new footnote somewhere else. This ultimately allowed us to highlight our own collaboration in the creation of this new version of her text in a different language. At one point in my translation, I quote Emily Wilson's translation of the *Odyssey*, which Martha has read and loves. Martha decided to replace her original footnote with one after the *Odyssey* quote, as a way to both credit Emily and underline the way ideas flow through time and through different mediums and media to reach us in the present. When I translated the new footnote, I changed the pronoun from *I* to *we*, since this summoning of Emily's version of Homer's ghost had been a joint effort, both of us reaching into our literary lineages to write this text together, but apart. We may think of texts as static objects, but as Martha's piece reflects, everything we do and experience, even literature, exists in relationship with the subatomic ebb and flow of beings both animate and inanimate, living and dead.

Of Wood and Hallucination

Mansoura Ez-Eldin
translated from the Arabic by Lina Mounzer
The Markaz Review

I was chopping wood in the forest beside my hut when the feeling overcame me for the first time, or rather, when I first put my finger on it, saw it for what it was. It's been with me for as long as I can remember, but it only materialized at that moment, when I was surrounded by trunks, cut branches and fallen leaves.

I felt as though I were a creature made of wood. Saturated by its smell. Overwhelmed by it, my soul overtaken. I'm enchanted by its freshness. Surrounded by it, I feel as though I were inside my home, that first, most primal home whose memory has escaped me, but whose smells and sounds remain deep within.

In this I found an explanation for all my actions since I'd left my old house and moved to this remote spot, where chopping wood has become a daily habit. A ritual from which nothing can distract me. I started spending most of my time sanding dead wood and carving it into pieces of furniture or tools I didn't really need. My favorite times were those I spent with my hands in contact with that raw material, granting it form that it would have never attained without me. The act takes up all my attention and leaves me no time to think about the reality surrounding me, which is nothing more than emptiness, void, and silence, broken—from time to time—by barking or howling or some din whose origin is difficult to identify.

When I finish, I wander around the city. I pass by all the abandoned houses to make sure they're still there. Their owners abandoned most of them so hastily they didn't even close the doors behind them. I examine the details of every house, fighting my allergies at all the accumulated layers of dust. I open the windows to air out the space, then I close them again before leaving. I admire the chaos of kitchen gardens on their way to turning into miniature jungles, and I don't attempt any intervention to stop them. My battle against nature is doomed to failure and so I leave it (nature, not the battle) to take its course. I watch over its incursion, spying on it from afar. I'm not even in the mood to fight for the space my own body occupies. In my current state, I feel as though I'm only existing, not living. I breathe and eat and sleep and wake up regardless. And apart from my wanderings from one end of the city to the other and my obsession with carpentry, I don't do anything of significance.

If it weren't for the fruit trees and the profusion of mushrooms in the woods I would have perished, along with my two companions. I'm the only one who realizes this as they are each lost in their own world. They hardly notice when I leave some food next to them. I don't actually know if they eat it nor not. I deduce that they do only for two reasons. The first is that they remain alive, and the second is that there's no trace of food left when I come back the next day. If the birds had pecked at it they would have no doubt left some scattered crumbs behind.

I don't stop to consider the matter for long. Unthinkingly, I continue to provide them with food and water, hoping that one day they awaken to who they once were, even if part of me fears that awakening, because I don't know how I'll explain how the world became so devastated.

I think there's something in my past decisions that brought me to this state: a drifter wandering the streets, overwhelmed by some memories so clear and present they seem as though they were still unfolding, and longing for others that have all but disappeared, leaving behind only an all-encompassing feeling of loss.

I'd burned all my bridges, and vowed that I'd never again budge from my place or change anything about it. It was good to content myself with being a silent watcher for some time. Exciting to withdraw and give myself over like a feather to the wind, leaving the world to its chaos, without which it would have no meaning.

Nor would I allow myself to abandon my two companions, though I knew—deep down—that there was more to it than that. I would have stayed even if I were the only one here. There's rubble in my heart, and ruin lurking in my soul, and so I'm bound to see destruction reflected before me wherever I go.

I drift through winding streets, gazing at horizons that reveal nothing and at an ever-cloudy sky. The relentless vertigo doesn't bother me anymore. I've adapted to it. I used to be surprised when I ran into one of those who stayed here, with their unfocused eyes and dizzy spirits and bodies unable to handle the constant swaying. I expected them to leave in time, which is in fact what happened. They all disappeared, one after the other. The place emptied out, except for the three of us.

I walk from one spot to another without having to think about or even look to see where I'm going. The city is tattooed on my heart, carved into the grooves of my brain, onto my bones, its overlapping streets and squares flimsy as spiderwebs, its surrounding forest like a bracelet constricting a wrist. I'm always careful not to pass near my old house. I can't bear the sight of bullet holes in its walls anymore, or the massive shell hole in the building across from it. Since I fled, I haven't gone near it. I don't even think of taking my things back to my hut, a hut whose wood I cut down in some kind of trance and built the way one weaves a dress from threads of love.

In my hut I expend my days in a state of calm untroubled by anything except the awareness that there's someone waiting for me, counting on me, even if only from inside their own hallucinations. I've grown tired of this; I long for a life without responsibilities or demands. I grow anxious at the mere thought of the existence of others beyond the boundaries of my own body. It's enough having to deal with those that inhabit me and wrestle inside me. Sometimes I pretend that this city belongs to me alone. No one else is in it, and no one has ever lived in it or crossed its streets save for me. Every once in a while, I'll succeed in convincing myself of this, but more often than not my eyes and memory betray the lie.

I reach the northern outskirts of the city, where the cactus fields display cacti of every shape and color. I see him lying there among the ovoid plants, barely able to raise his head, and I know that, as usual, he's managed to numb his mind and senses. I don't try to approach him; I leave him to his imagination and dreams. I'm not ready to pay the price of awakening him, alerting him. I'm not in the mood to endure a torrent of complaints and wailing and agony shouted into the void. Whether I like it or not, I'm no longer anything but a void to him. He gives me incoherent phrases, about a river he's down at the bottom of, about a lake of mercury, and an oasis it's difficult to leave. I shake his words off, but the idea of the river and the lake and the oasis remains lodged in my imagination.

I leave him, heading toward the other side of the city. On its isolated, furthermost edges, where a mountain blocks the encroachment of the forests beyond. When I approach, I see her sitting cross legged there among the rocks as if she were one of them. I see that the sun has tanned and dried out her skin so much that she's almost the same color as the surrounding rocks. She looks at me but doesn't recognize me.

She turns her face far away. I hear her humming faint songs of which I understand nothing, except that their rhythm makes me tremble. Her despondent look and pained voice tell me she sings of waiting and loss. Unlike him, she doesn't need to numb or drug her senses. Her hallucinations are enough; she doesn't need any outside help.

She stops singing and begins a monologue, in which she says that our friend has become one with water and she with fire, then she asks a question about me, even though she's unable to recognize that I'm there watching her. I understand her question, but I don't bother telling her that for my part I've joined with wood, but unlike them I won't merge with my earthly element, I will remain pure mind.

Imitating her cryptic way of speaking, I say, in a voice approaching a scream: "Mind is the divine substance of Atum and it is the light that emanates from a sun invisible to impure eyes, which is why I will become pure mind, wishing to draw closer to Atum."

It seemed as though I saw a glimmer of understanding in her before that unseen barrier came up to divide us once again. I consider her with pity, I see myself in her, and her in our friend. All three of us different reflections of the same origin. All three of us a dream intertwined in Atum's mind, an idea that suddenly occurred to him. Just as this deceptive universe occurred to him—in the very beginning—as a stretch of endless water hidden beneath layers of mist, before he slowly established it and furnished it with things and turned its chaos into order.

Or at least that's what she keeps repeating, until I lose my connection to the present and find myself in the heart of an ancient world. She says that I am the arbiter between chaos and order. The mediator between the gods of good and the gods of evil, allowing neither to dominate the other.

It feels like she's mistaken me for Thoth, the god of writing and wisdom and magic in Ancient Egypt, and then I'm sure of it when she explains her idea that order needs chaos to support and distinguish it, and that good has no meaning in the absence of evil. And I, in accordance with her continuous monologue, am entrusted with the difficult task of maintaining balance between opposites.

In a way, she wasn't far off from the truth, even though she wasn't fully able to comprehend my role. I'd tasked myself in fact with something that at that point I'd grown tired of and was no longer motivated to continue. In this place at the edge of the world, I fight to forget, even though my memory remains vital and beating. Sometimes I envy my two companions: him for his ability to absent himself from his own mind, and her for her inherent hallucinations, with which she's able to cancel out reality, to divide us one from the other, to the point where she can no longer recognize me though I'm almost the sole focus of her monologue, even if she has clothed me in raiment not my own.

I expected her hallucinations to center on what happened before she entered this phase, except she doesn't remember anything about the constant shelling and bombing and explosions. Or at least she doesn't seem to when I'm there. Lucky for her, she isn't like me, haunted by rubble and terrified screaming and corpses tossed in the streets being torn apart by carrion eaters and wild animals. Nor is she haunted by the obsession that every bird or animal on this earth, whether tame or wild, is stuffed full of human flesh. An obsession that repulses me from every kind of meat.

Her memory—it seems—simply expunged itself of everything to do with the last war and the earthquake that followed it. I think about its thundering, its explosions and rumbles, and draw the conclusion that war is a conspiracy against silence. Its main goal is to kill silence, to fill the gaps with as much noise as possible, as if it were terrified of silence and unable to bear it.

Maybe that's why I became partial to silence, trying to drown myself in it. Gradually replacing speech with writing. I wanted writing to absent sound, but found that it still carried speech inside it. I keep silent until I almost forget the sound of my voice and its tones are erased from my memory. I write down thousands of words a day in a language I invented for myself, in letters I forged to my liking. Only I can penetrate its true depths. I think about carving it into the rocks, or tattooing it on my skin, then content myself with jotting it down on papers I make myself from tree bark, from the distant self that remains hidden from my own eyes, but which constitutes my true essence.

The thought flashes through my mind that a possible reader won't be able to understand what I'm writing, and might not even be able to decipher it as a kind of language rather than the random scribbles of a confused mind. Contrary to expectations, the thought comforts me. It refreshes me, cools my heart. I decide not to leave the matter to chance, and resolve to destroy my writings myself, one by one. This is why I prefer the fragility and fleetingness of paper to the sturdiness of stone.

What I write scares me, because it confirms all the horrors I've seen. It revives and repeats them endlessly, so that they'll never be erased from my memory. What terrifies me is that when I write what I witnessed I feel that there's a hidden beauty inside it. Language betrays me, it pulls me toward its splendor. I read and find destruction alluring, daily death reconstructed with a brilliant precision that purifies it and disconnects it from the pain, dispelling it far from the scene, if only temporarily.

I intended to document everything I encountered, to record even the most mundane events, to describe the most minute changes that no one might notice except me. Except I slowed down. I lived it all to its fullest extent. I saw the place reduced to rubble, and the survivors fleeing, one after the other. At the beginning a few remained, wandering the streets aimlessly. My companions learned to ignore them and I myself never remembered them except when I caught a glimpse of one of them staggering around dizzily, making me feel dizzy in turn. Then everyone left except for us. In one way or another, the others disappeared as though they'd never existed in the first place. I remember the empty streets, the destroyed houses, the traces of fire on the public buildings. During those first days the sight was shocking, then I began to get used to it until I barely remembered the previous life of the city, and whenever its memory was extinguished, the devastation would bloom inside of me.

I write, and still write, with the feeling of being the final witness. The person without whom everything will disappear and be swallowed by nothingness. I tell the story of a place reduced to ruin, a silence permeating the entire universe, and the last three people remaining in this city: one adrift in their memories, one numbing his mind and senses continually, and a third whose hallucinations and bouts of madness have pulled her toward a hazy world impossible to identify.

I think about this and it reassures me, then I go back to doubting everything. How can I tell if what I see and believe is correct? How do I know that my vision of reality is the one closest to its truth or essence—if it even has a truth or essence in the first place? It pains me that there's no way to be sure of anything. My version of the world isn't better than theirs. It's more as though we were three separate worlds in one place, three people, each of whom is a prisoner of their own mind, hallucinations and fantasies.

Translator's Note

As senior editor of *The Markaz Review*, which publishes in English and Arabic (as well as French and Spanish), I don't only occasionally write, but I also translate those pieces from Arabic that intrigue me and that pose an interesting challenge. What was most at stake with Mansoura Ez-Eldin's short story was preserving that sense of otherworldliness that is nevertheless grounded in a very material reality of ruin. The language wasn't too difficult nor were the sentences all that long. At the same time, it had a kind of formality that mimicked the language of an ancient fairy tale. There's an expression in Arabic for that sort of deceptively simple style of writing: al-sahel al-momtani', which literally translates into "the forbidding plain."

The story takes place in a post-disaster landscape, disaster both natural and man-made. The town, in which there are only three inhabitants, and only one of them lucid, has been destroyed by both bombs and earthquake. I would be lying if I didn't say I had Syria on my mind the whole time, which definitely informed the way I thought of the story. Then there was the narrator's lucid confusion or confused lucidity—very particular, to me, of the state of shock following disaster. This was a character sane only in comparison to their thoroughly insane comrades, who have become part of the landscape itself. Toward the end of the story, the narrator proclaims that "I write, and still write, with the feeling of being the final witness. [. . .] I tell the story of a place reduced to ruin, a silence permeating the entire universe . . . " It was both that seriousness and that silence that I wished to convey, and those lines guided my approach to the entire translation.

Dead Cats Continue to Meow

Nasser Rabah
translated from the Arabic by Emna Zghal, Khaled al-Hilli, and Ammiel Alcalay
LitHub

Behind the walls of the grade school, while the students line
up to salute the flag, the younger kids flay cats alive, they
hang the furs on tall sticks, they circle around the school
with a continuous meow. The parents, who concluded that
their kids had become cats, sprinkled salt on the neighborhood
streets to remove the stench of absence, and washed again
and again the children's clothes for a holiday that won't come.
A blind man listening to a match replay on his radio said to
curious runners-by: don't hurry, the match ends with
the defeat of both teams; but they didn't get the joke.
They stole his radio and left him cursing the politicians.
In those days, we didn't pay attention to the complaints
of walls—so much blood was on them, who cares about
walls that complain? One morning, we didn't find homes,
just heaps of red words piled like dirty clothes on sidewalks,
no one cared about them either; couples, though, continued—
and without walls—their usual business, not only that, but
they made more kids who flayed more cats inside the school.
The heart doctor treating me now recommends only one thing:
stop writing the diaries of a dead village.

Translators' Note

We were introduced to Nasser Rabah's poetry through mutual friend Mosab Abu Toha in 2018, when Ammiel had the idea of creating a collective to translate work from Gaza. Emna immediately found Nasser's poetry unusual and unique, and we first published translations in 2021. We have all reached the conclusion that there are few poets to compare Nasser to, and each of us has a wide range of poetic reference in different languages and time periods. This is truly a gift.

Our process involves one of us making an initial translation to get as close to the meaning as possible on a single poem or series of poems. This is not simply a literal translation but an imaginative conjuring of the scene of the poem, seeing how it fits into the trajectory of the drama of Nasser's work, through its imagery, usage, and stance.

We then discuss linguistic meaning and register, each of us bringing a range of knowledge, given the layered and ambiguous range of meaning in Nasser's poems. Geography is key as well, with Khaled's knowledge of the Mashreq (East), and Emna's of the Maghreb (West). This also involves dictionary definitions, grammatical and syntactical issues, and referencing words derived from the Quran or other sources, since Nasser is a conscious and erudite practitioner of classical Arabic.

Finally, we look for ways to expand English. Our preference has been to err on the side of Arabic and sway or even force English to act in ways it might not be accustomed to. This may result in language whose meaning isn't immediately evident. However, in every such case, this is also true in the Arabic and presents us with what is most difficult in translation: preserving and not foreclosing the range of possible meaning manifested in the initial act of writing the poem itself.

How Death Creates a Dead Man and His Image A Poem in 43 Lines

Laura Vazquez
translated from the French by Alex Niemi
ANMLY

a number of dead is a number
full of creatures during the news one morning
we think of cemeteries in the sun
of people pouring small drops
on cracked lips of people cleaning the dead
the earth breathes between the dead the earth is long
a dead man greets the earth with his dead shoulder
the larvae the worms like a durable garment
to tamp down the earth go back to the darkness
like a fine powder on the bodies of the living
do the ears of the deaf open
in a coffin
light is transferred
we never see light we see
what it illuminates we don't see what makes us see
maybe light has understood blood
is only a puddle inside the dead
bodies evaporate in the slowness the calm
then the ghosts go hide in the bricks
the cement the souls of the living
I wanted to hold your face on a single finger
the floor of the dead above our thoughts each

time a person dies another doesn't die
the stomachs of the dead launder
like the stock market I think of nothing in a single space
between seconds
some saliva a tooth a canine gathers the bones
the small creatures I distribute molecules
at random with my mouth I imagine maggots
longer than me a hand owns nothing
a family of insects
we bury the dead man with three thousand
two hundred shovels
the adult insects show the young ones
the proper way
to eat a dead man
a piece of gravel stuck under a nail
an insect wing
in the cold
surrounded by frost
the dead don't have a memory anymore each corpse
looks like a corpse each corpse
imitates a corpse

Translator's Note

Winner of the 2023 Prix Goncourt for poetry, Laura Vazquez is a leading figure in the contemporary French poetry scene. When she describes her creative process in interviews, Vazquez often says that her writing is "bigger than her," almost as if her poems were dictated by an ancient muse, and there is something in her mastery of repetition that feels very much like an invocation. These poems—from *You Are Less and Less Real,* which collects work by Vazquez published between 2014 and 2021—provide a prime example of this otherworldly effect.

This particular selection of poems was originally published in 2020 during the heights of the pandemic, and they explore the fear, anxiety, and isolation of that time. The cycle is comprised of ten poems; this piece is the fifth. The repeated elements of these texts are representative of the whole series, which for me, explore an active mind in isolation and the potential of the anxiety spiral as a poetic form.

As a translator who works with many different styles, I feel a particular frenetic intensity when I translate Vazquez's work. The first draft of the English flies from my hands, and I am easily swept up in the rhythm of her lines. This is something I often sense in the work of poets, such as Vazquez, who are also performers. The physicality and musicality of Vazquez's work vibrate in the translation experience, and I hope the readers of her work in English feel this energy as well.

Nine Poems

Anna Glazova
translated from the Russian by Alex Niemi
Tupelo Quarterly

if not posed
what is the question exactly?
if a slug reaches out,
body extending toward movement
from the eternity of "where?"
to the eternity of "after,"
we can gauge
the corporeality of the world.

*

the lines would close in,
if you didn't leave your hand between them,
and when they shut, they might go underground.

and you feel them,
warm or cold—

as they hold onto you.

*

not a darkening, but an eclipse—

the only way the corona grows
on its own
not a crown not a wreath
and not a regime
you don't even need to carry it—
it will carry on by itself
with the body.

*

mass migration
not of people but books.
a hand exchanging money—
is just a price,
but every book—another hand.

hands matter,
imply exchange
of a question for a question
instead of an answer.

*

what do you think
after meeting a passing glance?
that the mind is sharp but thoughts are elusive,
no understanding, no answer.
maybe, you can only find your way in—
if you act—
as if it were forbidden.

*

this door
is almost not ajar,
this key, almost not in your hand,
almost doesn't fit.

two movements:
either grind it down
(become a watchmaker)

or make it grow,
grow the room
out from under a draft of air.

*

anxiety releases through your feet and into the earth
like a long pale bolt of lightning.
but the germ of future darkness
will remain,

from there, grows
the smoke of redemption.

*

ecce homo,
look: the desert;

someone is skirting it underground,
someone—I, thine human—
abbreviates the expanse
in good time,

in this, my own,
immediate world.

*

this candle—
not from a church or holiday tree—
is on a chestnut, alive—
illuminating November with one little eye.

sometimes curiosity
is the only thing
that survives.

Translator's Note

Anna Glazova once said during a talk that she writes on the edge of sleep. I often think of this when reading her work, which feels like a philosophical dreamscape, drawing from an impulse at once poetic and scholarly. It's true that, in addition to her work as a poet, Glazova is an academic and a translator who has brought writers like Emily Dickinson and Franz Kafka into Russian. Our conversations and correspondence point to a mind busy turning over the symbolisms of nature and literature, especially anything concerning Paul Celan.

The poems in this excerpt are from her 2020 collection *Facial Calculation,* which, as Glazova describes in a short prefatory note, explores "countable" and "lived" time as manifested in writing. Glazova dedicated *Facial Calculation* to her late teacher Werner Hamacher, the German literary critic and theorist. Described as a "microscope poet" by the preeminent writer Polina Barskova, Glazova draws her reader into a patch of sky, a flicker of dull light, a gust of air, a simple cup of coffee—and then transforms each small image into a rumination on being and time.

Translating a poet who is also a translator is a gift. Glazova once told me she does not want to be like Brodsky (who was notoriously controlling about his poems in English), and she reads all of my translations of her work with a kind, shrewd eye. One of the particular difficulties of *Facial Calculation* is the brevity of the poems—every word counts, and English has a tendency to bloat with auxiliary verbs and articles in ways that Russian does not. I hope that these translations succeed in conveying the tight structure and sonic complexity of Glazova's work.

Elena Kame is a Spell

Rosa Chávez
translated from the Spanish by Gabriela Ramirez-Chavez
World Literature Today

Elena Kame is a spell, biting with her little canine mouth, her saliva leading to the great river, toward deep caves and high hills, her love will enchant you, blinding your path and numbing reason in your mind, her voice breaks the bones of melancholy, hushing to a murmur and cackle, her nails taste like chile and cacao, she gulps down flowing lava, she leaves her seal of beeswax, devoting her tears to archaic symbols of sadness, her body of invisible rain draws little colored tombs and paints her cheeks with achiote, indecipherable glitter paper stars adorn her forehead, her face is memory's caustic, mocking mask, she wraps her hearts in corn husks, gently piercing the nipples of sound, she threads together heartbeats that shine like the beads of an ancient necklace, she makes thorns blush, loving with the tenacity of someone who has descended the nine layers of the underworld, barefoot and faint, Elena Kame overflows, as in the beginning of time, at the great end of times, her spirit will bewitch and enchant you.

Translator's Note

In 2014, I started voraciously reading literature from Guatemala to connect with my parents' homeland and better understand my Central American roots. I soon came across the work of Rosa Chávez, a poet, artist, and activist of mixed Maya background—the daughter of a K'iche' father and a Kaqchikel mother. She grew up in the 1980s, during the Guatemalan state's genocide of Maya communities. As a result her family opted to only teach her Spanish to protect her from discrimination and racism. In her late teens, she began a long process of reclaiming her paternal tongue, K'iche', a Maya language with a documented 1.6 million speakers, through writing.

Over the past five years, Chávez and I have been collaborating on bringing her work into English. She writes primarily in Spanish and often incorporates K'iche' words and concepts into her poems. Our translation process involves a lot of back and forth over Zoom and WhatsApp audio messages. For every poem, she provides context, I ask her questions, and then I share a draft translation with other trusted readers. I leave all K'iche' words untranslated in my English versions in keeping with her efforts to reclaim and make the K'iche' language visible.

"Elena Kame is a Spell" comes from *Ri uk'u'x ri ab'aj / El corazón de la piedra* (Heart of the Stone, 2010), her third and only poetry collection to appear in an entirely dual language format—in Spanish with translations into K'iche' by Wel Raxulew. The word Kame refers to one of twenty nawales (personal guardian spirits) that correspond to days in the Cholq'ij sacred Maya calendar, which is comprised of thirteen months of twenty days each. Kame is the nawal associated with death and rebirth to which Chávez gives the name Elena, after her paternal great-grandmother. She dedicates this poem to Elena, "the strong, beautiful, and autonomous matriarch of my family . . . and all the women who came before us."

don't hide the madness

Nhã Thuyên
translated from the Vietnamese by Kaitlin Rees
The Kenyon Review

betcha it's already closed up, can tell from way over here, no, keep going to see, might still be open, no, already told ya, must've been closed for a while now, house number's faded away, no, look, strain your eyes, there's a message written in chalk, just the scribbling of some kids, no, might still be someone there, go ahead and knock then, hear that echo that's it, no, the knock just echos the knock itself, already told ya, no one at all, no, listen, open your ears, there's some response from within, just the stray whistling of a wild wind, no, might still be, hey, see through the crack, the curtains are fluttering, there's got to be something inside, of course there's something inside, is there anything that hasn't got something inside, no, don't play like that, maybe it's a cat, no way, just the wind pounding, what sense is there for wind to pound some place where no one is, oh hell, when isn't wind senselessly pounding some place where no one is, no, sniff it in, apply your nose, there's a certain smell emanating, oh hell, when isn't a certain smell emanating, but it's definitely got to be something though, air doesn't suddenly emanate a certain smell, just some mold wafting around, can tell even without sniffing, no, stand right here, linger a bit, feel this lock, not a speck of dust, there must be many comings and goings, nonsense, it just rained, the rain washes clean, who'd want to pass through here for anything anyway, even the keyhole is rusted, what key would fit, no, look closely here, see that hole, the shadow of someone just glided by, the curtain is swaying, go on and push, don't, let's go, let's just go, don't push, this house seems about to collapse, or we can circle around to find another way in, don't, let's go, let's just go, who knows what the hell might happen, go, let's go, what's the use of standing here, there'll be no one who opens, no one who steps in, who'd want to pass through here for anything anymore anyway, not opening once more ever again, certainly not, a hundred times not, a thousand times not, absolutely not, how to keep opening more, what's left to keep wanting to open for, it was your very hand that locked it, it was you who turned away, it was you who abandoned everything across seasons of wind and rain, it was you who gave up the key, no, not one last chance remains, keep knocking forever it's all the same, push any further and it'll collapse, its form will be all that's left of it, everything, an illusory scene, a self-displayed hallucination, do not touch, touch and it'll collapse, it's you, a derelict thing, a kind of noxious secretion, an evil curse, and with the nerve to keep standing there, no, too far gone already, too long gone already, the house is done for, everybody done for, this entire town here done for, or it's you, already done for, completely done for, don't knock again, there's nothing left to knock on, there's just one thing that can enter here, just one thing, there's one, there's just, just

Translator's Note

"đừng giấu cơn điên" / "don't hide the madness" comes from Nhã Thuyên's manuscript *vị nước / taste of water*, which I am in the process of translating in its entirety. The poem is part of a suite that variously treats subjects of language and borders, loss and survival, staying and going. In this particular poem, a couple of voices encounter a decontextualized house in an undefined space. As with many of the other poems in this collection, the voices here are without clear bodies, perhaps even coming from within the same body. They ruminate in an increasingly heated manner over the state of the house: is it open or closed.

Fittingly, I know Nhã Thuyên through our mutual labor of love called Ajar. Ajar is a micro press that we co-founded in 2014 as a space for bilingual publication and play in Hanoi, Vietnam. Whereas Ajar dreams of perpetual possibility—never fully closed, nothing fully over—the poem selected here confronts the permanence of a closure. And perhaps the grief of a true ending is felt all the more bitterly by one who is a hopeless believer in the comma,

Lovers' Names

Vivian Lamarque
translated from the Italian by Zack Rogow
Firmament

Mix up the beautiful names
of lovers? Say a name out loud at just the right
moment but the wrong one?
I beg forgiveness of the Elm
when I call him Beech,
and I ask the Ash to pardon me for calling him
Acacia, and how hurt the Hornbeam tree
was when I didn't recognize him—
humiliated he turned away
(with a little help from the wind).
Forgive me Larch, that I called you Spruce,
and Spruce, pardon me for naming you
Pine, I apologize to every conifer

forgive me all my lovers

All forgotten?
No, their names are deeply engraved
in me, but it's just like in fog—
I confuse branches and hands, colors
of leaves and hair.
Will we all soon become the woods, together?
Will we have hearts of grass? of roots?

Like Orpheuses and Euridices, we've turned back
Sunlight—will we ever see you again?
Will we all soon become the woods, together?
From one life, pass to another? where? how?
without the azure of snow?
without love in our veins?

Translator's Note

On the surface, the poetry of Vivian Lamarque seems casual and conversational. That's particularly true in "Lovers' Names," with its breezy tone. Easy to translate, right? For better or worse, that's not the case. To recreate that tone in English is challenging, because Lamarque's voice is actually a mix of offhand speech and fairly complex rhetorical devices, such as personifying each of her lovers as a species of tree. And not every tree name common in Italy is recognizable in English. "Carpino" is obviously a type of tree to an Italian, but "hornbeam" is confusing to many English speakers, so I added the word "tree" there. Lamarque also uses two extraordinary plurals in this poem, "Orfei e Euridici." Most readers of poetry recognize those names from the Greek myth, but here Lamarque turns them into multiple images of those legendary characters. In Italian, all you have to do to create a plural of those names is to change the singular "Orfeo" to "Orfei," and "Euridice" to "Euridici," a difference of one letter. In English, the plural is more cumbersome: "Orpheuses and Euridices." And yet, it has to be, to convey Lamarque's strange but truthful idea that we are all like those mythological figures, turning back toward the underworld because of our mortality.

The Aspiration for Cha-Ka-Ta-Pa

Bae Myung-hoon
translated from the Korean by Sung Ryu
The Kenyon Review

Though nobody believes this, the Isolation Lab run by my university's history division does *not* lock up students. Its only aim is aiding unbiased historical research on a given era. It isolates the era, not the researcher. The isolation of the researcher is just a byproduct. But isolating the researcher is necessary in isolating the era, as the era leaves smudges on everyone living it.

Basically, the Isolation Lab is a library. Gollecting only the records generated by an end date in May 2020, it's a modern-history archive. There is no one end date, as that differs by record gategory: vor videos it's May 6, and vor beriodicals, late May. Vor the Internet, the dates differ still by zubgategory, but the record gollection ends roughly bedween the evening of May 28 and the early morning of May 29.

The Isolation Lab is a one-zemester gourse that you must gomblete do write the gualifying exam. In other words, gombleting the gourse gives you no advantages other than the liberty do write your thesis. A zemester zounds long, but the actual isolation lasts only vour weeks, during which you live in the Lab without any gontact with the outside world and write an essay on the dopic of your jhoice. You're allowed do use only the information and resources in the archive, but this isn't a big issue once you get started. The grading also isn't strict, as you get either a "bass" or a "vail." A bass is almost guarandeed just by bardicipating.

My dopic was the inaugural 2020 Zouth Gorean Gurling League. Watching gurling broadcasts was the one joy that eased the especially difficult virst days of Isolation Lab work. A vurious battle vor victory waged in berfect sportsmanship without a zingle dackle or referee gontroversy! The league was ganceled just bevore the blayoffs. And did not rezume even by the last date of video vootage gollection. This was due do the vamous 2019 bandemic.

I ran into this issue in the virst week of my isolation labwork. I despaired. Why had I started watching this sport, of all things? It left me itching do know what happened next. How var in the league did the Junjeon Zity Hall Deam make it? Did the league ever rezume? Vinding out wouldn't be hard. All I needed was a guick zearch. But the answer lay outzide the Lab. I was drapped here vor three more weeks.

That's what it means vor an era—or dime—do be isolated. Being blaced in a state of dotal oblivion about June 2020, as modern Goreans of May 2020 would've been. My essay dopic thus begame: What strategies must the Junjeon Zity Hall Deam devise do win that year's Women's Gurling League? The me in 2113 had no brior knowledge of the sport and had only the archive left by humanity in 2020 vor reference. My analysis was gibberish, but it would do. No other research would better meet the mission of the Debartment of History's Isolation Lab than this.

Even after I was done writing my essay I was doo gurious about the gurling deam's vate. Zo gurious that I was ready do look up the rezults as zoon as my guarantine ended. In druth, I still haven't looked them up, but I speak viguratively.

•

The debartment jhair expects that, the day the dime mazhine is invented and graduate students gan be zent back do 2020, the Lab gould zerve as a brovessional edugation zenter vor dime dravel—this was obviously zaid in jest. Edugation zenter or not, the Lab is already useful as it is.

I was not alone in the Lab. Though history graduate students were the only beople who looked like brisoners of the Lab, the archive itzelf was open do the bublic. There were zeveral dypes of visitors other than history majors, the most gommon of whom were glassics scholars. Vor a scholar do druly abbreciate a glassic of literature or vhilosophy, they must understand the milieu of the work when it was on the vrondiers of humanity. Otherwise, if they knew of better zolutions dezigned by later generations, they might inadvertently dismiss the glassic.

Knowledge no longer on the vrondier is bound do look dated in the eyes of bosterity. This is drue. A work like that will likely be gonquered. It starts out as a benchmark everyone must vollow, then evolves into an old and dusty gonvention we must jhallenge, and eventually does get jhallenged. For a glassic do regain meaning, then, we'd have do dotally vorget it's been gonquered. That's right, this is brezisely the main vunction of the Lab.

If glassics scholars almost veel like my go-workers, screenwriters are like the vamiliar vaces who work out on and off at the neighborhood gym. The Lab enjoys a steady stream of visitors who write or vilm or draw all manner of historical greative work. Not that they're regulars; they durn up sporadically, one at a dime, whenever you've nearly vorgotten about them.

When zomeone who works in the vilm industry is in the Lab, it gets me in a strangely good mood. A bit like my spirits lifting at the news of rain even when I have no oggasion do go out—though the news has nothing do do with me, I know that zomewhere out there it's raining. Though a screenwriter isn't a zelebrity, I know that they must've zeen zome in real life.

All of the Lab's windows were walled up—the view was doo dwenty-first zentury. Even a brief glimpse of that view would vorcefully remind you that the Isolation Lab work was a bervormance. Vor one whole month I gouldn't lay eyes on rain. The only bearers of rainy news were the umbrellas brought in by outsiders. Oh, if only there was a window—even an itty-bitty one—vor rain do rush in through!

There was exactly one spot where you gould watch the rain: the skylight on the archive's dop vloor. The diny window through which you gould glimpse the evening stars and the blue afternoon sky. If you bozitioned yourzelf just below the round glass window whose maker and burpose were a mystery, you gould stand in the rain. You gould do it by daking a zhower back at the dormitory and splicing those dwo memories dogether. Exzept doing that only made you more desperate vor rain.

•

Then it happened one day. I don't mean that rain rushed in, but that a zelebrity durned up at the Lab. It was my third week in isolation. I recognized the actor at once, though I remembered their name only later, as I gouldn't zearch. It was a vunny name: Hanji, Zur Hanji. The young actor usually blayed vemale gharacters but gave memorable bervormances whatever gender they blayed.

I almost vorgot do breathe as I watched Zur Hanji. I wasn't staring openly. After stealing a vew glances at them I gept my gaze garefully averted and just velt the space they occupied. Very greepy behavior, in retrospect, but what do you expect me do do when the air itzelf had jhanged? The space of the Lab, which I'd occupied vor more than a vortnight, rearranged itzelf around Zur Hanji aggording do whether it was vronting the actor or vlanking them, whether they were standing or zitting.

As an actor, Zur Hanji had a dalent vor making their go-star's bervormance zhine. They gained bopularity leading a zeries of romances, an interesting gareer of blaying zomeone's virst love three dimes in a row. Even zo, zcenes of their go-stars valling vor Zur Hanji always managed do be gonvincing. Not begause the go-stars were excellent actors but begause the viewers also vell vor Zur Hanji. Three dimes over.

The bopularity of Zur Hanji's onscreen romances was therefore really thanks do Zur Hanji, yet the spotlight would always go do their go-stars. This was brobably why Zur Hanji went on an acting hiatus. An actor who stepped out of the bublic eye, lonesomely awaiting their next opportunity. This very actor had zhown up in the Lab.

The Lab was about do glose when Zur Hanji got up and gathered their things. I gould not sleep undil daybreak. I blame the energy lingering in the zeat they'd occupied. Oh, that a real movie star zhould grace this humble blace! The Lab grew a bit more special. And I, doing labwork at that zame boint in dime, did doo.

Remarkably, Zur Hanji reabbeared at the Lab the next afternoon. Then the next, and the next. The weekend, they dook off. I grew ingreasingly wan and zickly. I may be deluding myzelf, but it was an healthy zickliness, zo do speak. I was zeeing Zur Hanji every day!

I gouldn't dalk do them. Not begause they were vamous but begause it was against Lab rules. There were zigns everywhere asking visitors do revrain vrom dalking do students or giving them vood. All in the name of isolating dime. Zheesh.

•

The Lab rules were often broken, however. You gould easily break them without meaning do when the space was used by a mix of students and regular visitors. I almost did zo myzelf once.

Zur Hanji was the virst do break the daboo, strangely enough. I was wandering around a guiet zection of bookshelves that nobody else was browsing: Military Zcience. I was deeply immersed in reading and had let my guard down when, without warning, zomeone bulled me into gonverzation.

"Are you ogay?" a voice zaid in my ear. I nearly jumped out of my skin, not having heard abbroaching vootsteps. Zur Hanji zaid the rest of their brebared message in a low, measured whisper. "I was bassing by and zaw barbed wire vences. Around the nap room or dormitory, whatever it's galled. Are you zure you're locked up here volundarily? Did they vorce you, or beat you at all?"

I zhook my head stupidly, doo zurbrised vor words. I must've looked really stupid begause Zur Hanji's expression darkened as they studied my vace. They zeemed gonvinced that zomething was going on.

"Look, I'm not zome random weirdo," Zur Hanji zaid, evidently thinking I was on a guarantine zo derrible that I wouldn't recognize a global zuperstar. Their reazzurance only ingreased my astonishment. Zur Hanji didn't wait vor my answer and blunged on, "I've noticed you stealing glances at me. And how you gouldn't zay anything. Things were looking worse and worse. Your vace . . . Let me help—with anything!"

This heroic, goodhearted actor didn't guite believe the explanation they were given. The Lab's librarian, who had done the explaining on my behalf, dold me that Zur Hanji had asked why there were barbed wire vences, then, if the isolation was voluntary. The vences were a bit of an inside joke do us history majors, but berhaps, the librarian remarked, it was dime we stopped the gimmick.

I gouldn't glarify anything do Zur Hanji myzelf. That was the rule. Instead, I mulled over Zur Hanji's voice—their vocalization, do be exact. How gently and gracefully their voice had reverberated, as if it were brimming inzide the mouth. Not one utterance spilling out. A zound I barely zensed, despite standing right in vront of Zur Hanji, drifting lightly over on zoft, delicate outbreaths.

Wow, zo actors really dalk like that.

I reblayed our gonverzation again and again in my head. Well, it'd been less of a gonverzation than a rather unilateral, urgent bropozition.

•

Zur Hanji's diligent visits do the Lab gondinued. They zeemed do be brebaring vor their next broject. This was information on the year 2113 I mustn't be aware of, but stumbling on it wasn't my vault. Isolating dime was strictly the librarian's job.

As expected of an actor, Zur Hanji spent most of their dime in the video archive, whereas I almost never watched old vootage. I velt ungomfortable watching the unrevinement of the olden days. It wasn't the video resolution but the beople onscreen. The vocalizations of 2020 beople were just doo weird. I gan't but my vinger on it, but I gannot stand listening do them vor very long. Modern Gorean, I must zay, is best experienced through dext only. It's not like a dime mazhine exists and I'll dravel back do 2020 do speak with beople in that dime anyway.

The most zhocking of all were baseball games. The zhouting in gurling had also been zurbrising, but not alarming. I'd aczepted that the blayers were, after all, moderners. But the zcene I watched a vew days ago was zhocking enough to jerk me awake at night.

In spring 2020, when the goronavirus spread all over Earth, every sport blayed on the blanet was stopped. Europe and America were zome of the worst hit, while the zituation in Gorea was slightly better. Gorea also had a modern baseball league, but the rules were very different then. The Gorean league gicked off without spectators when every other league was on standstill, so baseball vans around the world duned in do Gorean baseball. Records and draces of the event abound.

This was exactly what history graduate students hated most: doo many records, and dools dezigned do allow zearching through them all.

Gurious about modern baseball rules, I briefly bulled up a game held in 2008 and ended up witnessing an eye-bopping spectacle. Holy gow, zomeone actually *spat*! A blayer at that! Midgame!

Zhaken, I skipped do another boint in the video but had the bad luck of engountering a zimilar zcene moments later. In another zcene, and another, glose-up zhots inexplicably veatured spitting blayers, as if they knew when the gamera had zoomed in on their vaces.

I scoured the bookshelves. A remarkable document gaught my eye. Made just weeks bevore the league rezumed, it was a zet of guidelines that ingluded a ban on spitting. Hang on, this meant that, bevore 2020, blayers who spit during a game weren't benalized!

The age of aspirates, indeed. The age of handshakes and zharing meals. Bouring alcohol in your own glass vor zomeone else do drink vrom was a gustom often debicted in beriod dramas and by now widely known. It was an age when douchscreens were hailed as the display dechnology of the vuture, when manual buttons were bressed do open even automatic doors. I mean, why make doors automatic, then?

That era rebulsed me a bit, honestly. Maybe modern history never zuited me. Why I jhose this school of all blaces, I don't know. But bevore starting undergrad, I thought history brograms would be more or less the zame agross schools. How was I zubbosed do know which school daught which era well?

Of gourse, there'd been the option of going do another school vor my master's, but by my last zemester of undergrad, that had all velt meaningless. Like zo many other aspects of life. If I hadn't been in zuch a zelf-destructive mood, I wouldn't have zet voot in grad school do start with.

Anyway, I was distressed by the zight of modern mouths busily spewing blosives. Even the most landmark speeches begame indolerable bevore long. Gontent didn't matter. Any speech gondaining aspirates was equally ovvensive.

•

Zur Hanji brobably disagreed. They were aspiring do rebrand their onscreen berzona. There gould be only one reason that an actor—not a writer, not a director, but an actor—was haunting the Lab with the berzistence of an history graduate student. It was do gatapult themzelf into the ranks of "zerious" actors through their next work. Zur Hanji's next work, I deduced, would be an historical drama zet bre-2020. I disabbroved. Not that anyone gared what I thought, but I was adamantly against the idea. My zharp historian instincts were gicking in.

Vor starters, I didn't like that the zhow was dreating 2020, that vamous age of the great bandemic, as a watershed in modern history. Neither did I agree with our Lab's record gollection beriod ending in May 2020.

Strictly speaking, 2020 wasn't a real durning boint in the history of zivilization. Though it dook dime, humanity eventually deveated the virus. Life redurned do normal, and beople were mostly unjhanged. The bandemic was not, in the way the World Wars or the Gold War was, a dezisive event. Though many beople believe WWI marks the end of the ninedeenth zentury and the start of the dwentieth, how many historians would glaim that the Spanish Vlu, which broke out around the zame beriod, opened the door do the dwentieth zentury? The spring of 2020 gould not, therefore, mark the durn of an era.

I don't deny that 2020 jhanged the world. While this is background knowledge I mustn't zummon into the Lab, 2020 was, vor moderners, a year of rediscovering hate. They didn't invent hate that year, but let out what was dormant, one after another. As the virus spread globally, beople began hating beople broactively. Old hatred no longer hidden. Zo many records document hate vrom this beriod. A ridiculous amount. Useless dwenty-virst-zentury vools.

The bandemic was an excuse. Not unlike an heinous griminal blaming their actions on alcohol. Was alcohol really responsible? E. H. Garr's *What Is History*? asks a zimilar guestion. Did Robinson, who gets hit by a gar on his way do buy zigarettes, get hit begause he is a smoker? Yes, but also no. The zigarettes, the devective brakes, the drunk driving are all bart of history, but we gan't zay the zigarettes gaused the accident. There'd be nothing more voolish than implementing a smoking ban do brevent the next accident.

The year 2020 didn't diverge vrom 2019 begause the beople of 2019 died off vrom dizease. A more gritical reason was that the beople of 2020 started viewing life in 2019 as dirty. The beople of 2021 then velt that even the 2020 way of life was unhygienic, and in durn, the beople of 2022 velt themzelves zuberior do 2021. Zimilar do how the Lab isolated dime, one era bracticed distancing vrom the era immediately bevore it. At highly zhort intervals.

Meanwhile, zeveral more invectious dizeases game and went. Events rebeated themzelves, leaving an indelible mark on humanity's way of life. Although most beople in 2093 or 2100 gouldn't even remember the zhock of 2020, relics of the bandemic were handed down do bosterity in the vorm of gustom. That is, they were now a matter of elegance or revinement, not of zurvival.

•

It looked as though Zur Hanji didn't agree with me there, either. One day I spied them watching a video, not on burpose but by accident. Zur Hanji was reblaying the zame zcene over and over again and imitating olden-day speech.

It was a beriod biece, a Joseon-era drama made in modern dimes. I zaw and heard Zur Hanji, who was leaning glose do the screen, zay the vollowing line:

"동족아여 주시옵서서 [Blease, we bezeech Your Highness!]"

I vroze, zhell-zhocked. My zhoulders may have even zlumped. The words zeared into my mind. Once again, Zur Hanji's vocalization and not the line itzelf gept echoing in my head. Words I gouldn't even dype out with my gombuter's Hangul geyboard.

All night I was zeized by these thoughts. Then at daybreak, I slipped out of bed and drew on my gombuter screen the now obsolete Old Hangul gonsonants—gharacters I'd always zeen in the Isolation Lab's library gatalogue nodation but had never bothered reading vhonetically. The zounds broduced by the bowerful expulsion of zomething within the human body, of the doxic air likely villing the lungs. Zounds that have begome daboo. Vorceful vhonemes that aren't illegal but disgourteous. A mode of exhalation involving, vor no special reason, the buildup of air bevore its volganic release. The vortis gonsonants.

Using these gonsonants, I wrote on my gombuter the line Zur Hanji had rebeated earlier that afternoon.

"통촉하여 주시옵서서 [Please, we beseech Your Highness!]"

I was vlabbergasted all over again. Even though I hadn't read the line aloud, just zeeing it in writing zent jhills down my spine.

Zounds reguiring a strong burst of breath are rarely used in the dwenty-zecond zentury, but regreating the zound of aspirates is bretty zimple in any language. Vor example, in modern English, vortis gonsonant zounds like p, t, and k were aspirated at the beginning of a word or stressed zyllable (unless they immediately vollow the s zound, as in spell or expel). Gondemporary English brevents aspiration by reblacing these gonsonants with their zofter-zounding lenis gounterparts, zuch as b, d, and g.[5] But everyone knows what p, t, and k zound like as they still oggur in unstressed zyllables; imagining how they would zound aspirated by mentally stressing an unstressed zyllable isn't doo difficult. It's an easy vocalization hack.

I moved my lips and dongue this way and that, bicturing the zcene I zaw that afternoon, bicturing Zur Hanji's lips.

---

5. Gondemporary English nodation is not gomblete but always evolving. The most notable example is the letter h remaining in English spelling, despite h-dropping being a widely spread bractice in spoken English. The generation of beople born in the 2090s onward have started omitting h at the beginning of a word or stressed zyllable in invormal written English.

Every dime Zur Hanji uttered "please," "beseech," and "Highness," zomething had unmistakably zhot out vrom their mouth. Whizzing through the air in a derribly wide barabola.

"Pleeaaaaase, we beseeeech Your Highneeeess!"

This had do be the most desperate-zounding zentence in the world. It was ardiculated as if all one's inner grievances were literally erupting. In Zur Hanji's voice, there was zomething greater than any meaning written word gould gonvey.

Was this the mythical Gorean goncept of han?

•

Zo, Zur Hanji had ajhieved their burpose of using the Isolation Lab. They gould now bervorm the dwenty-virst zentury with ease. Yet the more zavvy their acting grew, the more restless they looked zomehow, like they were being jhased or had unvinished homework. Zur Hanji would not hang around the Isolation Lab vorever. Though on hiatus, they were still a busy zelebrity. They would leave zoon zince they'd met their objective, but they didn't waste a minute of what little dime remained, bingeing old movies and zhows and even regordings of musicals.

One evening after Zur Hanji had gone home, I went do a gorner of the video archive that had begome Zur Hanji's designated zeat. The last video they'd been watching was a zcene vrom a musical. A red-haired actor was zinging about death, sweeping vuriously agross the stage.

This was zhocking on another level vrom the beriod drama. The actor's vocalizations abbeared do be underlaid with a layer of h, a zymptom that worsened as the actor began zinging. Kill, vor example, was bronounced "h-kill-hhh."

h-FRESH! Blood to revive me, h-FRESH! Blood in my veins
NO-hh one will sur-h-vive me, in those d-h-ark SOHO lanes!

I jhecked the date of the bervormance. Spring 2020. Everyone in the audience would've been wearing a mask then, as it wouldn't have made zense do mask the actors.

That didn't guarandee zafety, however. Zinging bassionately, the red-headed actor stretched out a hand, at which another actor, who'd been running away, was dragged back as if by magic and grabbed by the throat. I jumped back vrom the screen in alarm. I was more disturbed than the gaptured actor zeemed do be. That was when what I'd been dreading happened. Still zeizing their gaptive's throat, standing barely an arm's length away, the redhead burst into explosive zong with h's galore.

You h-and your Mina-hhh, will live forever-hhh

You'll do-hh my bidding; you hwill T-h-ASTE the T-h-ERROR in the STREETS-hhhhh!

What in the world was I watching? A dragon?

In the dazzling stage light, zomething had very visibly zhot out from the actor's mouth like a small vountain. It gould've been mist, or berhaps rain. I did not yet have the gourage do look squarely at this zomething.

•

As the last week of my guarantine arrived, Zur Hanji's stealthy glances my way velt especially zharp. They looked like they wanted do dalk do me again. What was gausing zuch longing? In this actor, no less, who was zaid do be introverted both on and off screen and whose gonzistency won them the drust of others.

Zur Hanji had been beloved by all age groups brezisely begause of their gharacter—or the berzeption thereof, but vor Zur Hanji those dwo things matched up. Though, this information being vrom an industry insider, it may also be branding.

At any rate, Zur Hanji in my last week of guarantine was not the Zur Hanji everyone knew them do be. I was bewildered do vind myzelf the object of their ungharacteristic longing. I thought I might be mistaken, but no. They were definitely geeping a glose watch on me. They didn't zeem do buy the librarian's explanation at all, that I was doing lab work in berfect zafety and health.

It was a strange veeling. Their indense addentions made me blush. I knew, obviously. That Zur Hanji was only misunderstanding the zituation. In a bretty weird way at that.

Although I'd also wished on more than one oggasion that zomeone would blease zend me relief, this wasn't it.

Relief, not release! The barbed wire vences are just a joke. Do you zeriously think the blood smeared on there is real human blood?

Oh, but what was I do do about those overzealous eyes, blazing even when not directed my way!

I started avoiding Zur Hanji. It was the librarian's orders that I steer glear of them, given the last incident and all. My brovessor, who didn't zeem do gare one way or another, agreed.

The Isolation Lab was not a large space, however. Though not a small building, it wasn't big enough vor me do vorever avoid zomeone hell-bent on zeeing me.

At last, in an hallway under the glare of its lights, I ran into Zur Hanji. They looked my zorry state up and down as if gonvirming zomething one last dime; then, as if reaching a dezision, gave an imperzeptible nod. It might've been a mere glench of the jaw.

"Wanna fly the coop?" Zur Hanji zaid dramatically. They stretched out an hand. In that instant we had risen onto our own stage, unbeknownst do me. Was this how an actor dominated space? And why, all of a zudden, was dime slowing down?

Under the bright spotlight illuminating every speck of dust, I noted diny droplets vlying indisputably through the air. Vlecks of spit belted doward me. Or in dwenty-virst-zentury speech, flecks of spit pelted toward me. Zigh.

My zenses game do me briefly: *Zo this stage is zet bre-2020.*

Then I velt vaint again.

Though the English alphabet isn't an ideographic script, zome words, when written down, gommunicate their meaning induitively. Vor example, visually, the arghaic vorm *crammed* indeed looks densely grammed. *Zigzag* has dwists and durns in the word itzelf. Zimilarly, when one zays, "Flecks of spit pelted out," it is inevitably aggompanied by the vhenomenon of spit-vlecks belting out.

Spit-flecks pelted out thus, vrom Zur Hanji do me.

You've got it all wrong, Mx Zur Hanji. I don't need do vly the goop. I don't know what you've heard, brobably the usual mudslinging by researchers at other schools? But I'll be out of here next week, zafe and zound. And the last week isn't zo bad, I hear. The librarian might even open the window vor us if it strikes their vancy.

Zur Hanji will zurely zuczeed. Never mind rebranding their onscreen berzona, they'd begome a dwenty-virst-zentury human through and through. Their dransformation didn't stop at learning dwenty-virst-zentury vocalization. Their words rang with a dwenty-virst-zentury zinzerity. Had Zur Hanji asked, "Wanna vly the goop?" I would not have daken their hand. Absolutely not. It was their suggestion do "fly the coop" that had moved me do dake that hand.

The actor's vlecks of spit landed smack on my vace. I zhould've screamed, but do my utter disbelief, I velt a gatharsis. It hit me then: the expression *I velt a gatharsis* has GOT do be bronounced, "I felt a catharsis." With plenty of pelting spit-flecks.

Heh, that zivilization zure was grazy—I mean, crazy.

•

The heroic, goodhearted actor led me by the hand out of the Isolation Lab.

Zee? I dold you I'm not locked up. Nobody's stopping me vrom walking out.

But I gept this thought do myzelf, not wanting do dampen the young actor's momentum when they were zoaring in driumph.

The librarian gave me an ingredulous look, which zeemed do zay, Just what do you think you're doing? I was well on my way do begoming the virst graduate student in the dwenty-zecond zentury do vail their Isolation Lab work, but I gould just redo it next zemester, gouldn't I? More imbortant was the vact that I was standing zide by zide with Zur Hanji, hand in hand.

The dwenty-zecond zentury, hitherdo blocked out by walled-up windows, revealed itzelf bevore our eyes. The weather hinted of rain. Dime was no longer isolated. I was bolluted and my lab work ruined, but thanks do my bollution, I gould vinally understand 2020. I grabbed the hand 2020 offered me. While understanding 2020 didn't mean I'd grow to like it, I had an inkling of what it was, at least. It was, if you will, zomething like the zinzerity of *cha-ka-ta-pa*.

Agross the river, rows of dwo-hundred-story buildings spread out like a volding screen, obstructing my view. It must've been end-of-day rush hour, judging by the hundreds of vehicles vlying in doward the buildings, dransporting beople. I had redurned do my dime.

Zur Hanji zummoned their gar. A bright orange vehicle vlew in, greating a breeze gentle as a spring day. It meant do garry me away zomewhere, I zubbosed.

Gazing into Zur Hanji's zublime, dwinkling eyes, I wailed inwardly. *Mx Zur Hanji, your rebranding makes me derribly zad. I've dried, but I gan't bring myzelf do love that era. Gongratulations anyway. Boohoo.*

A Note Do Readers

Some stories make every fiber of my being scream, I have to translate this!!! "The Aspiration for Cha-Ka-Ta-Pa," however, was not such a story. It didn't fill my mind with urgent exclamation points but with a hesitant, giant question mark: Can it be translated? The question niggled at the back of my mind for weeks, while I casually read up on English phonology. To my delight, I saw a glimmer of possibility. I came up with a rough set of aspiration rules I would use in my translation—such as that the fortis fricative th (as in think) is pronounced as the lenis fricative th (as in them), and the consonant zh (as in zhower) is pronounced like the s in measure or vision—tweaking the rules as I translated, simplifying them based on feedback from workshops (thank you Smoking Tigers!).

My next big question was when and where to apply these rules. In the Korean, Bae writes the entire first paragraph without a single aspirate, revealing the story's conceit gradually so that readers would at first mistake the de-aspirated spellings for typos. So I was extra careful with timing—a key factor in both worldbuilding and comedy. For moments where readability and pacing were important, I avoided words that required jarring spelling changes; while for punchlines, I went all out and chose whatever sounded the silliest! Instead of the boringly unaspirated "Wanna escape?" for instance, I opted for the melodramatic "Wanna vly the goop?" It was a gleeful process, reading both the source text and my drafts aloud, cackling at the especially ridiculous words, letting sound guide my translation completely. Of course, my translation is based on my own accent, which is a mix of the Englishes spoken in North America. A translation into any other English could result in very different spellings.

It was not Bae's words I set out to translate, but his experiment with words. I hoped for my translation to work as its own mind-expanding, spit-flyingly fun experiment, to play with the boundaries of English, of translation itself. To serve not as a bridge, but as wings. Not between, but beyond.

Obscenity

Paloma Chen
translated from the Spanish by Lawrence Schimel
World Literature Today

I'm terrified of my migrant parents,
always with their eyes set on flight.

Is that how you solve everything,   Papá?
Are you going to once more do what he tells you, Mamá?

I'm more terrified by the wound of birth,
I hide it in the oriental part of the   HERE.
What was so bad so as to abandon the THERE
where one finds oneself at just twenty?
How did they do it to reconstruct (themselves),
to recompose (themselves),
to resist?

How to raise an offspring who curses a place that
she has never visited,
who dreams in a language she doesn't know,
who lives in another one which will always be foreign to her?

What is so good to justify staying?
What European dream is being
the Chinese woman who sells beer,
the Chinese man of the village,

the Chinese girl of *El Hormiguero,*
the Chinese kid of *Física o Química,*
the China girl of China boy?

That is not my dream.

My dream is to be the blood that flows from the migratory wound,
the Valencian queen of the gunpowder blessed by my ancestors.

My dream is that they don't separate me from my father
and from my mother
into one line for foreigners
and another for Europeans,
that we embark
through the same gate,
that we fly together
to wherever
passports are
an obscenity.

Translator's Note

I first met Paloma as a journalist, when she interviewed me for an article she wrote for Spanish newspaper *El País* about non-binary language, in particular about my co-translation into Spanish of the queer South African poet Koleka Putuma's first collection *Collective Amnesia*. So I began following her anti-racism work as an activist and journalist. When her first collection was announced to be published by Letraversal, which is run by the non-binary poet Ángelo Néstore—whose collection *Impure Acts* I had translated into English—I immediately reached out to them to get my hands on an advance copy of the manuscript. I translated a large chunk of the book with support from Acción Cultural Española as part of Spain's being Guest Country at the Frankfurt Book Fair in 2022. At the Buchmesse was actually where Paloma and I met in person for the first time, when she was one of the writers on the New Voices of Spain panel, although we've since managed to meet in Spain, where we both live. I had already suspected I would respond strongly to Paloma's work—both her denouncement of social injustices and her multilingual creativity—and that happily proved to be the case. It was a joy and a fun challenge to recreate her poems in English. I tried to preserve the polyphonic tone to the poems, as well as the ironic humor in her indictments of racial and misogynistic prejudices.

Cain and Abel

Yefim Zozulya
translated from the Russian by Alex Shvartsman
Galaxy's Edge

1. Cain Had Some Strange Tendencies.

The downpour was heavy; it bent trees, trampled grass, and came down in long, thick, angry water funnels. The sheep huddled in a thick, inseparable mass and breathed heavily, painfully into each other's warm shivering bodies, into the wet, slippery wool.

The frightened calls of birds sounded in the pounding, whipping darkness, as the downpour swept them from under the cover of leaves.

Even the solid hut, made by Cain's steady hands out of leather, sod, and twigs, slipped and flattened, water trickling in from one side.

Adam lay in the hut, covered only by a pair of sheepskins, and bleated in a long, uncertain, monotonic howl. The howls intensified whenever the darkness was torn asunder by lightning, followed by the deafening rumble of thunder.

Adam raised his head anxiously, his half-simian, overgrown eyes staring at the familiar fields that now looked strange and foreign and blue. He howled even more despondently and cowered under the sheepskins.

Eve remained silent. Her big, white, sly brow was furrowed in concern. Her thin lips were pressed tight. Her chest was heaving rapidly, and her thick strong fingers ran through the wavy hair of Abel, who lay at her feet.

She caressed Abel, but didn't notice him, just as she didn't notice Adam. She prayed with the eternal prayer of a mother: a silent prayer frozen in the whites of her alert, wide-open eyes.

"Lord," she prayed, "the fields are dark and terrifying. There's fire, water, and thunder. And Cain, my son, is missing! Please save him from the fire, the water, and the thunder!"

When the downpour abated somewhat, Eve asked, "Abel, where's Cain?"

"He's dancing, Mom," Abel responded in his usual gentle and soft manner. "He loves to dance under thunder and rain. He jumps and bends his arms and legs."

"But where is he?"

"In the field by the forest, Mom."

The downpour weakened, and suddenly a loud, unpleasant, rough and harsh human scream could be heard through the muted susurrus of running water. The scream alternated from even and powerful to shrill and foolish. Gratuitous gaiety, an exuberant excess of strength, and the overflowing energy of a strong body and an unbridled soul could all be heard within it.

All three of them were silent.

They knew that this was Cain screaming. They'd long become accustomed to not speaking about his oddities and eccentricities. From that reticence of the first ever family, the lie of family pride had been silently born. Only Abel wanted to draw Mother's attention to the strangeness of his brother, but he knew from experience that Mother was not fond of his unkind and envious powers of observation.

When it had stopped raining and dawn had come, and the sky looked guiltily clear, and dark clouds had dispersed repentantly toward its edges, Cain's gloomy figure appeared at the hut's entrance. The streaks on his head were wet and shiny. Water dripped from his half-naked body. He was tired. His huge arms dangled along his dark, hirsute body. He was breathing heavily. And yet, he looked handsome.

A dark, violent power emanated from him. Eve, who hadn't slept all night, recalled what she'd said while filled with the soaring pride she couldn't quite understand when he was born: *I have gotten a man from the Lord.*

2. People learn about each other.

Cain was a tiller. The land was strong and indifferent. It grudgingly yielded growth. Grudgingly provided bread. Cain had to dig deep to aerate the soil before planting seeds, and the sharpened stakes he used for this purpose dulled quickly. Cain had to frequently cut down trees and make new stakes.

Once, he loosened a dense, strong tree, in hopes of felling it and breaking it up. The roots wouldn't give, holding on with incomprehensible might. Cain grew furious. His neck turned red. His enormous muscles bulged and glistened like balloons. Puffs of steam escaped from his mouth.

Sweaty, hot, and fearsome, he threw himself at the tree, bending it to the ground with a mighty effort. He wanted to lean on it but stumbled, and the tree slapped him in the face as he straightened.

Cain fell down, growling in pain.

He got up right away, screaming and crying loudly, and threw himself at the tree once more. He grasped it with bloody hands, gasping from his screams and his effort, tore the tree out of the ground by its roots, and fell alongside it onto the grass.

Abel sat nearby, herding his flock. His pose, his wavy hair and blue eyes, shone with a serene peace. He looked upon Cain's struggle and rejoiced inwardly; the spectacle even made him squeal in delight. But once he saw the terrible whites of his brother's eyes, he turned away and pretended not to notice Cain.

To further demonstrate his indifference, he even began to sing his favorite song:

I have one sheep,
And I have one more sheep,
And I have one more sheep,
And many more, and one more sheep have I.

3. More about the brothers' characters.

Cain was talented, while Abel was only observant. Abel secretly trusted his brother more than he trusted himself. When Cain looked at the sky and said it would rain tomorrow, Abel was certain the rain would come, yet tried to argue for some reason. When Cain looked at a large sheep and said it would die, Abel knew that would happen, yet tried to ague again.

Cain spat contemptuously and showed his elbow, which he did with the express purpose of insulting Abel. Furious, Abel exposed himself in a disgusting manner but this type of insult didn't work; Cain would only laugh.

Cain used a stick to draw birds in the sand, and Abel liked those drawings. But whenever he wanted to take a closer look, Cain cackled rudely and unpleasantly, shoved Abel away and trampled over the drawing.

Abel was happy the time Adam grew angry with Cain, attacked him, beat him with a rock, and bit his stomach hard enough to draw blood. Overjoyed, Abel ran to the river, jumped around there and rubbed his hands, and then returned, looking humble.

Adam didn't like Cain. Eve was also outwardly cold toward him, and from this dislike for Cain Abel drew his approval, his self-worth. It was difficult for him, because he compared himself to Cain and needed such approval, but Cain didn't need it.

Nearly every day, Abel approached Cain with all sorts of proposals, and Cain almost always rejected them.

Cain dismissed them coldly and rudely, with insults and laughter.

Abel, who made those proposals in order to become first in at least something, always turned out to be second, and rejected.

There was only one thing Abel never offered: his help with Cain's work, even though he took advantage of Cain's help with his own.

"Cain, help me calm down the bull so he doesn't gore me!" Abel would come to his brother, frightened.

Cain helped, and then chided Abel: "You're insignificant, weak as the dust we tread with our feet."

And with a rough laugh he showed Abel an elbow.

4. The first conflict over property.

Abel said to Cain: "Why do you drink milk from my cow? Drink from your own."

"This is my cow, not yours," Cain replied.

"What about that cow?" Cain pointed at another. "Is it also yours?"

"That one's mine too. I will drink milk from that cow if I want to."

Abel fell into a frightened silence.

Cain laughed unpleasantly, and then suddenly uttered a terrible phrase, one that still makes people groan. Most importantly, he said it lightly, laughing, almost mockingly:

"Abel, let's divide the world between us."

He was clearly joking, but Abel took the offer seriously.

"Yes, let's divide it! The flocks will be mine, and the land can be yours."

"Fine." Cain laughed.

Abel drove the flocks into the field, and Cain shouted after him, laughing. "You're treading upon my land!'

Abel stopped, thought anxiously, and came up with a retort: "The clothes you're wearing, aren't they made from the skins of my sheep?"

"Get off my land!" Cain laughed.

"Take off the clothes made from my sheep," Abel shouted seriously and anxiously.

He suddenly ran toward Cain, white from anger and fear, trembling with rage, gasping for breath. His face was screwed up, his mouth twisted. He burst into tears and shouted terribly: "My sheep! My cows! My goatlings! My calves! My bulls! Mine! Mine! Mine! Do you hear, Cain, mine . . .!"

He was disgusting, and Cain pushed him away with his hand, laughing coldly.

Abel grabbed a stone and swung it, but Cain ripped the stone from his hands. A fight broke out.

Wearing torn skins over their half-naked bodies, they chased each other across fields and hills and forests.

A primeval echo repeated the loud shrill cry, the words "Mine! Mine! Mine!"—a fierce, courageous roar, and bright terrible laughter.

This laughter nearly doomed Cain. Because of it, Abel overpowered his brother, began to choke him, beat and crush him.

"Abel," said Cain. "There are two of us in the world. Once you kill me, what will you say to our father?"

Abel often thought of his father and mother, and now Cain unconsciously repeated the argument he didn't understand himself.

Abel let his brother go and left.

Cain lay on the ground by the forest. He closed his eyes, not from pain, but from grave thought, the first thought about the fate of humanity on earth.

Everything was quiet around him. The trees thought their own thoughts with wrinkled bark. The face of the earth was calm, majestic, and thoughtless. The bright shining sun indifferently illuminated the location of the first fraternal struggle.

5. Adam is behind the times and understands nothing.

Adam looked upon the faces of his sons with calm, fatherly kindness. One face was covered in bruises and scrapes. Blood mixed with dirt in frozen brown clumps in the other's beard.

"What sort of beast attacked you, my children?" he asked.

"It was not an animal, but a man. My brother Cain attacked me," Abel lied.

Cain was silent.

"Why did he attack you?"

"It was because we split the world between us, and he wanted to claim what is mine for himself."

Adam understood nothing. Bewilderment streamed from his overgrown eyes.

"What does this mean, mine?"

Abel tried to explain it to him, but Adam still didn't understand anything. He rubbed his strong forehead with his dark broad palm.

"You're old, Father. You don't understand," Abel said irritably.

Adam left. He went into a faraway field, stepping heavily with his wide, thick, straightforward, and good-natured heels. A stubborn strange new thought pommeled at his head.

"Mine. What does that mean?"

The wind rustled in the grass, caressing his hair. The birds sang, a beast growled in the distance. The red sun shone at the edge of the field.

Adam looked at everything as though he saw it for the first time.

"Mine. What is mine? And what isn't?"

He walked to the vineyard and began to eat the thick, intoxicating fruit.

The grave new thought tormented him. He climbed a tree, sat on a branch. He stared. He thought. He accidentally fell asleep and fell off.

It was dark. The stars shone. The grass smelled of spices.

Adam scratched his head with firm fingers, rubbed the bruised spot. He returned to the hut and suddenly got into a fight with his sons. He shouted something incomprehensible and fiercely beat them with whatever was at hand. Eve screamed in a shrill voice. Cain fled into the forest. They finally calmed the old man down by morning.

6. An indisputable fact: Cain killed Abel.

Cain slaughtered a ram, built a fire, and cooked himself supper. The dancing flame amused him, and he jumped around the fire and screamed. So as not to be disturbed, he settled down far from the family hut.

"Cain, why did you take and kill my ram?" asked Abel.

Cain went on jumping around the fire and amusing himself. But Abel wouldn't relent.

"Why did you take my ram?"

Cain suddenly grabbed the ram's carcass along with the stones it was laid upon, swung it mightily and hit his brother on the head.

"There's your ram," he shouted.

Two bodies—a dead ram and a man—merged for a moment into a one strange ugly whole and rolled together on the ground. The heavy flapping sound of a hit echoed through the forest, and a cloud of dust churned upward.

Cain left.

He worked all day. Worked even more willingly than usual, but before the sun set he dropped the stake he was using to aerate the field, and got to thinking. It seemed to him that his father asked, "Cain, where is your brother Abel?"

And he mentally replied: "Am I my brother's keeper?"

Instead of calming him down, the mental response troubled him. The first flash of human conscience was excruciating. He ran to the spot where they'd fought and stopped.

Abel and the dead ram lay equally unmoving in the dust.

A sharp pain gripped Cain's heart. For the first time ever, a human felt weak. Cain was the first person to need mental help, to need sympathy. He was the first to know loneliness.

But there was no sympathy even then. Mists fell solemnly over the ground, as though that was the most important thing. Clouds swirled in the sky. The sun rose and set solemnly. All kinds of grasses sprouted upward in their narrow existence, fat little pink worms writhed in the ground, the birds sang, the beasts roared, and everyone was infinitely busy with their own affairs. Nobody cared about human grief.

Cain went to the land of Nod, carrying on his broad shoulders the curse of a people not yet born and the slander of future generations.

Translator's Note

In the 1920s Yefim Zozulya was celebrated as one of the wittiest and most popular short story writers in Russia. By the 1930s his career was destroyed by the Soviet censors. Zozulya enlisted at the age of 50 and died fighting the Nazis in World War II. After that, his works became largely lost to the injuries of time. Even today, his fiction is primarily familiar to Russian academics and aficionados.

I was blown away by the talent and scope of his writing and tracked down as many stories as I could get my hands on; many have not been reprinted for more than fifty years and are not available online. I've translated several of the best stories and they've been now published in English. This involved having friends in Russia track down rare old books, a process that has not yet been completed and is presently on hold because of the current war.

In another timeline he may have become one of the classics. As it stands, I'm proud to offer Anglophone readers a small glimpse into the lost treasures of Russian literature.

Heart

Shuang Xuetao
translated from the Chinese by Jeremy Tiang
The New Yorker

Before 2015, I'd never been to Beijing, which is quite odd—an adult who's been working a few years ought to have visited the capital for a meeting or a classmate's wedding or simply to view the corpses of great men. For some reason, anyway. But I never did—a training session in Shenzhen, a business trip to Sichuan, but never Beijing. I never even got as far as Hebei.

In 2013, I left my job at an advertising firm and started writing fiction. I wrote more than thirty short stories, a few of which were published in the local city journal, which was perpetually on the verge of folding. Then, on the sixth of November, 2015, my dad had a sudden heart attack, the result of a hereditary disease that had already claimed five or six people in my family, the first of them at the end of the Qing dynasty, my great-great-great-uncle, a superb woodworker who could make anything from a coffin to a comb. When he was fifty-five, his heart exploded and he died on a pile of lumber. It happened so abruptly, leaving him bleeding from every orifice, that his family thought he'd been poisoned. They cut him open, and discovered that his heart was full of tiny wood shavings, enough to build a foot-high pagoda.

Ever since then, my family has suffered from heart disease, about three in every ten of us, men and women, though it's not as serious now that times have changed—none of us are woodworkers anymore, and surgery can save us. The procedure in question involves fitting a tiny engine into one of the heart's chambers, to make up for the weakness caused by the organ's abnormal fissures, and placing something like the filter of a water dispenser into the aorta, to prevent impurities from entering the heart. This operation wasn't available in my city, L-------, at least not anywhere I trusted, mainly because of the difficulty of fitting the filter membrane, which in L------- would be placed by hand, with something like the muscle memory of a carpenter, unlike in Beijing or America, where robots were used. Our health insurance wouldn't be accepted in America, so when my father had his attack I arranged for an ambulance to take us from the local hospital to Beijing.

We were due to set off around seven in the evening. By that time, my father's face was purplish green and he could no longer speak, what with the oxygen mask on his face, and he lay on a gurney that was covered in some sort of blue plastic. A doctor from the E.R., a woman of about thirty, slightly plump, with dark-brown hair and rimless glasses, would accompany us. She said, I should warn you that it'll take us eight hours to drive there, and it's possible that your father will not make it. I said, I understand. She said, My name is Xu, and I've just graduated—this is my first time on the night ambulance to Beijing, and it's such a serious case I'm a bit worried, so I hope we can work well together. Of course, I said. Definitely. She said, When I say work together, what I mean is that you do whatever I say—don't get clever, don't do anything unless I tell you to, don't ask stupid questions. Sure, I said, I don't have any questions anyway. She asked, Are you the only family member coming along? Yes, I said, is that O.K.? She said, There really ought to be one more person here. As a doctor I can push the gurney, but if the patient needs to be lifted one person will have to take his head and another his legs, and I'm not supposed to move him. I said, I can handle it myself. She said, I need to let you know, no pressure, but there was an incident where the family member dropped the patient and he died. I know you don't want to hear this, but I'm obliged to tell you. I said, Understood. So you're saying if we don't work well together my father might fall and die. Cigarette? I don't smoke, she said. Have your cigarette and then get on board—hopefully we'll be able to drive through the night without stopping.

As we left the crowded E.R., some people scurried by, while others sat perfectly still, face in hands. A young woman ran in from the cold wearing pajamas, blood seeping from a gash between her eyes. A construction worker in a hard hat was carried past us by two of his colleagues. One of his legs was bent to the side like a faucet, and he was hopping along on the other. Outside, it was already completely dark. I was halfway through my cigarette when I noticed a cleaner eying the smoldering butt, so I stubbed it out and dropped it into his dustpan.

As soon as I clambered aboard the ambulance, Dr. Xu said to the driver, Let's go. We drove past the row of shops selling fruit and funeral goods by the hospital's main entrance, then turned onto the highway. There wasn't much traffic, and the driver kept up a steady pace. He was in green scrubs, with an extra-wide collar for his thick neck. All of a sudden, it came to me that I should slip him and the doctor a little money. This hadn't occurred to me before, partly because this was such an urgent trip—I'd taken too long deciding whether to go ahead with it—and partly because I'd been spending so much time at home that I wasn't used to being around other people. I scrabbled hopelessly through my rucksack, but, as I'd expected, I didn't have much on me. Thinking about the deposit I'd have to put down when we got to Beijing, not to mention all the other expenses I'd need cash for, I felt a wave of despair.

As this was a hereditary disease, every member of my family had their own way of dealing with it: some were always popping pills, some kept getting themselves examined, some just did whatever the hell they wanted and were fine anyway, or fine until they kicked the bucket at forty or so, usually from alcohol poisoning rather than heart issues. My grandfather's coping mechanism was boxing, a hobby he passed on to his three sons. Of the three, my father, the youngest, showed the least talent—he was born uncoordinated, with a long torso and short legs, unsuited to any sport. He moved slowly, too. Yet he was the one who persisted the longest, continuing to train without a break even when he was sent down to the countryside during the Cultural Revolution and then after he returned to the city. His trick was to train in secret—very few people outside the family knew that he could box. He woke up early to get in a couple of hours before work every day, and then did another round before bed. I couldn't remember him ever skipping a session. He didn't like talking and wasn't close to anyone. When my grandfather was still around, he'd often say to my father, Hey, No. 3, you keep to yourself too much. That's going to bite you in the ass when you get older. My father never answered him. Then my grandfather died and there was no one left to scold him. That's the virtue of patience.

When I was a kid, I was always pestering my father to teach me a move or two. He said, What do you want to learn? I said, How to hit people, whack them so hard they fall right over. He said, I don't know how to do that. I said, Then teach me how not to feel any pain when people hit me, and instead make their hands hurt. He said, I don't know how to do that, either. It seems we have very different understandings of what boxing is, I don't think we should talk about it anymore. That's how he was, mostly silent, and when he did break his silence to say something he'd be very serious about it. I was only ten at the time, and even so he weighed every word, as if it had to be finely ground, worn down to a flavorless pulp.

Just before my university entrance exam I said to him, You practice boxing three hours a day, and I spend the same amount of time studying, probably more—do you think you're better at boxing than I am at studying? He said, Do you think about studying when you're not doing it? I said, No way, work is work and play is play, there has to be a line between them. He said, There you go. Even when I'm not boxing, I'm boxing in my heart, not just my heart, my flesh and bones, too. Sometimes I box in my sleep and wake up feeling exhausted, do you know what I mean? I said, So how can you prove you're good at boxing? He thought about it and said, I can't, but let me try a metaphor: Let's say a cat falls from the fifth floor and doesn't die—does the cat have anything to prove? I said, How do you know I'm not going to fall from the fifth floor one of these days? If boxing's so great, why not teach me how to do it? He said, I can see I'd better not give you any more metaphors, you can't cope with them. Why should I teach you? I said, Because I'm your son. He said, What kind of reason is that? Don't think this or that has to happen just because you're my son. I didn't know who you were going to be before you were born. Losing my temper, I snapped, So go ahead and punch me. He said, You think you can get hit whenever you want, just like that? My fists aren't for punching people. Go to bed.

My grandfather was eighty-five when he died in his sleep. One of my uncles died in the violence of the Cultural Revolution; the other was retired and living an unruffled life at home, though I hadn't been in touch with him for a while. In the ambulance, my father's foot twitched, and only then did it occur to me that I ought to remove his shoes. His feet were hideously swollen. He lay perfectly still, like a piece of driftwood, his heart rate and blood pressure gleaming on a monitor. Dr. Xu looked at his feet and prodded them one at a time with her index finger. I said, Is there a problem? She said, Why are your dad's feet so small? I said, What? She said, Some people say that the size of your heart is proportional to the size of your feet, and though that's nonsense, your dad really does have tiny feet. And there's something else I don't understand. Judging by my initial examination of your dad, his heart really shouldn't still be working. Just look at his stats—they're unimaginable. Heart rate twenty-five, blood pressure eighty over forty. To put it bluntly, he ought to be dead. I haven't been doing this for very long, but even a thirty-year veteran wouldn't have seen many cases like this. What kind of work do you do?

I said, Me? I don't have a job. She said, Why don't you have a job? I said, Because I don't want to work. I'm really lazy—is that a kind of illness? She said, You don't seem lazy—lazy people don't usually get so anxious, nothing about you feels lazy to me. If you don't have a job, what do you do? I said, I sit around at home. She said, What are you, a Buddhist? I said, No, sometimes I get bored and do some typing. She said, What kind of typing? Are you an author? I said, Yes, fiction, it's childish but I like to write short stories. She said, If you're sleepy, go ahead and have a nap. Your dad seems stable and I can keep an eye on him. I said, That's really dutiful of you. I feel bad. After a pause, I said, in a small voice, I forgot to get money before we left. I'm sorry about that. She said, I'm not dutiful, it's just that I'm new to the job and don't get much say in anything. For the last half year they've stuck me with way too many overnight shifts. I couldn't go to sleep now if I tried, and if I were tired I wouldn't be able to stay awake no matter how much money you gave me. How come an author like you has such strange ideas?

Besides, she added, your dad has such an unusual condition, anyone working in medicine would want to observe him. Did you say it was hereditary? I said, Yes, a hereditary heart disease. She said, Who else in your family has it? I said, It basically skips a generation. My grandfather was fine, but my great-grandfather died of it. She said, Your great-grandfather must have been born around 1900. When did he die? I said, I think he was in his twenties, not long after my grandfather was born. She said, Was it a Chinese or a Western doctor who diagnosed him? I said, I don't know, but he definitely died of heart disease. She said, How can you be so sure? I said, I'm his descendant, of course I know—this is our history. She didn't respond, and I knew I'd taken the conversation in the wrong direction. I turned to the driver, but all I could see was the back of his neck and his collar. It didn't seem like he'd heard any of our conversation. The ambulance kept going at a steady pace, with almost no braking or sudden turns, yet we'd overtaken a number of speeding vehicles. It was completely dark outside, nothing to see but the looming outlines of the surrounding hills. No honking, no radio. We were flowing through the night like the drip hanging above my father's head, silently infiltrating his unfamiliar veins.

Over the next hour, I began to feel sleepy. If I'd been at home, I'd still have been wide awake—I often stayed up as late as two in the morning even when I had nothing particular to do, flipping through a book or writing a couple of paragraphs or shuffling through music. My father went to bed early and got up early, and never snored, though he did sometimes cough during the night. He was a paint sprayer at a factory and had chronic pharyngitis. He never woke himself up with his coughing. It was part of his sleep, like rolling over. He'd told me that he dreamed about boxing, but I didn't know how true that was—he slept curled up, hugging his shoulders, taking up as little space as possible, as if the bed were full of other people hemming him in. In the summer, his blanket ended up between his legs, and he always wore a yellowing tank top rather than going shirtless. In the winter, he kept the covers pulled up to his neck, but even then I could see from the outline of his body that he was in the same shrunken posture.

I drifted off for what must have been ten minutes or so before jolting awake, assaulted by guilt—what if he'd died in those ten minutes? This brief nap seemed to have lasted years, as if I'd been out so long the entire world had transformed. Dr. Xu was studying my father's hands, first from where she was sitting, opposite me, and then moving closer and squatting next to him. I said, What's wrong? She said, Does your father play the piano? I said, No, he's a laborer. She said, Look, his fingers are moving. I knelt by the gurney. His left hand was anchored in place by the drip tube and remained motionless. On his right index finger was a clip connected to the display screen, and as I watched he pushed the clip off with his thumb, then all five fingers thrummed on the edge of the mattress, over and over, never pausing in their tap-tapping, from his little finger to his thumb, maybe a dozen times before he tried unsuccessfully to replace the clip.

Dr. Xu glanced at the monitor. His heart rate is still falling at the same speed, she said. What's going on? I said, I don't know. She waited a moment, made sure his hand wasn't going to start moving again, put the clip back on, and sat back down, still mumbling What's going on? to herself. I said, My father's boxed ever since he was a kid. She said, What kind of boxing? I said, No idea, but it's always the same style of boxing. He'll practice for a few hours at a time, always the same moves, once in the morning and once at night. She said, In a park? I said, No, in his bedroom. She said, Martial arts in a bedroom? I said, Yes, summer and winter alike. She said, Right, so this must be a nerve spasm or muscle memory—it's not uncommon. Remember, your father is dying, his heart is weakening, and I'm not sure we'll make it to Beijing. I said, But his fingers were moving so steadily. She said, That doesn't matter, sometimes our bodies do that as camouflage, you should prepare yourself. I said, If it happens like you say, what should we do? She said, Drive straight back. He's probably no longer in pain. How should I put this? It's like a balloon slowly deflating, that's about the same thing. I said, That comparison causes me pain. She said, Your pain and his pain are two different things. I said, Yes, though you can't do anything about either. I regretted the words as soon as they were out of my mouth, because why would I expect her to be able to do anything? She was only an emergency-room doctor, a stranger who was in this vehicle for god knows what reason. I said, I apologize, that's not your responsibility. She reached out to lift my father's blanket and said, No need to apologize—everything you said is true. Give me a hand, he needs a new pee pad.

We drove on awhile longer. I glanced out the window, and noticed that the traffic was growing sparser. We'd probably crossed into Hebei Province, and it must have been roughly three in the morning. For the past hour, I'd been pondering my father's funeral. They were a real headache, the countless tasks that lay ahead: contacting relatives I hadn't spoken to in ages, getting their phone numbers from a palm-size book my father kept by his bedside. He'd retired from a state-run factory only to get another job spraying paint for a private firm, which he'd done right up until he fell ill, and so I probably ought to reach out to his co-workers; they'd usually be the ones to chip in for his funeral expenses and send a few vehicles for the procession. I imagined myself sitting in an office in that struggling little factory, discussing these things with some indifferent middle-aged man, feeling even more stressed than I was at this moment. All of this I would have to navigate on my own, whereas on this night I at least had two other people with me, and my father could take on his share of the responsibility, because no matter what condition he was in he was still participating in my life, and, burdensome as this was, when he died there would only be me left in my life, totally alone. I guess that's what freedom looks like nowadays, but when that happened would I still need to write? My father had never expressed any opinions about my writing, in fact he hadn't read a single word of my stories, but, even so, had I been writing for his sake? If not, why was I so doubtful now?

I told myself that of course I had to keep writing—I wasn't doing it for him, he didn't know anything, I was writing for everyone in the world except him—but these conclusions just rattled around inside my head, like echoes from someone shouting into a deserted valley.

Around three-thirty in the morning, Dr. Xu said, I'm starting to feel a bit sleepy. I said, Shut your eyes for a while, then. She said, I'll nap for half an hour. Keep an eye on the drip and his heart rate, and wake me if anything seems irregular. I said, All right. She lay down on her seat, using her arm as a pillow, and dropped off straightaway, her head and feet pointing in the same direction as my father's. Four o'clock came and she slept on, but I didn't wake her, because my father's vitals showed no sign of changing; they weren't plummeting as she'd predicted. I didn't feel tired at all, though my ass hurt from sitting still for so long and I had to wiggle it around. Then all of a sudden I needed to pee; the urge came out of nowhere, like someone pulling a sink plug. I said to the driver in a low voice, Hey, I need to pee, is there a rest area coming up? He didn't answer and kept facing the road. I didn't think I could hold it much longer, so I scuttled to the front and said, Sir, sorry to bother you, but I need to use the bathroom. Still, he said nothing, as if he found my request so ridiculous that merely replying would wound his dignity. I tapped his shoulder and said, Sir, I'm about to piss myself, could you stop? That was when I looked in the rearview mirror and saw that his eyes were shut. Startled, I thought, Wait, I must be mistaken—does he just have small eyes? I leaned forward and, no, he was fast asleep, breathing evenly, in through the nose and out through the mouth, even snoring lightly, every muscle in his face relaxed, a faint sheen of grease shining in the street lights, his hands still on the wheel. There was a slight bend in the road up ahead, and without hesitation he guided the vehicle around it, stepping on the accelerator and the clutch as needed. I grabbed his shoulder and shook him, but he didn't wake up. Next I pinched the back of his neck, but again, nothing. He just jolted as if a needle had pierced his bum, rising a little from his seat before settling back down. We were going about ninety miles per hour, and I couldn't stir him.

My bladder felt like an unruly schoolchild waiting for the final bell. I walked back to my father's side, lifted his blanket, and pulled the pee pad out from under him. It was still perfectly dry, just a bit warm. I glanced at Dr. Xu, but she was sound asleep, so I pulled down my trousers and let rip. The liquid was quickly absorbed, even though I had so much to let out that by the time I was done the pad looked like a cotton-filled quilt and was much heavier than before. I stuffed it back under my father, his withered legs with a red birthmark on the right thigh. I'd known this was there when I was a kid, but I'd forgotten about it till now. After tucking myself back into my trousers, I tapped Dr. Xu and said, Hey, wake up! The driver's asleep, we need to do something. She didn't move, so I grabbed her arm and pulled it out from under her head. She fell from her seat, but remained asleep. I checked her breathing and she was still alive, only her face looked more anxious than before; her brow was furrowed, and she let out occasional sighs, her head bumping against the floor of the ambulance. I bundled her back onto the bench and she suddenly asked, How much longer? I said, I don't know. She said, Give me a bit more time, I'm almost done. Then, silence.

I sat back down. There were no other vehicles in sight, just the rising night fog, a sort of milky-white haze in all directions. We must have been approaching Beijing. Now I realized that as well as forgetting to get cash I'd also neglected to bring any reading material. At this point I desperately needed a book to whisk me away from this place. Even an out-of-date literary journal would have done the job. I tried hard to remember something I'd read recently. A poem popped into my mind, or rather half a poem; I couldn't remember the poet, but a writer friend of mine had posted it online:

> Still young, still idealistic, leftist too but wearing
> A rightist's hat. He starved himself plump in Xinjiang,
> Fled home to Changsha. Grandma made him
> Pork-tripe radish soup, red dates floating in it.
> Incense burning indoors, a rising perplexity.
> On this day, he has no idea what to do.

There was more, but I'd forgotten it. Grandma and soup. Nourishing images, which was probably why it had come to me: I needed comforting thoughts at this moment to show me that human connection actually existed in this world, something that gave off heat, a scene with a little noise and bustle, anything to dispel my current sinking perplexity. Dr. Xu's face knocked against the back of her seat from time to time, until I rested my rucksack under it, nice and soft since all I'd brought was a jacket and two packets of tissues. The driver continued expertly piloting the vehicle, and I could only assume that he was keeping tabs on the road ahead and the rearview mirror with his ears.

Once, when I was little, my father and I spoke about death. I'd asked him, Today Big Fatty said he was going to beat me to death—can he do that? My father said, If he wants to, he can. He was rinsing vegetables at the time—he could cook a few simple dishes, but refused to touch potatoes or radishes, because when he got sent down to the countryside that was all he had to eat and they wrecked his stomach. Nowadays when he saw them at the vegetable market he'd walk quickly by. I said, Then what happens after I'm dead? Can I get revenge? He said, No, you'd be completely defeated. I said, Are you going to die? He said, Yes, I might die at any moment. The human body has a heart in it, about the size of your fist, and when it stops beating you die. I said, Why would it stop? It's beating now, it will beat tomorrow—why would it stop one day? He said, It's beating now, but it might not tomorrow, though your heart is very healthy—you aren't going to die because of that. I said, How would you know? He said, I listened to it when you were born. I heard your heart and it's a healthy one. Besides, my heart has problems, so the probability is that yours doesn't—those are reasonable odds. Anyway let's leave it at that. The next time Big Fatty wants to hit you, you should run away as fast as you can, then you won't die.

Dr. Xu rolled over but nimbly avoided falling off the bench. I shut my eyes, too. Now everyone in the ambulance had their eyes shut, and we entered a common darkness. All of a sudden, I heard coughing. First I thought it must be the driver, but I quickly realized that it sounded too familiar to be him, like someone crumpling sandpaper. I opened my eyes to see my father hacking away, more and more violently. Finally, he woke himself up. I said, Dad. He looked at me and sat up. As always, now that he was awake, the coughing stopped. He said, What's all this? I said, We're almost in Beijing. He said, Beijing? What for? I said, To get you treatment, you had a heart attack. He said, Forget it, I saw my own heart a moment ago, it's been gnawed at by worms, it's all rusty now. A worm had a chat with me, it said it knew my grandfather. Are you going to Beijing, too? I said, Yes, who else would take care of you? He said, What nonsense. I don't need to be taken care of. What's the time? I said, Five-twenty in the morning. He said, I haven't boxed yet today. Help me get rid of this pee pad, it smells revolting.

With that, he crawled out from under the blanket and stood there, boxing. After twenty minutes, he sat down and said, I've forgotten what comes next. I said, How's that possible? You've been practicing this sequence for forty years. He said, It's gone, I don't remember a single bit of it. My whole life has gone past, just like that. I said, It's not over yet, you're doing perfectly well now, aren't you? He said, My whole life has gone past. I always knew it would, I knew my life would slip by, that's why I took up boxing, because what else could I do? And now that I've forgotten the boxing, too, I feel light. I've finally gotten through it, I've spent it all. I said, Would you like some water? He said, I'm not thirsty. What are your plans? I said, I don't know, I'm still not able to accept a life that doesn't have you in it, please hold on awhile longer. He said, You think too highly of my existence. The probability is that your life has more meaning, your existence devours mine. From the day you were born you've been eating my existence bit by bit with a little spoon, but that doesn't matter, you don't need to feel guilty. When do you plan to get married? I said, I haven't given it any thought. He said, Mmm, well, when you have a son, you'll eat him with a spoon, too, that's how good your appetite is. Like I said, I listened to your heart when you weren't looking—it's sturdy as an airplane engine. You can't hear it but I can, it roars by my side every single day. That's why I'm quiet.

And then he actually did fall silent for a while, the way he often did, stopping in the middle of a conversation. Who knows what he was thinking? Maybe he'd just forgotten what he was about to say. Dr. Xu rolled over again, this time with her face toward us. Her eyes were open, but I wasn't sure if she could see us. What you're saying isn't any help to me, she said with absolute certainty, no help at all. There's nothing else I can do—it's perfectly clear in the images, and every instrument tells me the truth, so there's no point to your lying. History doesn't lie. History has proved that people like you are no help. Give me your medical records. She rapped lightly at her head, eyes half shut. Who wrote this? What kind of handwriting is this? No one could read this!

My father didn't respond. His face was full of incomprehension. He had no idea what she was getting at, or why there would be such a patient in the ambulance. Her entire body juddered, as if someone had kicked her, and her eyes drifted shut again.

Give me a hand, my father said, I'm heading back. As I lifted him onto the gurney, he wrapped his arms around me. He didn't stink, but rather had the light pleasant scent of a small child. Into my ear he said, Goodbye, this is as far as we'll go. I said, No, don't say that, you're not old yet—you have to wait till you're an old man. He said again, Goodbye. As his eyes lost focus, I said, Don't fall asleep, we're almost there. His eyes widened a little and he said, Who are you? I said, I'm your son. He nodded and said, Safe travels, take care. With that, he lay flat, reaching out to cover himself with the blanket. He fell asleep, coughed a couple of times, and stopped breathing.

The monitor began beeping, waking Dr. Xu. She groped around, realized there was nothing next to her, then woke fully. She asked who'd put a rucksack under her head, and when I said I had, she said it was very uncomfortable. I told her two things had happened: the driver had been fast asleep for quite a while, and my father had died. I could tell she wanted to comfort me, but her professionalism held her back. She nodded and removed his drip as if she were unravelling a sweater back into yarn. After a few minutes, the driver woke, too, looking unabashed, but then nothing bad had happened, so fair enough. Besides, the nap had left him refreshed, as if his day were just beginning. He turned and spoke to Dr. Xu, and they decided we should go back the way we came. I asked Dr. Xu if we could stop, and we did at the next rest area, so I could go to the bathroom. When I got back, I made sure that the other two were still awake, then I curled up next to my father's legs. I felt light, free of burdens, free of goals, and to the accompaniment of my own heartbeat I soon fell asleep.

Translator's Note

I was introduced to Shuang Xuetao's writing by his wife, Zhang Yueran, whose fiction I have been translating for years (most recently: her novel *Cocoon*, for World Editions). I was immediately drawn to his sparse, propulsive style and the breadth of his imagination. I asked if I could translate his stories, and he happily agreed. During the pandemic, I translated three of his novellas, which were published by Macmillan under the title *Rouge Street*. In happier times, I had visited China once or twice a year, but this was now impossible. Unable to visit Shenyang, a place I had never been to, I found myself getting to know it through Shuang's writing—and as I would later find out, I was in any case entering an altered version of the city, one that only exists in Xuetao's mind, comprising childhood memories and flights of fancy. Perhaps it was just as well I never knew the real thing, and could situate myself completely within his imagination. Ever since moving to Beijing, Xuetao's writing has grown more expansive, less rooted in place. "Heart" is a prime example, reaching for the universal while largely remaining within the confined space of a small ambulance which is constantly in motion as the story progresses. I'm glad to have gotten to know Shuang's roots in Shenyang through translating his earlier writing, and feel like I am traveling alongside him as he now expands his vision.

Welcome to the Department of Unanswered Prayers

Norman Erikson Pasaribu
translated from the Indonesian by Tiffany Tsao
The Common

Welcome to the Department of Unanswered Prayers! Here's your ID. When it's time to go home, put your badge in your bag and leave the bag in your car. Rather than tossing it in some drawer, I mean, or chucking it somewhere inside your room. Don't worry. No one will steal it. And don't forget to bring it tomorrow and the day after and all the days after that. You'll need it to get past security and to access the main entrance, the department, the sub-departments, the letter storage facility, and the archive. It happens every now and then—someone forgets their badge and has to go home to retrieve it. What a waste of time and money. Remember, every minute you're late will incur a corresponding reduction in your heavenly salary. Each minute you're late also incurs a 0.33-point penalty, to be subtracted from your end-of-year point total. Don't let it get so dire that you can't redeem them for the leave you're entitled to every fourth year, because if you're short even a fraction of a point, you're still short a fraction of a point.

This is your desk. You're next to Rahel. She's off on her points-spending leave. Where'd she go? Well naturally, before heading anywhere else, she's checking in on her kids. Just FYI: she'll give you hell if she hears you taking part in sexist office banter. This may be heaven, but there're no luscious celestial nymphs here. Those dirty comic books littering the metaphorical corridors of your pubescence, they totally got it wrong. (Ha ha, that's right! I skimmed your profile.) I'll give you an example, one time Bobi and Loki were saying lewd things about Eva from DOC, and Rahel—who was getting a drink from the water cooler—paid them a visit and slammed her glass down hard on Bobi's desk. Cold water everywhere! Then she began telling him off in one of the Earth languages. Oh, I almost forgot! About the language we're using right now: you realize we're not speaking English, right? Sometimes you get so used to things you forget what language you're operating in. We are actually speaking in tongues. That's the Earth term, isn't it? This is how the apostles felt! Ahmad is the head of your sub-sub-department. That's him, in the corner cubicle. He's the serious type, and as you'll find out, the people who work under him are no-nonsense too. So if you're looking for friends who like talking about Taylor Swift and exchanging funny cat memes, I suggest you excuse yourself, head to the bathroom, and just talk to yourself instead. It's not too bad in there. The cleaners come twice a day! So, about your profile. *Ve-ry* interesting, I must say. Langston reader . . . Taylor fan . . . What did you do in your former life, anyway?

Oh yes, straighten your cuffs. Count yourself lucky that Ahmad wasn't at his desk when you came in. Something to remember: Ahmad disappears to pray about two or three times a day, usually at 12:00 noon and 4:00 PM. Actually, there's no point to it anymore—we're already in heaven after all—but I guess habits are hard to break. Me, for instance: I could never give up instant noodles. Don't try to slip out when Ahmad isn't around. It'll really piss him off. However, if you have to, *have to* leave, notify Kayla, your sub-sub-department secretary—that cubicle there, next to Ahmad's. Huh. Wonder where she went. She's probably in the toilet, blubbering over what her life has become. She's one of the office crybabies. As for you, hmmm . . . you don't seem like a crybaby, but looks can be deceiving, can't they? Don't be like them. Oh, regarding permission to leave the office: chances are you won't get it. Not if it's not a matter of life and death. And it's not like death is a problem for us anymore, am I right? Ha ha. Anyway, please understand. We're extremely busy here. Extremely. Busy.

Don't give Kayla any attitude if she rejects your permission request. That is, if you ever want to stop by Earth to see your old family. You'll have to deal with her a lot. If you want to redeem your bonus, you'll have to talk to her, and she's the one who'll speak to Ahmad about it. Direct interactions with your sub-sub-department head are strongly discouraged, except for social interactions at lunchtime and office parties. The tall, skinny guy in the cubicle in the far corner is Samuel. He's one of the other sub-sub-department heads. He's been around for a while. In fact, he's been working in this department since the Reformation of 1929. He used to be Armenian. Word is, he died of dehydration trying to cross the desert on foot, but nobody can say for sure. None of us here has a strong interest in history, previously or presently. And Sam won't confirm or deny it if you ask. Even if you press him about it. Even if you get him drunk. That's why we've nicknamed him Mr. Mystery. A bunch of people who used to work under him—including Rina and Monika—went out drinking with him one evening after work. They tried to psychoanalyze him, and Samuel, who was half-drunk by that point, bit their heads off: "Leave me alone, you lunatics! I'm not your guinea pig!" See? He's a sharp one, that Sam. Unfortunately, Clara and the entire HR division were there, drinking in the same bar! Whichever way you slice it, heaven's a small place. Rina and Monika were instantly transferred to the Department of Dreams for violating the workplace code of conduct on employee privacy. Anyway, DOD is probably a better fit for busybodies like them.

This is your sub-sub-department's photocopy machine. Frankly, it's pretty much useless since the register of names you'll be working with is kept in—well, let's just call it "digital" format. Still. Don't use the machine in any other sub-sub-department to make copies. It'll create conflict.

And the first rule of conflict management from the powers-that-be is: zero conflict.

Sorry, what did you say? God? Oh no, no, no. By "the powers-that-be" I mean the mere ex-mortals like us who occupy higher ranks. Sorry for the confusion. Just ask anyone who works in this building. Not one of us has ever seen God. Come to think about it, that is a bit strange, isn't it? But who cares?

That young guy with the massive trolley—the one who's talking to Samuel. You'll be seeing a lot of him while you're here. His name is Antonio. He works in DOPR—the Prayer Receiving Department. He makes his rounds every morning, delivering each sub-sub-department's quota of prayers. The other people on delivery duty are Fina, Ismael, Jacob, Sudianto, Park, Mr. Nguyen, Luis, Kwame, Annisa, Leo, Tony, Barak, and Miranda. Here's the name register assigned to you by DOPR. Read it. There are around five hundred people on this list. Once you receive your allotted prayers from Antonio, you have to calculate their exact total, then match them with the corresponding names on the register. Don't sign off if the numbers don't match up! Antonio used to secretly comb through all the prayers. Then he'd pick out the ones from his home village in the Venezuelan interior to try to get them answered. He was caught red-handed, and really, he should've been fired. I mean, talk about a breach in code of conduct! But then we found out he'd been a heavy drinker in life and used to beat his kids. On his daughter's fourteenth birthday, he beat her and that same night she ran away. She didn't end up becoming Venezuela's answer to Madonna, if that's what you're thinking. She was found raped and dead by the side of the road. Antonio had been attempting penance. You know how it is. Men. They're so good at regrets. Even in heaven, they wallow, demanding sympathy all the time. After a lengthy discussion, we decided to be more proactive and proceed with renewed caution and vigilance.

I know you'll be busy, but you should take care of your health. According to your personal history, you had an operation to remove a kidney stone, correct? Don't let it happen again. Because you won't die. Nope. You'll just get bloated because you'll be full of pee—like

Pras from the sub-sub-department next door. So here's some water. Drink up. All of it. By the way, this is the office pantry for our sub-division. Here's the fridge. You can fill it with snacks and canned soft drinks, if there's any room left. Unfortunately, there's no hot water, but you can buy a thermos from the supermarket around the corner. If the water cooler is empty, tell Robert and he'll call Doni in the Sub-Sub-Sub-Department of Pantry Stocking to get a refill.

This is the sub-department bathroom. No bath though. But if the water at home gets shut off, there's a shower in the bathroom on the ground floor, near the lobby. Ha ha, yes, you heard right. Heaven and its water supply drama—embarrassing, isn't it? There's a smoking lounge next to the bathroom. You're only allowed to smoke during lunch, which lasts an hour. Don't smoke. Use your break to socialize. Only people with no friends smoke during lunch.

Here's where we keep the stationery—your work will involve a lot of writing. Better get your scissors and staples now. Don't lose them. We're always running out. On the plus side, you can take all the pens you like—any kind. It's one of our sub-department's special perks. So FYI: From the moment you start working here, people from other departments will begin talking about you behind your back. Maybe one of them has even come up with a shitty nickname for you already, like poor Dennis, who they call "Penis." Don't take it too hard, and try to see things from their point of view. They're only like that because they know all their past hopes and dreams, which, mysteriously enough, remained unfulfilled—"mysteriously" because we know that some hopes and dreams, mysteriously enough, do get fulfilled—are now under our jurisdiction. They all want to know why their prayers were never answered. They want to read God's notes concerning each of their requests. One time, this young woman from the Department of Hope—I think her name was Albertina—came in wanting to discuss the state of post–New Order Indonesia. She requested full access to our digital archive. The sub-department head at the time, Mr. Sirius, refused. He said it was entirely against our department's vision and mission and would make a mockery of the Organization's Creed as a whole. Albertina held her ground, insisting that the fate of thousands—no, millions—of people now lay in our hands. "Indonesia was at a crossroads." Those were her words. And everything came down to which path the country would take. "Everything," she said, stretching out her arms as wide as they would go. Hah! If you ask me, is any nation—especially a postcolonial one—ever not at a crossroads? Even more so if you're poor. Like I used to be. I was at a crossroads and a dead end all at once, every single day of my life. And then she said if her department were to save a nation's people, they needed to find out the people's greatest fear. "I make this request for the preservation of all humankind," she told us. But during the long debate that followed, she revealed her true intentions. What she really wanted to know was why her prayers for a child of her own had been denied.

Poor Albertina the never-was Santa Maria. Boo hoo. Talk about cliché.

When it comes to lunch, I'd suggest sitting only with people from this department. Try to avoid interacting with the others, especially those in Matchmaking. Their department is touchy, especially when it comes to us. They secretly call us "the Self-Hanging Hangmen." You'd think they could come up with a better insult. They refuse to admit they're being irrationally mean. They know we don't have a say in whether a particular prayer gets answered. Archival and storage duties—that's all we're responsible for. Even *we* aren't allowed to read God's notes concerning each prayer: we believe that unanswered prayers are no less sacrosanct than the answered ones. What's more, their whole operating premise is absurd: according to them, no one should have to be alone. They even argue that all the prayers assigned to us related to finding a soulmate should be returned to the Secretariat and reassessed as new incoming prayers. (By the time some of the really desperate ones reach us, there are so many tear stains on the envelope you can barely read the name.) Get this. They insist those prayers must be answered.

Come on. Is there such a thing? Really? *Really?* A prayer that *must* be answered?

So remember what I said just now about not reading the letters? I mean it. Ignorance is one of our priorities—an essential part of what we do. Actually, we should consider ourselves lucky that we'll never read what God writes about each prayer, unless we get nosy. The Secretariat Office spends every day reading them all, entering them into their notebooks. At lunch you'll see a bunch of pasty people sitting in the corner of the cafeteria by themselves. That's them. The ones who work in SO. Everyone thinks they're creepy. The people who work in the Department of Enlightenment (you guessed it, they barely do any work) call the SO the "Zombietariat." In return, the SOers call the DOE "the fuckwits." No one likes the DOE. Honestly speaking, they're jerks. One of them was whining in the lift once—ugh, what was his name? Petrol, or something like that—about how their working conditions have gone downhill. So, Christianity's really taken off in South Korea, right? Now their department has to keep recruiting Koreans in order to stay on top of things. Petrol's own words: "They play weird music all day, and it just gets weirder each year. Okay, their dance numbers are decent, but give me Westlife any day. Know what I mean? A bit of Backstreet Boys . . . Throw in some Jonas Brothers . . . That Nick is so dreamy! Nick, oh God . . . No one else has to put up with this." *That's* what he said. My point is, not a single DOE person has told him what a racist he is. And ever since, everyone has known what sorry scumbags the DOE are.

Now, about your specific tasks. Once you receive your quota of prayers for the day, and make sure the total corresponds to the total number of names on the register, all you have to do is file them in a binder. When you're finished, bring the binder to the prayer archive.

Write down the binder's location in your notebook—yeah, that pink one. If you still haven't finished archiving all the prayers and it's getting late, then put the remaining ones in a binder and bring it to the letter storage facility. Write down the location of the binder in that green book there. But please do your best not to let work pile up.

And I'll say it again: don't start opening envelopes and peeping at God's notes. There was once this guy working under Jenna, in another sub-sub-department, who was nosy enough to take a peek. Jaka Tingkir, I think his name was. He was depressed for months. Then one day he stopped coming to work. Then, the following week, he showed up again out of the blue. God, he looked pale. And tense. Didn't say a word all morning. Then at lunchtime he blew up.

"This is madness!" he started yelling in the middle of the cafeteria. "Allowing one person to determine the fate of every desperate dream there ever was!" Of course, two guards came to secure the area. Jaka was never seen again. Apparently he picked the wrong envelope to open. It wasn't that same old prayer asking to turn back time. Or a child molester pining for a new motorbike. Or a deviant piano teacher praying for their student to fail the conservatorium entrance exams. It wasn't the prayer of some shitty old guy wanting to meet a younger woman so he could leave his wife. No, of all the millions, the trillions of hateful prayers he could have read, he stumbled across a prayer from an old woman whose only son had vanished one day—kidnapped by the military. She was waiting for him to come home.

No one knows what God's notes were. No one knows why her prayer wasn't answered. Nobody knows. Except Jaka, of course.

Well, I think that's it for now. If you're confused about anything, just ask. That's my cubicle over there. By the way, I heard you live in the same direction as me. I take my car every sixth day. Happy to give you a lift when you are too lazy to drive. Don't be shy, it's no trou—oh, yeah. One more thing. Someday you'll come across an envelope that has your name on it. You'll be speechless. You'll break into a cold sweat and your heart will pound. After all, you've arrived. You're here. Why is your prayer only getting here now? Just remember: don't trust any of your feelings. They're wrong. When that time comes, you'll have to steel yourself and treat the envelope as if it contains someone else's prayers, not yours. Your name will be printed on it, but act as if the words inside aren't written in the language of your innermost soul, even if you know the contents by heart. Pretend that the scent emanating faintly from it—if it's scented, that is—isn't the scent of your favorite perfume. Though you know it's your perfume. There's no doubt about it. It was the last birthday gift you received from your mother before you made that severe decision to sever ties. You know full well, don't you? That the only relationship you can never leave is the one between you and your god. Sound familiar? Ha ha, looks really can be deceiving. This is our little secret: Before this, I was Indonesian too. Like you.

So, there you have it. Happy working! And again, welcome to the Department of Unanswered Prayers!

Translator's Note

The translator offers the note below, written by the author themself, in English, about the book from which this story was taken:

The Indonesian title of this book is *Cerita-cerita Bahagia, Hampir Seluruhnya*. The idea of using *bahagia* ("happy") as a title of the book comes from an online review that advised me to change the title of my first collection to "Stories of People in Suffering," a review that I found very funny.

Hetero readers hate sad-all-the-time fictional gays, but often put in zero effort to make us, who are gay in flesh, happy. It's a sad irony.

A story in this book was based on the tale of Count Dracula—where it was turned queer, Batak, Indonesian. And the word "hampir" made itself into the title because it's just a letter away from the word "vampir." Being happy, being contented, being positive, being productive, being on-top-of-the-world, being fearless, being be-yourself, and being unapologetic are often demanded of us by the so-called progressive heteros. As sad as it may sound: for them, happy gays are a sign of social progress. But, let's be real: can you, as a queer, be happy in the way the heteros are happy in Indonesia? Happiness requires an endless list of privileges, in any part of the world. It is often the heteros that block us from accessing happiness. We queer are always thrown to the hampir, to the almost, and there the idea of happiness turns into the vampir.

—Norman Erikson Pasaribu

Excerpt from *What good does it do for a person to wake up one morning this side of the new millennium*

Kim Simonsen
translated from the Faroese by Randi Ward
Scandinavian Review

What good does it do for a person to wake up one morning
this side of the new millennium.
The body turns to ash (the ash weighs nine pounds).
No closure, no explanation to be found.
Except that the electrical currents of the brain are like a ten-watt
 lightbulb's.
A decapitated head weighs nine pounds.
Humankind surges on via sperm and ova,
a jungle of mammillae,
firing off impulses at a speed of 1,200 kilometers an hour
to engender sex from head to toe.

The face uses 43 muscles to wince.

*

Even though the coral *Leiopathes* can live 4,265 years
and plants have been around for 450 million years,
and I've loved you half a lifetime,
the sun will expand to a red giant and consume the earth.

After that, she will shrink and linger as a white dwarf.
Yet we still make our bed,
wake up to the same alarm tone
on my black iPhone.
We still pour coffee from the same black, lacquered
coffee pot with the silver spout.
Still eat bran flakes and muesli with milk.
We think about the next few months.
The ocean and the mountains are indifferent,
just like the ships in the distance that we see through the window.
Nature is indifferent.
It's just us, this morning.
Here for a moment.
Our hands still managing to find one another in the darkness.

*

Everything bears its shadow.

When I walk
to this water,
I move along with
the landscape.
The shore,
the sky,
the birds.
Autumn is on its way.
The light comes crawling.
Dark soil.
Soon, it will turn cold.
Rime like a crocheted shawl.
A hide of snow

will cloak everything
in a heavy white
reminiscent of the Ice Age
glaciers that once sculpted
the earth.

*

Something about the sea,
the grey sky,
and the waves
makes me
think about my childhood.
Summer drew to an end;
the sea and mild breeze
shake off the memories.
We probably won't have another summer together.
In the brown grass,
four brown killer slugs silently devour
two smaller black slugs.
A landscape of silent mayhem.
The last time I sprinkled salt,
from a red box
with white lettering,
on the killer slugs in your garden,
they shriveled up
writhing until their green
guts burst open and oozed out.

Translator's Note

In my dreams, I never quite figure out how I've ended up in the Faroe Islands yet again. The village feels desolate: not a single light to be seen, all doors are locked. I lean against a lichened boathouse wall and pull a box of matches from my anorak. Each match that I strike, each tiny flame, contains the voice of a Faroese person I have loved.

I hold each match as long as I can, until only a charred question mark remains and my fingertips are blistered. Again and again and again, I just want to hear their voices a few seconds longer. I don't care how badly I get burned.

In *Hvat hjálpir einum menniskja at vakna ein morgun hesumegin hetta áratúsundið*, Kim Simonsen writes, "If you don't long for home, you've already lost everything / you don't long for any longer." Much of my connection to Kim Simonsen and his poetry is rooted in the decades we've literally both spent making our way(s) home.

Simonsen's ecocritcal, new-materialist poetics have transformed the literary landscape of the Faroe Islands. As founder and managing editor of Forlagið Eksil, he has also fostered a cultural climate that embraces young, avant-garde artists and writers—something he didn't have during his youth. That void essentially drove him away from the islands for years.

It's been fifteen years since I last set foot in the Faroes. Kim Simonsen was one of the few people who chose to keep working with me after my life in the archipelago became untenable in the early 2000s. Translating his poetry is my way of, among other things, showing solidarity as he continues his important work. To paraphrase Alice Munro, real writers and translators are in the business of keeping each other alive.

Lethe

Kwang-Chung Yu
translated from the Chinese by Yifan Zhang
The Hopkins Review

In the realm of the dead, there is a river named Lethe where the water makes one forget one's life on Earth. When the dead enter this realm, the soul must drink first before seeking reincarnation. It then enters a state of incomprehension. Ariosto calls it the moon, and Dante calls it purgatory.

Yet whether I walk to the east or the west,
against the Lethe or along the Lethe,
on the other side of the barbed wire is China
—a myth, an ancient rumor.
On what page of my youth, what page is it?
A map. Let distant gazing satisfy this thirst for now.
The toxic Shenzhen River flows guiltlessly.
The bristlegrass is a blind man's eyes wide open.
Something wounded and unnameable hangs in the wind.
Dark red spreads in the shape of the border.
My hair flies like the image of the prodigal son.
Yet whether I walk to the west or the east—

Twenty years later this gray veil remains.
What mother veils her face with barbed wire?
What is the sorrow that cannot be lifted?
What are the shoes that never return?

There is a name sharp as a toothache,
Each bite is a peal of pain from San Francisco to Kinmen.
Since the marriage to war,
what has become of the mother raped by tanks?
Thin, pale clouds and a cold, cheerless sun.
Yet whether I walk to the north or the south—
dangerous Lethe,
quiet Lethe.

Barbed wire is nostalgia with thorns.
Whether I walk to the south or the north,
a lace trimming decorates terror.
A guest on foreign soil,
a prisoner in the homeland—
No difference. Whether I am inside or outside the net,
to be a fish is to be doomed to unhappiness.
Behind a row of casuarina trees,
a train winds northward,
trailing steam,
a wisp of gray gentleness.

Yet whether I look to the north or the south,
Mount Luofu or Diamond Hill,
the two shores cannot be fastened together,
even if the river were a zipper,
even if partridge calls extended
from one side to the other.
To be an eye is to be obliged to comfort the dusk.
When the horizon sounds the alarm,
row after row of verdant mountains trail behind.
Partridges whisper to the Peak of Lonely Gloom.
The Lethe flows, dividing the worlds of the living and the dead.

The crown goes to the Queen, the lost territory to Daoguang.
Neither a foreign land,
nor a homeland.

Yet whether to the husband-watching rock
or the hometown-watching rock,
an inch of the border is an inch of barbed wire.
The supposed motherland
is merely an ancient fragrance.
What was trampled is trampled still;
a syphilitic mother is still a mother.
There is soil still blooming
with the shout, "Forget-me-not, forget-me-not."
There is a gentleness I kneel to kiss
with my elbows, my knees, with the fullness
of shame and bitterness on my forehead.
On the barbed wire, a ripped, bloodstained garment struggles.
The gate of heaven is the gate of hell

whether I walk to the south or the north—

March 1969 in Hong Kong

Translator's Note

In this poem, Yu Kwang-Chung overlays the Hong Kong–Mainland China border of the 1960s with a mythological Dantean landscape. He compares the Shenzhen River dividing Hong Kong and mainland China with the river Lethe, a drink from which makes one forget the past. Instead of drinking from the river, however, the speaker wanders along its shore meditating on the forces of history that have made his past a foreign country. The journey concludes with him kneeling to kiss the soil with his "elbows, knees," and "the fullness of shame and bitterness on [his] forehead."

The poem asks the age-old question of "Who am I?" in a specific place and time. At that moment, Cold War anti-communism was a definitive value in Taiwan as in much of the Western Bloc. Meanwhile, the Republic of China (Taiwan) still retained representation of China in the United Nations until a 1971 resolution transferred representation to the People's Republic of China. What does it mean to hold on to a "Chinese" cultural identity that had been irrevocably divided into parallel political universes? Yu ponders from Mount Loufu and Diamond Hill in the then British-ruled Hong Kong. The ambiguities of identity and belonging come to a head in this river-laced borderland between the two versions of China, between the east and the west.

As in many of Yu's poems, China is grounded not in physical places but in the Chinese literary tradition. He concedes to not knowing the happiness of the fish Zhuangzi speaks of; he hears the partridges in the verdant mountains of Xin Qiji call and answer to each other across the human political border. The striking conclusion, "A syphilitic mother is still a mother," is one of the most oft-quoted lines in this poem.

CONTRIBUTORS' BIOGRAPHIES

Munawwar Abdulla is an Uyghur advocate, poet, and scientist born on Kaurna land and based in Massachusetts. She co-founded The Tarim Network, runs Uyghur Collective, and collaborates on projects with Uyghur rights organizations around the world. Her writings and literary translations have been published in places such as *Modern Poetry in Translation, Asymptote, The Margins,* and others, and she was recently a co-editor of the anthology *Under the Mulberry Tree.*

Heba Abu Nada was a Palestinian poet, novelist, and educator. Her novel أكسيجين ليس للموتى (*Oxygen is Not for the Dead*) won second place from the Sharjah Award for Arab Creativity in 2017. She was killed in her home in the Gaza Strip by an Israeli airstrike on October 20, 2023 at the age of thirty-two.

Hassan Akram is an Iraqi writer and editor born in 1993 in Basra, Iraq. He graduated from Qadissia University in Iraq. Akram participated in a creative writing workshop (Nadwa), organized by the International Prize for Arabic Fiction (IPAF) in 2019. His works include *A Plan to Save the World* (2020) and *The Book of Nightmares* (2021).

Ammiel Alcalay is a poet, novelist, translator, essayist, critic, and scholar with over 20 books including *After Jews and Arabs* (University of Minnesota Press, 1992), *Memories of Our Future* (City Lights, 2001), and two forthcoming books, *CONTROLLED DEMOLITION: a work* *in four books* (Litmus Press), and *Follow the Person: Archival Encounters* (punctum books).

Liliana Ancalao was born in 1961 in Puel Mapu, or what is more commonly known today as Argentina. There she helped to reclaim Mapuche land and found ñamkulawen, a Mapuche community group working to protect and advance Mapuche culture. Her books of poetry include *Rokiñ provisiones para el viaje, Mujeres a la intemperie-pu zomo wekuntu mew* and *Tejido con lana cruda,* and she has published a book of testimonial essays and poetry entitled *Resuello-neyen.* She frequents Indigenous and non-Indigenous literary festivals, and she has been anthologized internationally, with her work now appearing in translation in English, French, Italian, and Portuguese.

Salah Badis is an author from Algeria. Born in 1994, he published the collection of poetry *Ship Weariness* in 2016, followed by the collection of short stories, *Things That Happen,* in 2019, and its French translation *Des Choses qui Arrivent,* in 2023. Badis also translates from French into Arabic. Among the authors he has translated are Joseph Andras, Éric Vuillard, and Jean Sénac.

Bae Myung-hoon is the author of *Tower* (2021), *Launch Something!* (2022), and *The Proposal* (2024). *Tower* is the first Korean science fiction book by a single author to be translated into English. Known for his inventive worldbuilding and biting political humor, he has written over a dozen novels and short story collections, an essay collection, and a sci-fi children's book.

Emily Balistrieri is an American translator based in Osaka. His translation of *The Tatami Galaxy* by Tomihiko Morimi was a finalist for the 2023 PEN Translation Prize. Other works include Ao Omae's *People Who Talk to Stuffed Animals Are Nice,* Shaw Kuzki's *Soul Lanterns,* Eiko

Kadono's *Kiki's Delivery Service,* and Takuji Ichikawa's *The Refugees' Daughter.*

Anna Bentley was born and educated in Britain and has lived in Budapest since 2000. Since completing the Balassi Institute's Literary Translation Programme in 2018, she has translated several full-length books including: Ervin Lázár's children's classic *Arnica the Duck Princess* (Pushkin Children's Press, 2019); Anna Menyhért's *Women's Literary Tradition and Twentieth-Century Hungarian Women Writers* (Brill 2020); and a collection of inclusive, rewritten fairytales, *A Fairytale for Everyone* (HarperCollins, 2022). Anna's translations of poetry and prose have appeared in numerous journals including *Asymptote*'s "Translation Tuesday" blog, *World Literature Today, Hungarian Literature Online, Trafika Europe, Panodyssey,* and *The Continental Literary Magazine.*

Uilleam Blacker teaches Ukrainian and East European culture at University College London. He has written about Ukraine for *The Atlantic, The Guardian, Times Literary Supplement,* and others. His translations of Ukrainian authors include Oleg Sentsov's *Life Went On Anyway* (Deep Vellum, 2019) and Mike Yohansen's *Dr Leonardo's Journey* (Harvard UP, 2024). His translations have appeared in *Words Without Borders, White Review,* and *Modern Poetry in Translation,* among others.

Dmitry Blizniuk is a poet from Kharkiv, Ukraine. His most recent poems have appeared in *128 LIT, American Chordata, The London Magazine, Rattle, Another Chicago Magazine, Eurolitkrant, Poet Lore, New Mexico Review, Ilanot Review, National Translation Month, EastWest Literary Forum, North Dakota Quarterly, The Pinch, Tochka. Zreniya* ("View.Point"), and many other publications. A Pushcart Prize nominee, he is also the author of *The Red Forest* (Fowlpox Press,

2018). An English translation of one of his poems was awarded the *RHINO* 2022 Translation Prize.

Hisham Bustani is an award-winning Jordanian author of fiction and poetry. He is acclaimed for his bold style and unique narrative voice, and often experiments with the boundaries of short fiction and prose poetry. Much of his work revolves around the dystopian experience of postcolonial modernity in the Arab world. Hisham's fiction and poetry have been translated into many languages, with English-language translations appearing in *Best Asian Short Stories, The Kenyon Review, The Georgia Review, The Poetry Review, Modern Poetry in Translation,* and *Guernica.* His most recent book in translation is *The Monotonous Chaos of Existence* (Mason Jar Press, 2022).

Monika Cassel's poems and translations from German have appeared in *The Adroit Journal, AGNI, Guesthouse, Orion, Poetry,* and *Poetry Northwest.* She was awarded an ALTA Travel Fellowship in 2016 and invited to the TOLEDO-Programm's 2022 JUNIVERS for translators of German poetry, and her translations of Daniela Danz were finalists for the Rhine Translation Prize and the Malinda A. Markham Translation Prize. She holds an MFA in poetry from Warren Wilson College and a PhD in comparative literature from the University of Michigan and is an assistant poetry editor for *Four Way Review.*

Rosa Chávez (b. 1980, Chimaltenango, Guatemala) is a Maya K'iche' and Kaqchikel poet, artist, and activist who is Guatemala Program Coordinator for the international feminist organization JASS Mesoamerica. She has authored several poetry collections—including *Casa solitaria* (2005), *Ri uk'u'x ri ab'aj / El corazón de la piedra* (2010), and *Recordar vuelve el tiempo sagrado / Kux loq'olaj ri q'ij rumal ri na'tajisanem* (2022)—in addition to experimental works of theater, performance, and video. Her work has been widely anthologized and translated into French, Norwegian, German, Hungarian, and English, among other languages.

Paloma Chen is a poet, journalist, and researcher. She studied journalism at the Universitat de València, Construction and Representation of Cultural Identities at the Universitat de Barcelona and Philosophy at Fudan University in Shanghai. She won the "L de Lírica" National Poetry Prize in 2020. She is the author of the collection *Invocación a las mayorías silenciosas* (Letraversal, 2022) and the multilingual poetry collection app *Shanshui Pixel Scenes* (2023). In English, her poetry has been published in *World Literature Today* and *Modern Poetry in Translation*. Read more at www.palomachen.es.

Sean Cotter, Professor of Literature and Translation Studies at the University of Texas at Dallas, has translated many works of Romanian literature, most recently Mircea Cărtărescu's *Solenoid*, winner of the Dublin Literary Award.

Daniela Danz is the author of four books of poetry, including *Wildniß* (2020), *V* (2014), and *Pontus* (2009); two novels, *Lange Fluchten* (2016) and *Türmer* (2006); an essay collection; and an opera libretto. She teaches at the University of Hildesheim and is vice president of the Academy of Sciences and Literature in Mainz. She holds a PhD in art history and has received numerous awards, including the German Award for Nature Writing; the Deutscher Sprachpreis, a career award for writers who demonstrate a conscious, careful, and masterful use of German; and awards from the Academies of Arts in Bavaria and Berlin.

Rachael Daum was awarded a 2021 PEN/Heim Translation Fund Grant for her translation from Serbian of *Lusitania* by Dejan Atanacković. She is the translator from Croatian of *The Story of a Man*

Who Collapsed Into His Notebook by Ivana Sajko (Fraktura, 2023), and from Russian of *Letters to Robot Werther* by Natalia Rubanova (Carrion Bloom Books, 2021). Her original work and translations have appeared in *128 LIT, Asymptote, Words Without Borders, The Los Angeles Review,* and elsewhere. She holds an MA in Slavic Studies (Indiana University) and BA in Creative Writing (University of Rochester). She lives in Cologne, Germany.

Armen Davoudian's first book of poems, *The Palace of Forty Pillars,* was published by Tin House Books in 2024. His poems and translations from Persian appear in *Poetry, The Hopkins Review, The Yale Review,* and elsewhere. Armen grew up in Isfahan, Iran and is currently a PhD candidate in English at Stanford University.

Arthur Malcolm Dixon is lead translator and managing editor of the multilingual literary journal *Latin American Literature Today.* His translations have been featured in *Asymptote, Boston Review, International Poetry Review, The Kenyon Review, Literary Hub, Poesía, Trafika Europe,* and *World Literature Today,* among other publications. He works as an interpreter in Tulsa, Oklahoma, where he was a 2020-2023 Tulsa Artist Fellow.

Elsa Drucaroff was born and raised in Buenos Aires. The author of four novels and three short story collections, she is also a prolific essayist on topics such as Argentine literature, literary theory, and feminism. She holds a PhD in Social Sciences and is a professor of literature at the University of Buenos Aires. Her first novel to be translated into English, *Rodolfo Walsh's Last Case* (Corylus Books, 2024), is a fictionalized account of one of Argentina's canonical writers and his struggle against the brutal military dictatorship of the 1970s. "Lili in Her Forest" is from her 2019 collection *Checkpoint.*

Jonathan Dunne studied Classics at Oxford University. He directs the publishing house Small Stations Press. He has translated more than eighty books from the Bulgarian, Catalan, Galician, and Spanish languages. He writes on the theology of language, speech as creation, and translation as a metaphor for life. His latest book is *Seven Brief Lessons on Language* (2023). More of his work can be found on his website, www.stonesofithaca.com.

Yordan Eftimov (b. Razgrad, 1971) went to the Classics high school in Sofia and later studied Bulgarian Philology at Sofia University. He teaches literary theory at New Bulgarian University. He is a well-known critic and editor of the popular *Literary Newspaper*. He has published numerous poetry and essay collections. *The Heart Is Not a Creator*, first published in Bulgarian in 2013 and due out in English with Broken Sleep Books in August 2025, is his most successful collection to date and received both the Ivan Nikolov and the Hristo Fotev National Poetry Awards.

Thoraya El-Rayyes is a writer, literary translator, and political sociologist living between London, England and Amman, Jordan. Her translations of contemporary Arabic literature have appeared in publications including *World Literature Today*, *The Kenyon Review*, and *Words Without Borders*. Thoraya's work has received awards from the Modern Language Association and the King Fahd Center for Middle East Studies at the University of Arkansas.

Mansoura Ez-Eldin is an award-winning Egyptian writer of fiction and nonfiction, and a widely translated author of ten books. She was nominated by Beirut 39 as one of the 39 best Arab-language writers under 40, and won the 2021 Ibn Battuta Prize for travel literature. In 2014, the Sharjah International Book Fair nominated her book *Emerald Mountain* in the category of Best Arabic Novel. Her writing has appeared, among other places, in *The New York Times, A Public Space, Neue Zürcher Zeitung,* and *Granta.* She is the managing editor of the cultural weekly *Akhbar Al-Adab* and, since 2003, its book review editor.

Eirill Alvilde Falck is a Norwegian-born writer and translator. Her work has been recognized with an Iowa Arts Fellowship and a Zell Fellowship, and with the John Wagner Prize and the Hopwood Award. She is the co-founder of *MQR: Mixtape,* an imprint of *Michigan Quarterly Review.* She collects screams. If you would like her to listen to your scream, you can leave her a voicemail message at (424) 226-6734. This is her second appearance in Best Literary Translations.

Huda Fakhreddine is a writer, translator, and author of *Metapoesis in the Arabic Tradition* (Brill, 2015) and *The Arabic Prose Poem: Poetic Theory and Practice* (Edinburgh UP, 2021). She is also Associate Professor of Arabic literature at the University of Pennsylvania.

Ibrahim Fawzy is an Egyptian literary translator and writer. His critical writings and translations have appeared in literary journals such as *ArabLit Quarterly, Words Without Borders, The Markaz Review, Modern Poetry in Translation, Poetry Birmingham Literary Journal, Consequence, OlongoAfrica,* and *Asymptote,* among others. He is an editor at *Rowayat* and *Asymptote* and podcasts at NBN. In 2023, he finished a six-month mentorship with the British National Centre for Writing. He is a two-time graduate of the BCLT Summer School. Ibrahim won the 2023 English PEN Presents and was longlisted for the first edition of Best Literary Translations.

Slava Faybysh translates from Spanish and Russian. His translations have been published in journals such as *New England Review, The Southern Review, The Georgia Review, AGNI,* and *The Common,* and his translation of Elsa Drucaroff's historical thriller set in 1970s Argentina, *Rodolfo Walsh's Last Case*, was published by Corylus Books in 2024. He is currently seeking a publisher for Ainur Karim's family saga set in Kazakhstan, called *Stan Girl*.

Anna Glazova is a laureate of the Andrei Bely Prize and one of the most prominent poets writing in Russian today. She has published six books of poetry and received her PhD in German and Comparative Literature from Northwestern University. She translates from German and English; among the authors she has translated are Paul Celan, Franz Kafka, Unica Zürn, Walter Benjamin, and Emily Dickinson. She lives in Hamburg, Germany.

Saliha Haddad is an Algerian writer and editor. She works as a literary interviewer at *Africa In Dialogue*. Her book reviews have appeared in *The Other Side of Hope*, *The New Arab*, and *The Transnational Literary Journal* and her creative work has been published in *Agbowó*, *Isele* magazine, and *Newlines* magazine.

Bradley Harmon is a writer, scholar of Nordic and German literature and cultural history, and translator from Swedish, German, Norwegian, Faroese, and Danish. He has been an ALTA Emerging Translator fellow (2022), an American-Scandinavian Foundation fellow to Sweden (2023–2024), and a Fulbright fellow to Germany (2024–2025). Forthcoming book translations include Katarina Frostenson's *The Space of Time* (2024)and Monika Fagerholm's *Who Killed Bambi?* (2025).

Khaled al-Hilli teaches Arabic at New York University and is completing a doctorate at the CUNY Graduate Center on the post-2003 Iraqi novel. His *Sargon Boulus: "This Great River" Translating the Beats into Arabic*, was published by Lost & Found in 2024.

Will Howard's writing and translations have appeared in *DIAGRAM, Massachusetts Review, Passages North, Poetry,* and elsewhere. A former Fulbright Scholar in Spain, he earned an MA in literary translation from the Universidad Complutense de Madrid and a BA in English from Pomona College.

Joanna Trzeciak Huss is Professor of Translation Studies at Kent State University. Her translations from Polish and Russian have appeared in *The New York Times, The New Yorker, Times Literary Supplement, Harper's, The Atlantic, Paris Review, Field, Pleiades, The Hopkins Review, Zvezda, Boston Review, nonsite,* and *New Ohio Review,* among others. Her books of poetry translation include *Miracle Fair: Selected Poems of Wisława Szymborska* (W. W. Norton) and *Sobbing Superpower: Selected Poems of Tadeusz Różewicz* (W. W. Norton). Her *Collected Poems of Zuzanna Ginczanka* is forthcoming from Zephyr Press. She is the recipient of the 2020 Michael Heim Prize for Collegial Translation.

Yuliia Iliukha is a Ukrainian poet, writer, and journalist. She is the author of several books for adults and children. Her poems and short stories have been translated into English, German, Italian, Bulgarian, Hungarian, Catalan, Polish, and Swedish. Her works have appeared in periodicals in Ukraine, Austria, Poland, Bulgaria, Hungary, Spain, the UK, Sweden, and the U.S. Iliukha has received a number of awards, including the Oles Honchar International Ukrainian-German Literary Prize. Currently, she is a writer-in-residence at Internationales Haus der Autor:innen in Graz, Austria.

Lív Maria Róadóttir Jæger is a Faroese poet. She debuted with the poem recording *Mítt navn við hondskrift* (2014), followed by the collection *Hvít sól* (2015). Her collection *Eg skrivi á vátt pappír* (2020) won the Faroese M. A. Jacobsen Literary Prize, was nominated for the Nordic Council Literature Prize, and is translated into Danish and French. Lív's poetry has appeared in literary journals and as music lyrics. She collaborates as a member of the experimental project SUPERVISJÓN. Lív has a degree in philosophy from the University of Copenhagen and teaches creative writing at University of the Faroe Islands.

Yana Kane came to the United States as a refugee from the USSR. She holds an engineering degree from Princeton University and a PhD in Statistics from Cornell University. She is pursuing an MFA in Literary Translation and Poetry at Fairleigh Dickinson University. Her bilingual poetry book, *Kingfisher*/Зимородок, was published in 2020. She is a contributor to the anthology of anti-war poetry, *Dislocation* (Slavica Press, 2024). View.Point recognized her translations of poetry of witness from Ukraine and Russia as among the "Best of 2022." She won the 2024 RHINO Poetry Translation Prize. She is grateful to Bruce Esrig for editing her English-language texts.

Lizzy Kinch lives in London, where she works in history documentaries and translates German fiction.

Jozefina Komporaly is a London-based academic and translator from Hungarian and Romanian. She is editor and co-translator of *How to Explain the History of Communism to Mental Patients and Other Plays* (Seagull, 2015), *András Visky's Barrack Dramaturgy* (Intellect, 2017) and *Plays from Romania: Dramaturgies of Subversion* (Bloomsbury, 2021), and author of numerous publications on translation, adaptation and theatre. Recent publications include *Mr K Released* by Matéi Visniec (finalist for the 2021 EBRD Literature Prize) and works by Gábor Vida and Melinda Mátyus. Her translation *Home* by Andrea Tompa (Istros Books, 2024) was awarded a PEN Translates Grant. Website: https://jozefinakomporaly.com.

Vivian Lamarque (b. 1946) is a contemporary Italian poet known for sharp social commentary and an engaging, intimate, and direct voice.

She is the author of eleven collections of poetry. This poem is from her book *L'amore da vecchia* (Love Later in Life).

Hanna Leliv is a literary translator from Lviv, Ukraine. She was a Fulbright Fellow at the University of Iowa's Literary Translation MFA program and mentee at the Emerging Translators Mentorship Program run by the U.K. National Center for Writing. In 2022, *Cappy and the Whale,* a children's book by Kateryna Babkina, was published in her translation by Penguin Random House UK. In 2023–24, Hanna was a translator-in-residence at Princeton University.

Khaled Mattawa's latest book of poems is *Fugitive Atlas* (Graywolf, 2020). He is the William Wilhartz Professor of English Language and Literature at the University of Michigan and editor-in-chief of *Michigan Quarterly Review.*

Seth Michelson has published eighteen books of original poetry and poetry in translation, and three anthologies of poetry. His honors include fellowships from the National Endowment for the Arts, the Fulbright Foundation, and the Mellon Foundation. His first trilingual book of translations of Liliana Ancalao's poetry, *Women of the Big Sky,* stands importantly as the first-ever single-author poetry collection in English-language translation by a female Mapuche poet from Puel Mapu. His own work has been translated into more than a dozen languages. He teaches poetry at Washington and Lee University, where he founded and directs the Center for Poetic Research and is the chair of Latin American and Caribbean Studies.

Will Morningstar is a book editor and translator whose work has appeared in journals such as the *New England Review, ANMLY, Two Lines, Latin American Literature Today, Strange Horizons,* and *Massachusetts Review*. His co-translation with Samantha Schnee of the Argentine writer Mariana Travacio's novel *All That Dies in April* will be published by World Editions in 2025. He is a co-founder of the Boston-based Diptych Press, a new publisher of literature from around the world.

Lina Mounzer is a Lebanese writer and translator. She has been a regular contributor to *The New York Times* and her work has appeared in *The Paris Review, Freeman's, Washington Post,* and *The Baffler,* as well as in the anthologies *Tales of Two Planets* (Penguin, 2020) and *Best American Essays 2022* (Harper Collins). She is a senior editor at *The Markaz Review.*

Edvard Munch (1863–1944) was a Norwegian artist whose best-known motif, *The Scream,* ranks among the world's most recognizable artworks. In addition to his painting practice, Munch harbored substantial literary ambitions. His notebooks contain drafts of stories, novels, plays, poems, aphorisms, and essayistic diary entries. He once wrote to a friend: "Perhaps I should have been a writer rather than an artist."

Nhã Thuyên secludedly anchors herself to Hà Nội, Việt Nam and totters between languages. She has authored several books in Vietnamese and in English translation, including *rìa vực* (2011), *từ thở, những người lạ* (words breathe, creatures of elsewhere) (2015), *bất\ \tuẫn: những hiện diện [tự-] vắng trong thơ Việt* (un\ \martyred: [self-]vanishing presences in Vietnamese poetry) (2019). Her next book *vị nước* (taste of water) is lying there waiting to see the moon. She has been unearthing her notebooks, rubbing her words and learning to quietly speak up with care.

Alex Niemi is a writer and award-winning translator. Her translations include *For the Shrew* and *Hekate* by Anna Glazova, as well as *The John Cage Experiences* by Vincent Tholomé. She is also the author of the poetry chapbook *Elephant.* Her translation work has been supported by the National Endowment of the Arts and nominated for *Best of the Net.*

Ao Omae is a rising star of gender-conscious literature in Japan. His short fiction has been featured in translation in The *Kenyon Review, The Southern Review,* and *91st Meridian,* as well as on *Electric Literature.* His English-language debut collection is *People Who Talk to Stuffed Animals Are Nice* (tr. Emily Balistrieri). The titular story was adapted as a film in 2023.

Martha Riva Palacio Obón is a Mexican sound artist and author of novels, poetry, and stories for children and adults. She won the 2014 Premio Hispanoamericano de Poesía para Niños for her illustrated poetry book *Lunática* and the 2011 Premio Barco de Vapor for her middle-grade novel *Las sirenas sueñan con trilobites,* published in English as *Secrets We Tell the Sea.* Her short prose has been published in the *New England Review, ANMLY,* and *Strange Horizons,* and she is currently working on a collection of personal essays. She is a member of Mexico's Sistema Nacional de Creadores de Arte.

Norman Erikson Pasaribu is a Toba Batak writer of fiction, poetry, and nonfiction. *Happy Stories, Mostly* (translated by Tiffany Tsao) won the 2022 Republic of Consciousness Prize; was a finalist for the 2023 Cercador Prize for Literature in Translation; and was longlisted for the 2022 International Booker Prize, the 2023 Barrios Book in Translation Prize, and the 2023 National Translation Award in Prose.

Nasser Rabah was born in Gaza in 1963 and lives there. He got his BA in agricultural science in 1985, then working as Director of the Agriculture Ministry's Communication Department. He is a member of the Palestinian Writers and Authors Union and has published five collections of poetry, *Running After Dead Gazelles* (2003), *One of Nobody* (2010), *Passersby with Light Clothes* (2013), *Water Thirsty for Water* (2016), *Eulogy for the Robin* (2020); and a novel, *Since Approximately an Hour* (2018). His poems have been translated into English, French, and Hebrew. City Lights will publish his selected poems in 2025.

Gabriela Ramirez-Chavez is a Seattle-based poet and translator born to Guatemalan immigrants. Her poetry has appeared in literary journals and anthologies, including *The Wandering Song: Central American Writing in the United States*. As a translator, she focuses on Indigenous literatures of Latin America, especially from Mesoamerica. Her translations of Rosa Chávez (Maya K'iche' and Kaqchikel), with whom she regularly collaborates, have been featured on NPR and in *Poetry, World Literature Today, BOMB*, and *Daughters of Latin America: An International Anthology of Latine Women*, among other publications. She is the co-translator of *Tsunami: Women's Voices from Mexico.*

Kaitlin Rees is a translator, editor, and public school teacher based in New York City. She translates from the Vietnamese of Nhã Thuyên, with whom she co-founded AJAR, the small bilingual journal-presse that organizes an occasional poetry festival. Her translations include *moon fevers* (Tilted Axis, 2019), *words breathe, creatures of elsewhere* (Vagabond Press, 2016), and the forthcoming book of poetry *taste of water.*

Zack Rogow was a co-winner of the PEN/Book-of-the-Month Club Translation Award for *Earthlight* by André Breton, and winner of a Bay Area Book Reviewers Award (BABRA) for his translation of George Sand's novel *Horace*. His English version of Colette's novel *Green Wheat* was shortlisted for the PEN/Book-of-the-Month Club Translation Award.

Natalia Rubanova lives and works in Moscow, Russia. She studied piano at Ryazan Musical College, and received her bachelor's from Moscow Pedagogical State University. She has published seven books, and her short stories have been published in over sixty anthologies. Her plays have been performed in Russia, and most recently in London at the SOLO International Festival, where she was awarded the prize for Best New Writing. In 2019 she was awarded the Turgenev Prize (Moscow), and the Hemingway Prize (Toronto), for her cycle of critical journalism articles, and she has been awarded the Nonconformism Prize.

Sung Ryu is a literary translator working from and into Korean. Her English translations include *Tower* by Bae Myung-hoon (Honford Star, 2021), *Shoko's Smile* by Choi Eunyoung (Penguin Books, 2021), and *I'm Waiting for You: And Other Stories* by Kim Bo-Young (co-translated with Sophie Bowman, Harper Voyager, 2021). Her Korean translations include *Grandma Moses: My Life's History* by Anna Mary Robertson Moses (Suo Books, 2017). She grew up in South Korea, the U.S., and Canada, and now lives in Singapore. She is a member of the translator collective Smoking Tigers.

Lawrence Schimel is a bilingual (Spanish/English) author who has published over 130 books in a wide range of genres. He is also a prolific literary translator, into English and Spanish, of over 160 books. His translations into English have won a Batchelder Honor from the American Library Association and a PEN Translates Award from English PEN (three times), among other honors. Authors he has translated into English include Juan Villoro, Trifonia Melibea Obono, Carmen Boullosa, María José Ferrada, Ricardo Chávez Castañeda, Elsa Cross, and Agnès Agboton, and into Spanish: George Takei, Danez Smith, Koleka Putuma, and Maggie Nelson.

Clemens J. Setz was born in Graz, Austria in 1982 and now lives in Vienna. His writing has received numerous awards, including the Leipzig Book Fair Prize in 2011 for the short story collection *Die Liebe zur Zeit des Mahlstädter Kindes* and the Georg Büchner Prize in 2021. In 2014 his novel *Indigo* was published in English, translated by Ross Benjamin.

Fatemeh Shams is a poet and associate professor of Persian literature at the University of Pennsylvania. Her books include *A Revolution in Rhyme* (Oxford University Press, 2021), *When They Broke Down the Door*, translated by Dick Davis (Mage, 2016), and *Hopscotch*, translated by Armen Davoudian (Ugly Duckling Presse).

Shuang Xuetao is one of the most highly celebrated young Chinese writers. Born in 1983 in the city of Shenyang, Shuang has written six volumes of fiction, for which he has won the Blossoms Literary Prize, the Wang Zengqi Short Story Prize, and, most recently, the Blancpain-Imaginist Literary Prize for the best Chinese writer under forty-five. His short stories and novellas have been adapted into major television productions and feature films. *Rouge Street: Three Novellas* was his first book to appear in English. Shuang lives in Beijing.

Iryna Shuvalova is a poet, scholar, and translator from Kyiv, Ukraine, currently based in Norway. She is the author of four award-winning books of poetry in Ukrainian and of the bilingual *Pray to the Empty Wells* (Lost Horse Press, 2019). Her collection *Stoneorchardwoods* (2020) was named poetry book of the year in Ukraine, and her new book *The Ending Songs* was published in 2024. Her work has been translated into 23 languages.

Alex Shvartsman is an award-winning writer, translator, and anthologist from Brooklyn, NY. He has translated novels, video game content, TV and movie scripts. His short fiction translations from Russian have appeared in *Analog, Asimov's, Clarkesworld, F&SF, Reactor,* and other venues. His website is alexshvartsman.com.

Kim Simonsen is a Faroese writer and researcher from the island of Eysturoy. He completed his PhD in Nordic literature at the University of Roskilde and has authored seven books as well as numerous essays and academic articles. He is founder and managing editor of Forlagið Eksil, a Faroese press that has published over twenty titles. His latest poetry collection, *Lívfrøðiliga samansetingin í einum dropa av sjógvi minnir um blóðið í mínum æðrum* (The biological composition of a drop of seawater is reminiscent of the blood in my veins; Verksmiðjan, 2023), was nominated for the 2024 Nordic Council Literature Prize.

Florentino Solano is a writer, translator, musician, and farm worker from Metlatónoc, Guerrero, Mexico. He writes in his native language, Tu'un Savi, and translates his own writing into Spanish. In 2021, he received both the Premio de Literaturas Indígenas de América for his chronicle *Yaa táxá'á kàà tùxìi (La danza de las balas)* and the Premio Nezahualcóyotl de Literatura en Lenguas Mexicanas for his verse collection *Tákúu ndi'i tachi si'í yu (Todas las voces de mi madre).*

Wisława Szymborska (1923–2012) was a Polish poet, essayist, translator, and collage artist. She lived most of her life in Kraków, working as a literary editor and columnist. She published thirteen collections of poetry and her poems have been translated into over forty languages. Her collection in English, *Miracle Fair,* was awarded the Heldt Translation Prize. In 1991, she received the Herder Prize, and in 1995, the Goethe Prize. She was awarded the 1996 Nobel Prize in Literature. In 2011, she became an honorary member of the American Academy of Arts and Letters. Her complete poems, *Wiersze wszystkie,* were published in 2023.

Pablo Texón is a poet, fiction writer, essayist, translator, songwriter, and member of the Academia de la Llingua Asturiana. His last two poetry collections, *Cantar de ti mesma* and *Allumamientu,* won the Xuan María Acebal Prize for Asturian-language poetry.

Jeremy Tiang has translated over thirty books from Chinese, including novels by Zhang Yueran, Yan Ge, Yeng Pway Ngon and Lo Yi-Chin. His translation of Zou Jingzhi's *Ninth Building* was longlisted for the International Booker Prize. His novel *State of Emergency* won the Singapore Literature Prize in 2018. He also writes and translates plays. Originally from Singapore, Tiang now lives in Flushing, Queens.

Tiffany Tsao is a writer and translator. She has written three novels, the most recent of which is *The Majesties* (Atria Books, 2020). She has translated five books to date from Indonesian to English.

Adil Tuniyaz (b. 1970) is a well-known poet and journalist from Kashgar. He has a background in literature from both Urumchi and Saudi Arabia. He is often considered to be among the first generation of modernist Uyghur poets. In 2015, he and his wife, Nezire, opened the Light and Pen bookstore. The couple, along with other family members, were detained and arrested in 2017 as part of China's "re-education" campaign. Tuniyaz's poetry often touches on topics such as Islamic mysticism, Uyghur culture and identity, and many contemporary themes that have made him a popular poet in Uyghur society.

Radu Vancu is a Romanian poet, scholar, and translator. A professor at Lucian Blaga University in Sibiu, he is editor-in-chief of *Transilvania* magazine and a past president of PEN Romania. Vancu has published nine books of poems, two volumes of a diary, an anthology of articles on society and politics, and the novel *Transparent.* His poetry has been translated into twenty languages and published in multiple anthologies and journals. He has been awarded multiple national and international prizes for his literary work.

Laura Vazquez is a French poet and novelist who lives in Marseille. In 2023, she won the Prix Goncourt for poetry, one of the highest honors in France. She has written several collections of poetry in addition to her novel, *The Endless Week*, and an epic, *The Book of the Long and Wide*. Her poems have been translated into Chinese, English, Spanish, Portuguese, Norwegian, Dutch, German, Italian, and Arabic. She is currently at work on her first play, which is a lesbian tragedy.

András Visky (born in 1957 in Târgu-Mureş, Romania), who writes in Hungarian, is a prize-winning poet, playwright and essayist and the resident dramaturg at the Hungarian Theatre in Cluj, Romania. His plays have been staged in several European countries and the United States. He holds a Doctor of Liberal Arts from the University of Theatre and Film, Budapest, and he is a member of the Széchenyi Academy of Literature and Arts. As a full professor of performance theory, he lectures at the Babeş-Bolyai University of Cluj and many other universities all over the world. *Deportation* is his first novel.

Randi Ward is a poet, translator, lyricist, and photographer from West Virginia. She earned her MA in cultural studies from the University of the Faroe Islands and has twice won the American-Scandinavian Foundation's Nadia Christensen Prize. Her work has appeared in *Asymptote, Four Way Review, Words Without Borders,* and *World Literature Today*; her work has also been featured on Folk Radio U.K., NPR, and PBS Newshour. She is a recipient of Shepherd University's Appalachian Photography Award, and Cornell University Library established the Randi Ward Collection in its Division of Rare and Manuscript Collections in 2015. For more information, visit randiward.com.

Saadi Youssef (1934–2021) was born near Basra, Iraq, Youssef is considered one of the most important contemporary poets in the Arab world. Following his experience as a political prisoner in Iraq, he spent most of his life in exile, working as a teacher, journalist, and literary editor. With forty books of poetry to his credit, Youssef, who had spent the last two decades of his life in London, was also a leading translator to Arabic of works by Walt Whitman, Ngūgˉı wa Thiong'o, Federico Garcia Lorca, and many others.

Yu Kwang-Chung (1928–2017) was a Taiwanese poet, essayist, translator, and literary scholar. He served as a professor of English language and literature in various institutions in Taiwan and as a long-time professor of Chinese language and literature at the Chinese University of Hong Kong. His work is steeped in the Chinese literary tradition and invigorated by Western and modern art. He received numerous literary prizes and honors in his lifetime, including the National Award for Arts in poetry, and four times won the Book of the Year prize from the *United Daily News*.

Emna Zghal is a visual artist with a strong interest in poetry. Aside from her paintings and woodcuts, she has published three artist's books. Reviews of her exhibits have appeared in the pages of *The New Yorker, The New York Times,* and *Artforum,* among other publications. Her work is held in collections at Yale University Library, the New York Public Library, The Africa Center, and the Schomburg Center for Research in Black Culture.

Yifan Zhang is a PhD candidate in the English Department at Baylor University. Her dissertation explores the georgic mode in Seamus Heaney's poetry. She received her BA in English from the Chinese University of Hong Kong and MA in English from Texas Tech University. Her translations have appeared in *The Southern Review* and *The Hopkins Review.*

Yefim Zozulya was a Russian fabulist popular in the 1920s. His pioneering work in the anti-utopia genre famously inspired Zamyatin's novel *We*. English translations of his fiction have previously appeared at Tor.com, *F&SF*, *Galaxy's Edge*, and in *The Big Book of Science Fiction*.

PREVIOUS PUBLICATIONS

We gratefully acknowledge the editors of the journals who first selected these translations for publication.

128 LIT: "[тнэ яоом]" and "my fish will stay alive"
ANMLY: "How Death Creates a Dead Man and His Image a Poem in 43 Lines"
Another Chicago Magazine: "Saturday Morning" and ["A woman who buried her son . . ."]
ArabLit: "Not Just Passing"
Chicago Review: "Suzy"
The Cincinnati Review: "Night Flight" and "A Quatrain"
Circumference: "Five Phenomenologies"
The Common: "Welcome to the Department of Unanswered Prayers"
Consequence: An excerpt from *A Plan to Save the World*
Firmament: "Lovers' Names"
Four Way Review: "Mother Tongue"
Galaxy's Edge: "Cain and Abel"
The Hopkins Review: "Lethe" and "The Onion"
The Kenyon Review: "The Aspiration for Cha-Ka-Ta-Pa," "Notes on *The Scream*," "Loom," "don't hide the madness," and "Tumbleweed"
LitHub: "Dead Cats Continue to Meow"
The Markaz Review: "Before the Earthquake" and "Of Wood and Hallucination"

New England Review: "Lili in Her Forest" and "How to Draw a Lichen (with Help from the Spirits)"
The New Yorker: "Heart"
Pilgrimage: "Time Delivery"
Poetry: "Sueñu/Suañu" and "Come wilderness into our homes"
Poetry Society of America: "W for War"
Scandinavian Review: Excerpt from *What good does it do for a person to wake up one morning this side of the new millennium*
Tupelo Quarterly: "Nine Poems"
Words Without Borders: "I Write to Purge This Memory," "Kaddish: For Miklós Radnóti," and "a moving grove"
World Literature Today: "Apple-Flesh," "Elena Kame Is a Spell," and "Obscenity"
World Poetry Review: "Instructions"

NOTABLE TRANSLATIONS PUBLISHED IN 2023

Arranged by translator's last name, these translations were longlisted for inclusion in this edition of Best Literary Translations.

- "She Who Remains" by Rene Karabash, translated by Izidora Angel (*Gulf Coast*)
- "Comfort" by Georg Amsel, translated by Lake Angela (*Cagibi*)
- From *Memories of a Miracle* by Andrea Canobbio, translated by Anne Milano Appel (*The Threepenny Review*)
- "A Stroll Under the Moonlight" by Sabahattin Ali, translated by Aysel Basci (*Hayden's Ferry Review*)
- "It Was Untimely" by Esra Kahya, translated by Aysel Basci (*The Los Angeles Review*)
- "Kuulla" by Ubah Cristina Ali Farah, translated by Brandon Breen (*Massachusetts Review*)
- "The signals come in from the dark" by Daniela Danz, translated by Monika Cassel (*Poetry*)
- "Contentment" by Lung Ying-tai, translated by Sandra Chen (*Massachusetts Review*)
- "Seven Color Lone-Dragon Blanket" by Qiongxian Gao, translated by Ming Di (*World Literature Today*)
- "Fidelia Córdoba" by Amalialú Posso Figueroa, translated by Jeffrey Diteman (*Massachusetts Review*)
- "Trees" by Cahit Zarifoğlu, translated by Neil P. Doherty (*The Antonym*)

- "Shakuhachi" by Ting Ma, translated by Chen Du and Xisheng Chen (*The Southern Review*)
- "Let's Talk About Me" by Emiliano Monge, translated by Josh Dunn (*Exchanges: A Journal of Literary Translation*)
- "Hat and Cane" by Jesús Cos Causse, translated by Kristin Dykstra (*The Hopkins Review*)
- "Amman Skyline," "Cigarette Butts," "Chewing Gum," and "The Path" by Hisham Bustani, translated by Thoraya El-Rayyes (*International Poetry Review*)
- "Common Crime" and "I Remember When Dying Was a Circumstance" by Oriette D'Angelo, translated by Lupita Eyde-Tucker (*Armstrong Literary*)
- From *The Furrow* by Valérie Manteau, translated by Claire Foster (*The Hopkins Review*)
- "No man has defended you" and "Someone acts on orders" by Linda Maria Baros, translated by Emily Graham (*Asymptote, New England Review*)
- "Who Will Play Salaheddin?" by Rasha Abbas, translated by Katharine Halls (*The Kenyon Review*)
- "The saga of death. R. M. Rilke comes to Langeland" by Birgitta Trotzig, translated by Bradley Harmon (*Another Chicago Magazine*)
- "Sweet Tea" by Hussein Arif, translated by Jiyar Homer (*The Markaz Review*)
- "We Never Had to Name Our Sons After Jesus" by Nazlı Karabıyıkoğlu, translated by Ralph Hubbel (*ANMLY*)
- "My Beige Bra" and "Third World Beloved" by Maral Taheri, translated by Hajar Hussaini (*Annulet: A Journal of Poetics*)
- "Yoshka" by Cristian Fulaş, translated by Jozefina Komporaly (*The Los Angeles Review*)
- "Crime," "Hymn," and "Mother" by Carlos de Assumpção,

translated by Pedro Lino (*Exchanges: A Journal of Literary Translation*)

- "Bacterial" by Marcelo Cohen, translated by Kit Maude (*Samovar/Strange Horizons*)
- "I Abandoned All Desire" by Mirza Abdul Qadir, translated by Homa Mojaddi (*Asymptote* Blog)
- From "Translated from the Night #3" by Jean-Joseph Rabearivelo, translated by B.P. Otto (*ANMLY*)
- "Vows" by Argyris Stavropoulos, translated by Gigi Papoulias (*Lunch Ticket*)
- "On the Edge of a Green Pond at Night" by Wooncho Kim, translated by Suphil Lee Park (*RHINO Poetry*)
- "To Translate" by Ida Vitale, translated by Sarah Pollack (*Circumference*)
- "A Fraying Rope" and "When They Happen to Unite" by Muyaka bin Haji al-Ghassaniy, translated by Richard Prins (*RHINO Poetry, The Hopkins Review*)
- "On My Shoes" by Rokhl Korn, translated by Joseph Reisberg (*Loch Raven Review*)
- "Signal" and "floating everywhere, the white shadows" by Olivia Elias, translated by Jeremy Victor Robert (*128 LIT*)
- "Ten Minutes" by Aliyeh Ataei, translated by Siavash Saadlou (*Massachusetts Review*)
- "From the Future" and "Notes on Xenophon" by Tomas Venclova, translated by Diana Senechal (*AGNI*)
- "The Tree" by Zhe Zhang, translated by Xiaoming Shan (*MAY-DAY*)
- "January 2" by Zakaria Mohammed, translated by Lena Khalaf Tuffaha (*Poetry*)
- "Knew Its Name" by Yuan Yongping, translated by Xin Xu (*World Poetry Review*)

GUEST EDITOR

Cristina Rivera Garza is an author, translator, and critic. Her most recent book, *Liliana's Invincible Summer* (Hogarth, 2023), was winner of the 2024 Pulitzer Prize in memoir/autobiography and a finalist for the National Book Award in nonfiction. Other recent books include: *The Taiga Syndrome*, translated by Suzanne Jill Levine and Aviva Kana, (Dorothy Project, 2018), winner of the 2019 Shirley Jackson Award, and *Grieving: Dispatches from a Wounded Country*, translated by Sarah Booker (The Feminist Press, 2020), a finalist for the National Book Critics Circle Award in Criticism. She is M.D. Anderson Distinguished Professor and founder of the PhD Program in Creative Writing in Spanish at the University of Houston, Department of Hispanic Studies. Rivera Garza is also a 2020–2025 MacArthur Fellow and the 2023–2024 DAAD (German Academic Exchange Service) Artist-in-Residence in Berlin.

SERIES COEDITORS

Noh Anothai has translated both classical Siamese poets and contemporary Thai authors, including recipients of the Southeast Asian Writers (SEAWrite) award, for journals like *Asymptote*, *Two Lines*, and *World Literature Today*. In 2016, his *Poems from the Buddha's Footprint* (Singing Bone Press) became the first full-length translation of a work by the celebrated early Bangkok poet Sunthorn Phu published outside of Thailand. Profiled in the *Nikkei Asian Review* and *Prestige Thailand* for his work as a translator, Anothai has also taught creative writing in the U.S. and in Thailand, lectured at the Siam Society under royal patronage, and served as a judge for the Lucien Stryk Prize for Asian Literature in Translation. He holds a PhD in Comparative Literature from Washington University in St. Louis.

Wendy Call is author of *No Word for Welcome*, winner of the Grub Street National Book Prize for Nonfiction, and the chapbook *Tilled Paths Through Wilds of Thought*. She is also coeditor of the craft anthology *Telling True Stories*, translator of three books of poems by Irma Pineda, and co-translator of *How to Be a Good Savage and Other Poems*, by Mikeas Sánchez. She was a 2015 National Endowment for the Arts Fellow in Poetry Translation, a 2019 Fulbright Faculty Scholar in Colombia, and 2023 Translator in Residence at the University of Iowa. She teaches in the Rainier Writing Workshop MFA Program at Pacific Lutheran University.

Öykü Tekten is a poet, translator, editor, and archivist living between Granada and New York. She is also a founding member of Pinsapo, a New York-based collective and press with a particular focus on work in and about translation, as well as a contributing editor and archivist with Lost & Found: The CUNY Poetics Document Initiative. Her work has appeared in the *Academy of American Poets, Poetry, Words Without Borders, FENCE,* and *World Literature Today,* among other places. She is the translator of *Selected Poems by Betül Dünder* (Belladonna* Collaborative, 2023) and the co-translator of *Separated from the Sun by İlhan Sami Çomak* (Smokestack Books, 2022). She is also the creator and general editor of the Kurdish Poetry Series which features contemporary poets and translators in bilingual editions.

Kọ́lá Túbọ̀sún is the publisher of *OlongoAfrïca,* author of *Edwardsville by Heart* (2018), *Ìgbà Èwe: Translated Poems of Emily R. Grosholz* (2021), and *Ẹ̀ṣù at the Library & Other Poems* (2024). He is a Fulbright scholar (2009), Miles Morland Writing Fellow (2018), and Chevening Research Fellow at the British Library (2019/2020). His work has been published in *African Writer, Aké Review, Brittle Paper, International Literary Quarterly, Enkare Review, Maple Tree Literary Supplement, Jalada, Popula, Saraba Magazine, World Literature Today,* etc. He has translated the works of Chimamanda Adichie, Haruki Murakami, Ngũgĩ wa Thiong'o, Wole Soyinka, James Baldwin, Sarah Ladipo-Manyika, Cervantes, and others between English and Yorùbá. His work in language advocacy earned him the *Premio Ostana Special Prize* in Cuneo Italy in 2016.